BLOOD AND DESTINY

Enchanted II

MALLORY WANLESS

Cover design by @AnjoleyDesigns

First edition

ISBN:

Paperback 979-8-9855733-2-9
Ebook 979-8-9855733-3-6

Also by Mallory Wanless

Enchanted series:

Storm and Flame: Enchanted I
Blood and Destiny: Enchanted II

Coming soon:
Reign and Ruin: Enchanted III

To anyone who has ever felt like they didn't belong.
To the black sheep.
To the outsiders.

You are not alone.

PRONUNCIATION GUIDE

Characters

Elena: eh-LAY-nah
Agon: A-gone
Quinn: qu-IN
Lyra: LIE-rah
Madame LaBelle: ma-DAM la-BELL
Zied: ZED
Roska: ROSS-kah
Demoni: de-MON-ee
Aiden: a-DEN
Aleerah: ah-LEER-ah

Places

Andover: ann-DOVER
Nexton: NEX-ton
Cyra: sigh-RAH
Riverayn: river-INE
Rolam: ro-LUM
Slyvestris: sill-VES-tree

PROLOGUE

*H*E'D SAT AT THE *chipped and aged wooden table for hours, watching them through the purple-tinted haze of his looking glass. He'd been watching them since their birth, checking in, making sure they were surviving and learning the skills they would need to stop what was coming. He didn't agree with how their mother had handled things, and it took every ounce of self-control he had—not to mention quite a few herbal concoctions and endless bottles of wine—to not step in and protect them when they needed it. He hated himself for letting them suffer so, but he knew their fates. He knew their separate and sometimes torturous paths would make them into the strong and powerful individuals they'd need to be in order to fulfill the prophecy and save the world of magic.*

These thoughts didn't make it easier for him, but he did what he thought was best. It was likely that was the same argument their mother used, but he knew that wasn't the whole truth for her. He'd watched her as she grew their children in her body, hoping to see her thrive and flourish in her new role as a mother. He was stunned when he realized how much she resented their children. She was self-righteous and arrogant, believing that the prophecy was about her. When she'd come to understand that she was not the center of it all, but in fact the literal creator of those who would remake the world, she reacted in the most childish and petty way, lashing out at the newborn babies by separating them and sending the boys away to end up in terrible homes. He'd foolishly thought that despite her beliefs that men should only serve one purpose, she would love her own children equally, regardless of their biological sex.

He huffed ruefully to himself. In reality, she did love them all equally, which was to say that she loved none of them.

Over time, as the children grew, he celebrated their victories with them, though they had no idea he was watching. He applauded Elena every time she succeeded in casting a spell. He cheered Roska in every one of his rebellions against the Brotherhood, no matter how minor. He watched proudly as Quinn stood up to his abusers and wrought ruination on their damnedable home.

Now, watching them finally connect, feeling the wave of power they released into the world, he felt immeasurable pride. And indescribable dread, because he knew they'd come for him next.

1

ELENA

THE SHOCK OF DISCOVERING she had brothers had been unsettling, to say the least. The following days passed in a blur, and Elena honestly couldn't remember what happened to her and her *brothers*. At some point, they were all relocated to a less populated area of Harbor Ridge, one of the neglected rooms in the southern tower that had once served as excess storage for their food supplies before the school had their new root cellar put in. The room was cold, musty, and damp. Not an ideal place to rest one's head, in her opinion, but she'd slept in worse places lately, and she refused to be separated from her brothers, for fear of what her mother might try to do to them.

Elena was confident that Quinn and Roska could have defended themselves from her mother's minions. Sorry, *guards*. But it wasn't a risk she was willing to take. Plus, Elena had a feeling they were stronger together. The shattered glass all over the floor in the old testing room was evidence of that. Her mother, no, wait, *their* mother, hadn't allowed them to socialize with the rest of the girls at the school. Instead, she kept them sequestered in the southern tower and the small clearing in the Dark Woods closest to said tower. Meals were brought to them by Madame LaBelle's guards. The servants weren't even allowed near them. Madame LaBelle was scared. If Elena weren't so frightened and confused herself, she would have reveled in her mother's clear discomfort and anxiety.

Based on the crescent moon winking at her from the night sky, Elena inferred that it had been about two weeks since their revelation in the testing room. She was sitting on the edge of her cot, Agon curled up into a furry blue ball on her pillow, while she toyed with the lightning flashing on her fingertips. Since their banishment to the tower, she and the boys had been taking every opportunity they had to practice controlling their powers. It was part of the reason her mother had allowed them access to the clearing outside the castle walls. Quinn nearly burned the school's cornfields to ash. Roska had been able to quell the flames rather efficiently, in Elena's opinion. Madame LaBelle was not impressed and told them if they insisted on using their powers, they needed to do it at a safe distance from the school. She never let all three of them out at once, however. She wasn't going to let them leave, and she made sure they didn't try to escape by keeping one of them in the tower while the other two were let out to train.

It was Elena's turn to stay behind this time. Her irritation with this system was evident in her endless sparks and flashing blue lights of rage.

"We need to get out of here," she muttered, mostly to herself.

"How do you propose we do that?" Agon's lazy drawl grated on her more than being trapped in their dank tower room.

"I don't muxing know, but we need to leave. Find Belladonna again and figure out how to stop the *turmio*. Why doesn't my mother understand that? We are the only ones who can stop it. She should want to save the magical world. She's part of it! Does she want to die?" Elena tossed a bolt of lightning at the stone wall, leaving a black scar across the cold stone.

"Do you think it's possible that she's trying to protect her children? I mean, I know she's a gods awful mother, but maybe this is her twisted attempt at keeping the three of you safe?"

Agon's question hit Elena like a punch to her stomach.

"It doesn't really sound like her, does it? She's never been bothered with my safety or theirs before. Why would she start now?" Elena asked, but even as she posed the counterargument, she wondered if there was any truth to Agon's theory. Could her mother really be trying to keep them safe after so many solar cycles of neglect and disinterest? Maybe now that Elena had become interesting, and brought her brothers home to Harbor Ridge, Madame LaBelle was finally ready to step up and be a mother. Or maybe she was just being a controlling bitch, trying to manipulate the situation to better suit her needs.

Yeah, that sounded more like the Madame LaBelle she knew.

Elena was about voice all of these thoughts to Agon when the thick wooden door scraped open, and the boys returned. Lyra led the way, bounding into the room with an enthusiasm that had started to become the norm for her. Since learning the truth about their connection, Lyra seemed to act as though a weight had been lifted from her little fox shoulders. If Elena didn't know any better, she might have suspected that Lyra had known about their relationship to each other long ago. Demoni crept in quickly after her, followed by Roska and Quinn. Elena was in awe of them. Since that day in the testing room, the two of them seemed to have completely changed their views of each other. They were friendly, bordering on playful. The way they talked and teased was adorable and utterly unexpected. Elena was more surprised by Q's behavior than Roska's, simply because Q had been so vehemently opposed to keeping Roska with them in the beginning. Now, the two were practically inseparable. She probably should have been jealous of their closeness and camaraderie, but she was so grateful that they were getting along and actually liked each other. She wasn't worried about feeling left out. Not to mention she had very special bonds with each of them. They were siblings, but they had all bonded before learning that information.

Hells, Quinn was the one who saved her all those moons ago. Nothing was going to change their bond. She wasn't as close with Roska as she was with Q, but Elena knew that would come with time. Until then, she still felt a strong connection to him through the shared trust and intuition that first drew them to each other in the cavern.

"How was it today?" she asked.

"Better than yesterday. I didn't freeze myself to the ground this time," Roska replied with a chuckle. Elena laughed with him. She still wasn't sure how he'd managed it, but he had somehow turned his ice on himself when she was training with him the previous day and had frozen both of his feet together and to the marsh-like grass they'd been working in. It hadn't been funny at the time. It had been quite terrifying, and one of the guards had to use her magic to melt the ice enough to free him.

"Well, that's definitely progress," she said, a grin still wide across her face.

Quinn collapsed onto his cot, propping his head up against his folded arm, lounging as though he didn't have a care in the world. Like the weight of the magical world wasn't resting on their shoulders while they were being held prisoner by their mother.

"It was a good day," he said with a nod to Roska. "It's pretty impressive how much control he's gained in just a couple of weeks. Frozen feet notwithstanding," he added with a smirk.

"Yeah, well, at least I'm not setting the food on fire," Roska poked back.

Elena loved having a family to pick on and play around with. It was still an adjustment, and she still caught herself forgetting they were all actually related, but it was a wonderful feeling. Knowing that they would have her back regardless, and she would do the same for them.

She waited until she heard the door locked from the outside—knowing that the guards wouldn't open the door again until it was time for dinner—and turned to her brothers.

"We need to figure out a way out of here." Elena's voice was a harsh whisper as she spoke quickly to her brothers. She prayed to the Mother that the guards wouldn't be able to hear her plotting. "We need to get to Belladonna. She's the only one who's been able to give us any real information about the *turmio*. The longer we're trapped in here, the more likely it is that we won't be able to undo it."

"Yeah, El, we know, but I can't see a way out of this place. Mommy Dearest is pretty good at keeping us locked down tight," Q grumbled.

"I actually had a thought about that..." Roska said, his voice barely above a whisper.

"A thought about what? The *turmio*? Or escaping this pit?" Q sat up, leaning closer to Roska, who had positioned himself in the middle of the tower, putting himself between the door and their makeshift fireplace.

"About escaping." He kept his voice low as he continued to lay out his plan. "I think I could use my ice to freeze the hinges holding the door, then Elena could zap them with her lightning. Break the hinges, and I think the door could come off pretty easily. I was studying it the other day while you two were out training. The hinges are sturdy enough, but the door itself is starting to rot along the hinges and at the base. I think we could take it down if we can break the hinges."

"That's brilliant!" Elena exclaimed, quickly clamping her hand over her mouth. They all froze, waiting to see if the guards heard them. Surely if they had, they would come rushing in to separate the magical triplets.

"That could work," Q said, as he walked over to examine the hinges himself. He looked at the door. "This wood is really damp. I couldn't set fire to this even with my strongest blasts. I imagine it would freeze really easily, though."

Elena rose from her cot and walked over to the door with Quinn. It was clearly neglected, but still fairly solid. She had to assume that their mother simply hadn't noticed the state of disrepair within the tower, or she wouldn't have placed them there. Studying the door and its hinges, Elena was very confident in their ability to break through the door. Perhaps Madame LaBelle simply assumed that they would be content to stay in this tower until she set them free. Gods, that woman drove her mad. She didn't hate her mother anymore; she had long since accepted that the Headmistress simply wasn't built for a maternal role. Still, Elena couldn't help but feel endless resentment and pity when she pictured her mother's face. Especially the look on her face when Roska had revealed the whole truth of their relationship.

No. She refused to think about that. Elena didn't need to feel anything more for her mother. She'd devoted sixteen solar cycles of her life to trying to make Madame LaBelle proud of her. Fighting to win her approval. Killing herself to make her mother notice her. No more. She was done.

"When are we doing this?" Lyra spoke up from her spot by the fire. She had appointed herself fire keeper in their tower, always making sure that they had enough firewood to last the night. The frost season was upon them, and it was getting colder each night. A part of Elena wanted to stay in the tower, simply because venturing out into the woods without the safety and comforts of a solid roof and walls did not appeal to her. Snow was starting to fall most nights, although it wasn't quite cold enough for it to stick around. By mid-day, the sun melted it to cold, mushy puddles. In another week or so, the snow would be a more permanent fixture in their landscape. Camping in the snow was something that Elena had never desired to try.

"The sooner the better, if we want to get to Belladonna before it gets too cold." Agon voiced her concerns for her.

Demoni chimed in. "Yes," she hissed, "cold weather does not agree with me. Let's get out of here and somewhere warm as quickly as possible."

Roska picked Demoni up and she curled around his forearm, presumably using his body heat to warm her own cold-blooded form.

"Then we'll do it tonight," Elena announced. She looked her brothers in the eye in turn. "We'll wait until after dinner, that way we have some food to travel with." Elena was suddenly grateful for their drafty little tower room because it had meant that Madame LaBelle had allowed Elena and Quinn to keep their respective enchanted cloak and bag.

Elena loved the cloak Amelia had given her. Its bottomless pockets were a magical wonder that never ceased to amaze or impress. The bag she had given Quinn had belonged to her magept husband and was equally impressive in its carrying capacity.

"We don't need to worry too much about that," Quinn said with a smile. "I've been stashing away food since they put us in this damned tower. The fruit will go bad faster, obviously, but the dried meat should last us quite a while."

Elena smiled back at him. He had been planning an escape the whole time. She loved that about him. She also mentally chastised herself for not thinking and planning ahead as he'd clearly been.

"It's decided then," Roska said. "Tonight, we leave this dreadful place behind and go find your all-knowing witch."

It was clear that he wasn't as enthusiastic about seeing Belladonna, but Elena was certain he would see the wisdom in their decision once he met her. Belladonna wasn't quite "all-knowing," but she was definitely very knowledgeable, and Elena was starting to believe that she was much older than she looked. Elena hoped that that meant she would have insight into their predicament and some idea of how they might stop the *turmio* from absorbing and destroying all the magic in their world. She couldn't let herself think about what would happen if Belladonna wasn't able to help. The possibility was too devastating to consider.

2
ROSKA

ROSKA WISHED HE'D NOTICED those damn hinges sooner. He hated feeling trapped, and being literally locked away in a tower was torture. Roska hadn't slept well since they arrived at the castle. He had nightmares every single night, flashbacks to when he was a little boy and the Brothers felt the need to punish him nightly simply for existing. He woke up in cold sweats, remembering the feel of their whips on his back and their canes on his forearms. On the first night in the tower, before they'd been given cots to sleep on, he had the worst, most vivid memory-dream of the night the Brothers had held him down and cut off Demoni's wing, cauterizing the wounds with a hot iron from the fire. That was the night of their one and only escape attempt. That was the night Roska had first started to realize that the way the Brothers treated him was not the way a loving family was supposed to act.

On that night, Roska had woken up screaming, blasted ice into the air, creating icicles on the ceiling and horrifying his siblings. The look of terror and pity on Elena's face had nearly broken his heart. The understanding on Quinn's had done him in. That was the first time Roska had felt truly seen by another human, he didn't know how to handle it. He'd cried like a baby. Elena held him in her arms, gently rubbing his back and whispering words of love and kindness in his ears. Q had carefully melted the icicles from the ceiling, managing to catch most of the water in buckets that he kept pulling out of his magical bag. They had plenty of fresh water to drink after that night.

When he'd first met them in the cavern, Roska hadn't been sure how they would handle the news of their connection. He had been shocked by their willingness to accept him into their little family. It had only been a couple of weeks, but Roska felt more bonded to these two than he ever had with any of the Brothers with whom he'd spent his whole life.

That wasn't terribly surprising though, since those men spent every waking moment reminding him that he was an abomination, pure evil, and that he didn't deserve to live.

Roska had felt more love in that first night in the tower than he had in his entire life. He knew he would do anything, fight anyone, to ensure that he never lost that feeling again. He wasn't thrilled about going to see a witch, but he *mostly* convinced himself that his anxiety was baseless and purely rested on the biased, ignorant teachings of the Brotherhood. He couldn't quite shake the feeling that they were missing something. A big piece of the puzzle that they hadn't put into place yet.

They sat around Lyra's fire, quietly stewing in their respective thoughts and not saying much to each other. The tower had small windows at chest height, evenly spaced around the circumference of the whole room. There were stairs along the eastern side of the room that led to a locked door. Elena had told them that this was an old food storage space. Roska assumed that upstairs held more shelves and cupboards to hold more food, but it had long been abandoned. As such, the door wouldn't budge. They'd tried that the first day they'd been tossed in here so carelessly.

Demoni stood watch from the stairs, peeking out through the slits, and alerted them when the guards were bringing out their dinner.

"We'll have to be quick about this. These are the same guards that protect Madame LaBelle," Elena informed them. Roska noted that she seemed to have stopped referring to their birther as Mom or Mother. "They are the best of the best."

A less-than-friendly pounding on the door announced the arrival of their dinner. Three guards entered their room, one holding a large platter of food, and two with spells at the ready to stop them should the siblings try to make any moves to escape while the door was held open.

Elena gave the women a tight smile, as per usual. She couldn't seem to stop being polite to these women, even though they were the ones holding her prisoner.

Once the guards backed out of the room, Roska heard the lock click into place and Demoni resumed her perch at the window, watching until the guard who'd delivered the food was out of sight. Quinn loaded all of the food into his bag, stuffing a couple of rolls into Elena's cloak pockets for easier access, then he nodded to Roska.

Demoni hopped down the stairs and quickly up the back of his leg to ride on Roska's shoulder. Agon took a similar position around

Elena's neck while Lyra bared her sharp teeth and braced for a fight Roska desperately hoped they could win.

He crept quietly up to the doorway and listened intently at the window closest to where they knew the guards would be standing. They were having a conversation about the upcoming Frost Festival. Elena had mentioned that the school always celebrated the changing of the seasons, not unlike the witches of old. He turned back to Elena and nodded, then he placed his hands on the two hinges holding the door in place. Roska reflected for a moment on the fact that a mere two weeks ago, he hadn't even known he had magical powers. Now here he was, trusting his powers to come at his command and work exactly as he had intended for them to. It was a foolish and arrogant plan, but they didn't have any other options.

Roska stopped himself from spiraling into the endless abyss of self-doubt and focused on the feel of the metal against his hands. He closed his eyes and called to the frost center of his chest. When he'd first called his power, in the testing room where they'd been unceremoniously dumped after being spelled and kidnapped, he hadn't known what he was doing, and he hadn't felt any control. Roska ruminated on that feeling for a moment, how it had happened so suddenly, and felt as though an icy dam had burst within his chest. He knew enough now—after training with Q and Elena over the last couple of weeks—to have some control and not freeze them all to death. Still, he was worried he'd do more harm than good.

He glanced over his shoulder at his siblings. Elena was watching him with hope in her eyes. Q was clearly just waiting to pound his way through the rotten door and wasn't paying much attention to Roska's existential crisis.

You can do this. Demoni's voice in his head was a welcome distraction from his own doubt-filled thoughts. *You are more powerful than we ever thought possible, and you can easily freeze a couple of rusted, old metal hinges.*

Roska pressed his cheek against her cool scales and turned his attention back to the hinges beneath his palms. He took a deep breath and felt the ice release from within him. He tried to channel all of the cold magic into his hands and directly into the metal blocking their escape. In seconds, the hinges were covered in a thick layer of frosty white ice.

"Nice work, little bro," Q whispered encouragingly.

"Thanks." Roska stepped back from the hinges and turned to face Quinn. "But how can you be so sure you're the oldest?"

"Just a feeling, I guess. You could call it my intuition." He smirked at his own little joke. Q didn't believe in intuition, and he had mocked Elena and Roska often for so blindly trusting their own. Roska no longer bothered pointing out that Q trusted his gut on all things, and "gut" was just another word for intuition. It wasn't an argument worth having.

Elena ignored them both and took her position in front of the door. If she was nervous, she hid it well. She raised both hands, took aim, and blasted the hinges to pieces.

Roska was a little surprised at how well his plan had worked so far. The hinges didn't just break, they shattered into a million tiny fragments. The door fell outward from the force of Elena's blast and landed with a deafening crash on the cobblestone courtyard.

The guards didn't hesitate, jumping into the doorway, casting combative magics, and throwing small fireballs at their prisoners. Unfortunately for the guards, Quinn jumped in front of Elena. Quinn—who was essentially fireproof—watched with casual amusement as their fireballs bounced off his skin and sputtered out on the cold stone floor. Then he raised his hands and shot a blast of fire at them, causing them to jump out of the way or be burned alive. Roska didn't much care what happened to the guards either way, and he was confident that Q felt the same way. However, they both knew that these women were people Elena knew and once cared for, so out of respect for her, the boys didn't try to cause serious damage.

Quinn led them out of the tower, continuously spraying his flames. Demoni jumped down from Roska's shoulder and sprayed the cobblestones under the guards' feet with a layer of thick ice. The women couldn't get their bearings and quickly fell on their asses. It would have been funny if they weren't still trying to recapture the siblings. Agon followed Demoni and jumped on the guard to the left of the fallen door, zapping her with a small blast of lightning and knocking her out. Elena rushed past Q and did the same to the guard on the right.

Without another word, they grabbed the last of their supplies, threw on their respective cloaks, and Q grabbed his bag. They raced out of the tower, away from Harbor Ridge, and off into the Dark Woods in search of a witch.

3
QUINN

IN THE WEEKS THAT they'd been stuck in that damned tower, Q had been studying the landscape and tracking the animals in the area every chance he'd gotten. When it was his turn to go out and train, he'd made a point to venture farther and farther into the woods around the clearing. The guards hadn't bothered to stick too closely to them, trusting that the siblings wouldn't try to get away when one of them would have been left behind in the tower. When it came time to escape, Q had a pretty good plan to get them to Belladonna's in a matter of days. Less, if they moved through the night, but he didn't think he could convince the others to go without sleep for too long.

They raced out of the tower and away from Harbor Ridge as though the beasts of Hells were on their heels, despite not actually being chased. Yet. The idea was to get as far away as possible before anyone could be alerted that they were gone. Quinn led them due east for the first few hours, before slowly venturing slightly north.

Quinn's breath exited his nose in little puffs of white clouds as they hiked through the woods. There were no paths or trails in this part of the Dark Woods, which slowed their movements as they fought against branches and roots in the pitch black of the near-moonless night. They couldn't risk lighting a torch or using their powers to light the way without drawing unnecessary attention to themselves.

The siblings didn't speak as they hiked. Q knew that was partly due to the drain of hiking through untamed woods. He also suspected that it was because they'd just escaped from a prison their mother had locked them away in, and that was some pretty mind-blowing shyt.

Q didn't let his mind focus on the word "mother." There was far too much trauma surrounding that word and the experiences of the last couple weeks that he didn't feel capable of dealing with, possibly ever. *Muxing heartless bitch.* He felt a wave of relief as the school disappeared from view behind the massive trees.

It was a few hours before dawn when Elena grabbed his arm and asked—more like *demanded*—they stop and rest for a couple of hours.

"Madame LaBelle knows we've escaped by now. I'm not sure stopping is the safest choice," Q argued.

"Maybe not, but hiking into exhaustion and passing out isn't a safe choice either. Unless you plan on carrying my unconscious body to Belladonna's," she countered.

"I could. It's not like you're heavy," Q quibbled, but he conceded her point. "Fine, we can rest. But only for a couple of hours. We need to keep moving as much as we can."

They found a small clump of saplings that weren't much taller than Quinn, and Elena threw her cloak across it, creating a small shelter that blended in with the surroundings, thanks to the magic in the fabric. As soon as the cloak settled on the small trees, it shimmered, and they stood in awe as it changed color to blend in seamlessly with their surroundings.

Roska reached out a tentative hand to rub the cloak between his index finger and thumb. "How does it do that?" he muttered, but since none of them had the answer to that question, Q assumed it was rhetorical. He pulled out a couple of rolls from his bag, tossing one to each of them before settling down on the forest floor within their temporary shelter.

"I know we're all tired, but I'm not entirely sure where we are yet, and we need to keep moving. I say we take a quick nap and get back to the hike before the sun gets too high. Lyra, you, Agon, and Demoni keep watch and wake me in about two hours, ok?" Q had taken up the mantle of group leader the instant they'd entered the woods. Neither Elena nor Roska knew these woods as well as he did. It just made sense for him to lead them. He would get his bearings soon, once he saw something he recognized, and then they'd be able to move more quickly.

Lyra said nothing, simply nodded her head—or the fox equivalent of a nod—and moved to stand guard outside their shelter. Agon slunk along behind her, taking a post on the northern side of their tent. Demoni followed Lyra to the western side. If anyone came after them, they would likely be coming from the west. Between Lyra's bat-like ears, Agon's keen eyesight, and Demoni's ability to feel vibrations of movement through the ground—an interesting skill Q had learned about during one of their training sessions—Quinn was confident that they would have plenty of notice if one of their *mother*'s guards tried to sneak up on them.

Q, Elena, and Roska finished off their rolls, took a deep swig from one of the waterskins in Q's bag, and crawled into the makeshift tent. They curled up beside each other for warmth and were all asleep in moments.

The feel of Lyra's warm, wet tongue sliding across his face woke Q with a start, causing him to nearly jump out of his skin and whack his head on one of the small tree limbs that made up their small roof.

"Ouch! What the hells, Lyra?" He moaned, rubbing his sore head.

"You said two hours. It's been two hours. How was I supposed to know you'd try to knock yourself unconscious the moment I touched you," Lyra responded with a casual air of disinterest.

"You licked me? Why didn't you just talk? Or nudge me? Shyt, girl, that was slimy and gross," Q said, before gently shaking Elena's shoulder and reaching over her to do the same to Roska. "See? *That's* how you wake someone," Q added as his siblings roused from their sleep.

Q was very sure that if she were capable, Lyra would have rolled her eyes and stuck her tongue out at him. Instead, she flicked her tail at him, flinging a spark onto his shirt sleeve and burning a small hole through the fabric. Without a word, she turned and left the tent.

"Has it been two hours already? I feel like we just laid down," Elena mumbled, reaching her arms up to stretch, only to be stopped short by the low-hanging limbs of their shelter.

"Yeah, sorry. I think we can make it to Belladonna's today. Or at least find my hut and get some proper rest before heading upstream to her godsdamned mist." Q crawled out of the tent and stood in the cold air of the late morning. It was going to snow soon, he could feel it. They needed to keep moving, to get away from Madame LaBelle's influence. Not to mention, being stationary for too long could easily get them killed. frost season wasn't something you muxed around with. Especially not out in the woods, exposed to all the elements.

"You know where we are then?" Roska crawled out from the tent and scooped up Demoni. He coiled her around his neck, and it occurred to Q that asking the cold-blooded reptile to keep watch in the frost might not have been a good idea. He was pretty sure that a familiar couldn't die if their human was still alive, but he certainly didn't want to make her any more uncomfortable than was absolutely necessary. He debated saying something to her for a moment, but he lost his nerve and instead moved on as though nothing happened.

Chicken. Lyra's voice echoed in his head.

Shut it, he thought back to her and gave her a wry wink.

"I don't know exactly where we are yet, but I know which direction to go. The river is east of here, and my hut is right along the river. If we keep going that direction, we'll run into the water, and I'll be able to get us to my hut or Belladonna's quickly. I'm just not sure exactly how far north we are. I've never been this deep into the woods or up the mountain range. I usually steer clear of this place." Quinn cast an investigative look around the surrounding trees, half expecting enchantress guards to jump out and attack.

Elena was the last to emerge from their tent, taking her cloak off the limbs and wrapping it back around her shoulders. "That sounds like a good enough plan to me. Let's get going. It's only going to get colder, and I don't want to spend another night exposed in these woods." Agon got a running start and jumped on the back of her cloak, making quick work of climbing the rest of the way to her neck and burrowing under her fur collar. Elena pulled the hood up over her head and turned to Quinn.

Q looked at his brother and noticed he was shivering. He didn't have a thick cloak to keep him warm, only the thin one they'd swiped from one of the guards as they made their hasty escape.

"Hang on," Quinn said, rummaging through his pack. He was pretty sure Amelia had packed a spare cloak. In case his was damaged or lost. Not that he lost things often anymore, but Amelia had raised him, and she knew he wasn't always the best at keeping track of his things. "Perfect!" he cheered, half to himself, as he pulled out a long, hooded cloak from the depths of his pack. He tossed it to Roska. "Here, bro. Put this on. Gimme that other one, and I'll stash it in my pack. We might need it later."

Roska looked surprised and a little embarrassed as he caught the cloak, but his expression quickly shifted to appreciation as he buckled the clasp at his neck and felt the thick cloak settle on his shoulders.

"Thank you, *veli*," he said with a small smile.

"What does that mean?" Quinn asked. "You've called me that a few times, but I don't know that word."

Q threw his pack back over his shoulder and looped the second strap across his other shoulder. With the weight of the bag balanced over his back, he started walking toward the east, looking out for familiar landmarks.

"*Veli*? It means brother," Roska answered, following in step behind him.

"Wait. If I understood that language, I would have known since we *met* that you're my brother?" Incredulousness seeped into Q's voice.

Roska chuckled. "Yes, you would have."

"What about me? You called me something before. What does that word mean?" Elena piped up from behind Roska.

"*Tyttö*. It means sister," Roska replied. Q glanced over his shoulder to see a smirk on his brother's lips. Elena laughed.

"Well, I feel ignorant and silly now. If only I'd known that language, we could have avoided a very awkward and destructive event in the testing room," Elena said.

Q looked back at her to see if she was upset by this revelation. He let go of the breath he hadn't realized he was holding when he saw the smile on her face. She thought all of this was amusing. Q wasn't sure he shared her feelings; he still felt like they'd been blindsided by the whole thing.

"If you knew all this time, why didn't you tell us sooner?" Q asked. He needed an explanation for all the shyt they'd been through over the last few weeks.

"Would you have believed me?" Roska asked. He wasn't defensive, and his voice didn't carry a hint of annoyance or anger. He was genuinely curious.

Q thought about it for a moment. When they first met Roska—just a few weeks ago—they'd assumed he was the enemy. Kick-starting the end of the world, destroying all magic, and ultimately causing the deaths of hundreds—if not thousands—of creatures including themselves. Q knew now that Roska had been brainwashed and willfully misled by their true enemy, The Brotherhood, but if Roska had told them in that cavern that he was their brother? That the three of them were all siblings? Not just siblings, but triplets? Q was certain he would have labeled Roska a nutter, just like Fàidh, and ignored everything he had to say.

Rather than admit all of that out loud, Q simply shook his head no.

"I didn't intend for the revelation to be quite *so* dramatic," Ros added, "but I didn't know what else to say. That woman, our *mother*," he spat the word out as though it left a sour taste in his mouth, "didn't give me much of a choice. I was hoping she'd tell you both herself when we all stood before her, but I should have known better. She is incapable of honesty."

Q felt the same way, but he wasn't sure Elena did. After all, the woman might have been a shyt mom, but she had at least been a part of El's life. Q imagined it would be hard for her to let go of that attachment. If he was being honest with himself, he didn't really want El to cut herself off from her mother. Their mother. Sure, she was an awful human being, but he knew how much she meant to

Elena, and he desperately hoped, for Elena's sake, that their mother had some redeeming qualities. Maybe she'd see the damage she'd done to her children and it would force her to change. Be a decent parent. Or at least not a completely wretched one.

4

BEATRICE

MADAME LaBELLE SLID OUT from between the silken bedsheets and slipped into her dressing robe, lightly tying the rope around her waist. She checked her visage in the mirror and caught the reflection of the man sprawled across her bed. Beatrice cringed internally. She didn't particularly enjoy sleeping with men, but she maintained this relationship with the King for obvious reasons. She also insisted that he always come to her. She often told him it was because she was trying to avoid the suspicious looks from his wife, the Queen, but in truth, her motives were far less altruistic. It was simply easier to have her guards kick him out by bringing her "pressing issues" than when Beatrice had tried to extricate herself from his grasp on the few occasions that she had visited him at the palace in the beginning of their physical relationship.

When she'd received his missive a few days prior, Beatrice had tried to delay his visit. She didn't want to tell him about her children but she couldn't come up with an acceptable excuse to postpone their regular tryst, so she had been forced to welcome him into her bedroom yet again. The fool always had the worst timing. Beatrice was certain that she would be able to get through to her children, explain her side of things, and convince them they were safer within the castle walls of Harbor Ridge, she just needed a few more days. And that self-important windbag had to insist on showing up in the middle of everything, keeping her from her children.

Beatrice was about to signal Zied to send in her perfectly timed interruption when one of her guards rushed in without warning. The woman had the decency to look embarrassed and averted her eyes. Beatrice tightened the robe around her waist, and the King stirred in the bed, grunting as he rolled onto his back and pulled the quilt across his lap.

"Apologies, Headmistress," the guard said, still staring at the floor. "We have an issue that requires your immediate attention."

The guard never looked up, but Beatrice could see the pink in her cheeks and she appeared to be slightly out of breath. Beatrice didn't respond to the guard, turning to the King instead.

"Darling, I hope you'll forgive me, but I must attend to the girls and my school. I'm sorry to cut our visit short. I'm sure you understand." She kept her voice light, lacing her words with a sense of apology and disappointment that she didn't feel.

"I do, dearest. Running a school is like running a country, on a much smaller scale." His voice was gruff, and his words grated on her. The level of condescension in his tone made her want to bash his brains in. Or, at the very least, use her magic to cause him to trip going down the stairs. She didn't really want to kill him—he was still quite useful to her—but breaking a limb might make him less smug.

Instead, she merely nodded and allowed him to plant a sloppy kiss on her cheek as he slipped on his leather riding pants, loosely tucked in his shirt, and carried his boots in hand as he left the room. The guards that stood watch outside her door would escort him out to the stables where he would mount up and meet his guards outside the walls of Harbor Ridge. The King was the only man permitted within the school, aside from the eunuchs who worked in the school as part of the maintenance crew.

Once the door was closed firmly behind his receding figure, Madame LaBelle turned to back to the guard.

"What's going on?" she demanded as she walked over to her wardrobe and selected a long, flowing black gown.

The guard stepped forward and helped Madame LaBelle out of her robe and nightdress, and into the soft fabric of the onyx dress. The guard seemed hesitant to answer the question, but Madame LaBelle simply held the woman's gaze in the mirror while the guard completed the final buttons of the dress at the back of her neck.

Cautiously, the woman cleared her throat, cast her eyes down to study her boots, and said, "The children have escaped."

Ice flowed through her veins as the words registered in her mind. Zied, sensing that something was amiss, forced her bedroom door open with his large, furry white head. His sharp teeth bared and his black claws left small scratches on the stone at the threshold of her room. He immediately calmed his face and sheathed his claws as he held her gaze. Madame LaBelle knew that she needed to keep her cool, be steady and appear almost unfeeling, in order to maintain the visage of a powerful woman in control. Internally, Beatrice felt as though her world were crumbling under her feet.

She said nothing for several moments as she tried to regain her self-control. To her credit, the guard didn't waver under Madame LaBelle's scrutiny or the deafening silence that filled the room. Finally, Beatrice spoke. "How?"

"It appears as though they combined their powers, freezing and demolishing the hinges of the door before knocking the guards unconscious and fleeing into the woods."

"When did this happen?" Beatrice questioned. She impressed herself with her ability to keep her voice level and unwavering.

The guard studied her boots again, shifting her weight from one foot to the other. Madame LaBelle noticed the snake wrapped around the guard's neck.

"I will not ask again." Madame LaBelle's words carried a heavy threat, reinforced by the presence of Zied as he came fully into the room, taking a seat at her side.

"It seems they escaped last night, Headmistress. Just after dinner was served."

Rage flowed off Beatrice in waves. The temperature of the room dropped as her anger and fear built up within. She stood still, frozen in place, processing the news and trying to contain her rage before she lashed out at this woman. This guard had not been one of the women keeping watch over Madame LaBelle's children. Taking her anger out on the messenger wouldn't be productive.

Beatrice felt Zied's head press against her thigh. Absentmindedly, she scratched behind his ears, distracting herself and calming her mind.

"Why am I just finding out about this now?" she asked the guard, her voice barely above a whisper.

"Apologies, Headmistress. We didn't realize they'd escaped until shift change this morning. The guards on duty last night were still unconscious when the morning shift arrived with breakfast. It seems your daughter's lightning is quite effective at knocking people out." The guard's last comment brought a feeling of pride to Beatrice's heart for a moment, but it was quickly quashed by the sense of dread at knowing that her children were loose in the world.

"The investigators have already been tasked with tracking them down," the guard continued. "They seemed optimistic that the children wouldn't get too far last night. Between the rapidly dropping temperatures and a lack of supplies, the investigators thought they'd have your children back home by the end of the day."

Madame LaBelle nodded and dismissed the guard, who practically raced out of the room, quickly closing the door behind her.

Beatrice remained standing in the middle of her room, staring out the window, watching the snowflakes as they drifted by. She didn't share the same confidence as the guard. Her children were resourceful. They would not be so easily captured again.

"They will find the triplets," Zied said, trying to reassure her.

"They will, but will it be too late?" Beatrice wondered aloud.

"They are strong, capable children. They will be ok." Zied rubbed his head against her thigh, trying to shake her out of her thoughts.

"I just wanted to keep them safe. I never wanted this for them." Beatrice released a breath that sounded eerily like a sob.

"I know," Zied cooed.

"I only ever wanted them to be happy and well taken care of. I never would have imagined their lives would take such turns and lead them to this." She took two steps backward and sat down hard onto her mussed bed.

Zied followed her to the bed, resting his massive skull on her lap, and cautiously licked her hand.

Beatrice had always known her children would change the world. She just never thought it would hurt this much.

5

ROSKA

H E DIDN'T KNOW WHERE they were or where they were going, but the one thing Roska did know was that when Quinn
handed him that cloak, he'd nearly buried his face in it and wept at
the small act of kindness. To Quinn, it must have seemed like such a
simple, casual action. To Roska, it was the first act of selfless kindness
that any man had offered him. Ever.

Rather than burst into grateful tears, he kept his eyes focused on
the ground before him and kept placing one foot in front of the
other. He didn't want Quinn to think him weak for crying over a
cloak.

Weakness has nothing to do with it, and Q would recognize that.
He heard Demoni's voice in his mind.

Perhaps, he thought back to her, *but I'd still prefer to keep my
emotions to myself. For all we know, my tears would come out as
tiny snowballs and attract Mother's guards.* It was a weak excuse for
locking down his emotions, but he felt like it was valid enough that
she wouldn't push it.

Perhaps, but bottling up your emotions isn't healthy or productive,
she replied. That was the end of it though. Demoni made a good

point, and they both knew it so there was no reason to discuss it further. If Roska took the time to examine why he felt instantly compelled to hide his emotions, and why he was worried that his siblings would view his tears as a weakness, he would have been thrown back into memories of his childhood and the abuses he suffered at the hands of the Brothers. That was not a mental route he felt comfortable going down.

He trudged along between Quinn and Elena, feeling on edge and yet oddly at peace. He'd finally found his family, and it wasn't anything like he'd expected. The Brotherhood had drilled into him that his siblings were pure evil. That they were all the product of pure evil and his siblings would be cruel and hateful to him because that was the nature of evil. Instead, they had been open and welcoming from the start. Roska felt more comfortable and welcomed by his siblings in the mere weeks that he'd known them than he had in the entirety of his tenure with the Brothers.

Roska was shaken out of his own thoughts by the sound of something cracking in the distance, to the north of their location. Quinn held up his hand, and they all froze in place. He turned to face them both, moving excruciatingly slowly, and held a single finger to his lips, signaling them to stay quiet, before motioning for them all to get low to the ground and try to blend in. As Q was signaling his directions to Roska and Elena, Roska saw Lyra slip silently off in the direction of the noise. Roska was amazed at how fluidly she moved between the low branches and avoided making a single sound as she crept quickly toward the source of the disruption.

After a few tense moments, Quinn stood back up and said, "False alarm. Looks like we spooked a family of deer."

Elena exhaled a sigh of relief, creating a large cloud in the cold air. "Thank the Mother. I don't know what we'd do if we ran into any of Madame LaBelle's investigators."

"I'd just set the woods on fire, and we'd run like the dogs of Hells were at our heels," Q said with a chuckle.

Roska admired his brother's levity in such a time of stress and tension, but he didn't share it.

"You would not!" Elena said, her voice held the tone of an irritated school teacher. Or, at least, what Roska imagined a schoolteacher would sound like when they were irritated. He never actually had schoolteachers.

"I absolutely would, and they would deserve any injuries they got." The levity had drained from Q's voice, leaving only anger and disdain.

"That's not fair, Quinn," Roska said. "They were simply following orders when they brought us to the school, and more orders still when they kept us there."

"Maybe so, but they should have known it was wrong and done something to help us. Blindly following orders isn't an excuse for being heartless and cruel. To anyone." Quinn's voice was harsh, but Roska knew his barely contained hatred wasn't directed at him. Quinn hated their mother and her guards, with good reason.

Roska had no argument against his statements. Instead, he merely nodded and opted to change the subject. "Any idea how much longer until we reach your hut?" he asked.

"I'm not entirely sure, but I think we should get there by sundown. I've seen a few trees and small landmarks that I recognize. We are getting close."

Roska nodded again, then glanced to the sky. He wasn't as comfortable in nature as Q, but he had a sense that it was late afternoon and would be getting dark in a couple of hours. More than anything, Roska was looking forward to sleeping somewhere warm and secure. Their midday nap in the woods had left him feeling more exhausted than he'd been before they stopped.

Elena dug around in her cloak and passed around some jerky and rolls for them to enjoy as they walked so they wouldn't have to stop for a full meal. They were all eager to put as much space between them and their mother as possible.

"I'll make a proper stew when we get to the hut if anyone is still hungry," Elena offered as she passed her waterskin to Roska, who nodded his thanks before taking a swig and passing the water to Quinn.

"That would be great," Quinn said

"Yes, please," Roska added. "A nice stew would definitely help warm us up."

"Well then, pick up the pace, slowpokes," Elena teased. "I can't make stew if it's too dark to see by the time we get there."

Quinn was right. They found the main road that led out of the Dark Woods and followed along next to it while keeping within the shelter of the woods themselves until they heard the sound of the river. Then they turned north, following the water upstream. Quinn stopped at the water's edge and began unloading his pack when they reached a mass of tree branches and undergrowth.

"What are you doing?" Roska asked, glancing around. "Why are we stopping here? I thought you said we'd make it to your hut tonight." Roska didn't like the idea of spending the night exposed to the elements. If they weren't going to make it to Q's hut, then they needed to find shelter for the night.

Quinn chuckled and stood from where he'd been kneeling at the edge of the river. He smirked at Roska, walking calmly over to the mass of overgrowth that had taken over the bottom half of a tree about ten paces from the river. Without a word, Q moved some fallen branches and revealed an entry into a small but cozy-looking space. Lyra bounded in behind Q and flicked her tail at the stone circle positioned in the center of the small room. A fire roared to life, giving Roska a clear picture of Quinn's quaint—but quite comfortable and secure—home.

Roska said nothing. His jaw hung open as he admired the space. Every nook and cranny served a purpose, yet it felt like there was plenty of room for the three of them and their familiars to stay without being cramped or uncomfortable. He took slow, careful steps into the room, feeling Quinn's watchful gaze follow his every movement. Q was waiting for his opinion, he realized.

"This place is amazing," Roska finally said, his voice a reverent whisper.

Quinn seemed to beam at Roska's small words of praise. Roska had no idea his words meant much to his newfound brother, but he watched Quinn's expression change from expectant to borderline exultant. Q was proud of his home, and he wanted to make sure that Roska appreciated his efforts.

Elena staggered in behind them, struggling under the weight of a large pot she had filled with water. "If you are done showing off your hut," she grunted, "would you mind helping me out here?"

"Oh, shyt, yeah! Gimme that." Q grabbed the pot from her hands and hung it on the hook attached to the cooking spit over the fire.

"What else do you need?" Roska asked.

"Well, I could use some herbs from the garden. Parsley, thyme, and some basil, if there's any left. Do you know what they look like?" Elena asked him.

"I do. The Brothers insisted on teaching me the basics of botany and herb identification before they gave me the task of cooking for the monastery." It was one of the few lessons that Roska had truly enjoyed and benefitted from. And Brother Liam was a very kind old man. Unlike most of the Brothers, he took the time to actually teach Roska and get to know him some. Of all the Brothers, Brother Liam was the only one who never once hurt or was cruel to him.

"Perfect," Elena said, though it was clear to Roska that she didn't seem to think anything about the Brotherhood or their influence on him was perfect. "Quinn will show you the way to the garden, but then I need you to check the traps and see if there are any rabbits waiting to be dinner." She turned her back to them then, pulling carrots and potatoes out of her cloak pockets and lining them up along the floor next to a large, flat rock Roska assumed would be their table for the evening. She pulled a small knife from her belt and began slicing the root vegetables and dropping them into the pot of water.

"Come on, the garden is back this way, up the river a bit." Quinn placed his hand on Roska's shoulder and guided him back out into the woods.

The sun was setting quickly, making it hard to see, but Agon accompanied them to the garden. The electric weasel allowed some of his power to leak out, causing him to glow a gentle blue and provided them with enough light to find all the herbs Elena had requested. Demoni, Agon, and Roska made quick work of collecting the herbs. Roska was impressed that they'd been able to find all that Elena had wanted this far into the frost season, but he reasoned that the snow hadn't fallen too harshly within the woods yet, so the garden hadn't been killed off.

They headed back to the hut, the smell of the fire and stew drifting out to guide them back. Elena was skilled with a knife. Far more so than Roska would have imagined, especially for someone who was raised in a castle filled with magic and servants to do all the mincing and dicing for her. He watched her slice and chop with practiced speed and skill. It was mesmerizing.

Roska wasn't sure how much time had passed, but at some point, while watching Elena cut up the vegetables, he'd drifted off to sleep. He awoke to the sound of Quinn saying his name and nudging his arm. Roska was leaning against the back wall of the hut, and based on the pain in his neck, his head had fallen forward to rest on his chest when he'd drifted off to sleep.

"Here, eat this." Quinn nudged him again, handing him a wooden bowl filled nearly to the brim with Elena's fragrant stew.

Roska took the bowl and the subsequent spoon, taking a deep breath of the steam rising from the bowl and letting loose a long sigh of relief. He filled the spoon with broth, a chunk of potato, and a sliver of meat, but he froze just before he lifted the spoon to his lips.

"Is this stew... spelled?" he asked cautiously.

Elena looked like she was trying to hide a laugh when she answered. "No, Roska, it's not spelled. I didn't want to wake you to ask, and I would never use a spell on you without your consent. Especially knowing how distrustful of magic you are. I promise. I will never spell anything for you without talking to you first."

Her smile was so kind and genuine that Roska felt a little foolish for questioning her about the stew in the first place.

"I appreciate that, *tyttö*." He returned her smile and spooned the stew into his mouth, not even minding that it was still quite warm and burned his tongue. He grunted his approval and appreciation for the dish through spoonfuls of the delicious meal.

"You do see the irony in your attitude about magic, right?" Q asked him, between spoonfuls of his own bowl. "I mean, you are literally magic yourself. A spelled stew shouldn't be a big deal."

"Hush, Q," Elena cut in. "He's entitled to his own opinions."

"Yeah," Q argued, "but these aren't his opinions. His hatred of magic isn't even his own issue. It was forced on to him since he was a baby by those damned Brothers."

"Yes, *veli*, that's true," Roska said, "but it's hard to undo one's upbringing so quickly. I spent cycles hearing and *knowing* that magic was the root of all evil in this world. I'm sure I'll let that mentality go at some point, but it will take me some time."

"I get that. I'm just saying, the best way to get over something is to try new things. Like spelled stew," Quinn said with a wink and a slurp of his dinner.

"I'll take that under advisement," Roska replied with a smirk and a slurp of his own.

6

ELENA

ELENA SAT BACK, RESTING against the wall of the hut, enjoying the gentle bickering between her brothers. *I wish we could just stay like this forever.*

That would be great, Agon's voice echoed in her head. *You know, until the* turmio *erases all of magic and we all die.*

Even in her head, his deadpan sarcasm made her chuckle.

Yes, fine, she thought back to him, scratching behind his ears as he lay comfortably in her lap. *I'm not saying we actually stay here forever, just that this is a nice change from the hells of the last few weeks.*

Annoying as it was, Agon made a good point. They still had a long road before them, and they really had no idea what they were going to do. They didn't know how to stop the *turmio*. They were blindly hoping that Belladonna would have insights that could help them. She'd been helpful before—in a sort of roundabout way—so Elena was optimistic that she'd be able to point them in the right direction at least.

"We're gonna be ok." She'd spoken the words aloud unintentionally, but her brother stopped eating and bickering, looking up at her with confused but amused smiles.

With both of them facing her like this, she could clearly see the family resemblance. Their coloring was different—Quinn being more olive-toned simply from having more exposure to the sun—but they had the same full lips, the same nose, and the same thick eyelashes curtaining dark eyes. It was astonishing to her now, knowing the truth of their parentage, that she hadn't noticed the physical similarities between the two of them sooner.

Well, we were in a bit of a rush when we first met Roska, Agon offered. He was the king of understatements.

"Of course we will," Q said, oblivious to her studious eyes roving his face.

"Yes, the witch will help. I know this is primarily my fault—" Roska started, but Elena cut him off with a glare. "What I mean is, I know the ritual that released the *turmio.* If we can combine my knowledge with the witch's insights, perhaps we'll be able to reverse the process before any permanent damage is done."

His logic seemed reasonable enough. Roska knew more about the *turmio* than she or Quinn, which meant Elena was left relying heavily on her blind optimism and arguably naive hope to save the world and stop the *turmio.*

"I'm still surprised that the Brotherhood was so willing to use a magical creature to cast what was essentially an insanely powerful spell, to release another magical creature to kill off magic," Elena mused, fiddling with her spoon in the dregs of her stew.

"It was a justifiable means to their ends, I suppose," Roska offered.

"I guess. Did they ever mention where they found the spell?" Elena asked. Maybe if they knew where the spell came from, they could find the reversing spell there as well.

"The Brotherhood wouldn't have shared that information with me," Roska said but with a hint of something mischievous in his eyes. He ate another spoonful of his dinner before continuing. "I remember the night it was delivered though."

"Wait, what do you mean, 'delivered?'" Q asked around a mouthful of carrots.

"I mean exactly that. The ritual, including most of the ingredients, was delivered by messenger a few moons prior. It was a full moon. I could clearly see the man as he rode in like the hounds of Hells were at his heels. He rode through the gates and met with Elder Fawn who immediately sent him with multiple guards to meet with the Grandmaster. I overheard the messenger's conversation with the Elder, telling him that he'd been sent by a friend with similar beliefs to deliver a cure to the scourge of magic. Within days of that delivery, I was taken from my daily chores to begin my training to complete the ritual."

"Do you know where the messenger was from? Was he wearing any distinguishable colors or symbols?" Q asked.

"On the shoulder of his armor there was a symbol of a sun with a rose blooming in the center of it," Roska explained. "I've seen the symbol since that night, but I don't know what it represents. Is it familiar to either of you?"

All the blood drained from Elena's face.

She knew that symbol. She'd seen it at least once a month, every month for as long as she could remember. It was the symbol the royal soldiers wore on their tunics, carried banners of, had embroidered into their horses' saddle pads.

It was the symbol of the King and Queen. A symbol of their royal union. The fire of the Sun King, as he liked to call himself, and the gentle but fierce protective love of his Rose Queen.

"Are you absolutely certain that is the symbol you saw?" Elena pressed, hoping against hope that Roska had gotten it wrong somehow.

"Yes, I'm certain. Why? Is this bad?"

"Oh, man, it's more than bad," Quinn answered. "That's the symbol of the King."

Roska's shocked gaze shot between the two of them.

"Why would the King want to destroy magic?" Elena wondered. "I mean, I know he's a pompous ass sometimes, but he's not stupid. Mother's magic is the only thing keeping him in power half the time. He would be an idiot to kill her now." Elena couldn't fathom the sheer arrogance it would take for a man like the King to try and murder the most powerful enchantress in Waverly.

"Maybe he thinks he doesn't need her anymore? Maybe he thinks erasing all magic from this world would free him from her control as well as weaken his enemies and keep him in power," Quinn suggested. He spoke to his bowl, clearly not too bothered by the conversation as he finished off the last of the stew. He froze mid-bite and looked up at her, locking eyes for a moment in an unexpected fit of tension and raw nerves. "Maybe he thinks that this is the only way to kill her and rid the world of magic. Making him the strongest, most powerful person in Waverly."

As the gravity of his words sank in, Elena was gripped with a new wave of anxiety and undeniable terror. If there was no one there to stop him, the King would overrun not just Waverly, but the whole world. He'd never been very good at keeping his ambitions to himself. Madame LaBelle was the only thing keeping him from starting a war with Rolam, their neighbor to the west who had considerably better fishing and access to warm water seaports cycle-round. Elena hadn't cared much for her geography lessons as a child—and she was loathe to admit it now—but they actually were relevant to her life.

"He wants to build an empire. If magic is removed from the world, it would be a much smoother path for him. I imagine he'd start with Rolam and quickly go from there to expand overseas, likely enslaving as he went. He hated that Mother made him end his slavery practices. He always said how much cheaper it was running the castle before Mother insisted on freeing the slaves and offering them paid positions in the capital." Elena had lost track long ago of how many times she'd listened to the King whine and complain to Mother about the increase in the castle maintenance costs once she'd convinced him to release his slaves. It was one of the few genuinely kind and selfless things Elena had witnessed Mother do.

But that was nearly ten solar cycles ago. It didn't seem quite fitting that he would decide to end her life and her power over him after all that time. They were missing something. Elena didn't know yet what, but she prayed to the Mother Goddess that Belladonna would have some useful information about stopping or reversing the *turmio*. If they were really lucky, she would also have insights into why the King would choose to eradicate magic now when he'd been so thoroughly benefitting from it for so many solar cycles. Elena knew that the King was a power-hungry, arrogant bastard, she also was fairly confident that he was thoroughly in love with Madame LaBelle. Wasn't he?

7

QUINN

T HE SUN SHONE BRIGHTLY through the branches of the evergreens that surrounded his hut by the river. Q had awoken before dawn to run through his morning rituals. He checked his traps for fresh meat, stoked the fire, collected more wood to keep it burning throughout the morning, collected water from the river, and checked the nets he left in the flowing water overnight, in the hopes of having fresh fish for breakfast. He and Lyra worked through their morning routine with practiced ease, even though it had been many moons since they last followed it. They'd spent so much time at Amelia's since Elena had arrived that Quinn was impressed by his own muscle memory and subconscious actions. He didn't even have to pay attention to what his hands were doing while he was completing his morning tasks. It gave him plenty of time to focus on the larger problems that lay before them.

Belladonna would probably help them if she could, but Q wasn't confident that she would have much insight that she hadn't already shared. She didn't seem to know too much when they'd seen her last, and he found it hard to believe that she would have willingly kept useful information from them. Not when their quest and the *turmio* put her life at risk too. If nothing else, Q trusted the witch's sense of self-preservation to keep her honest and upfront with them. That didn't mean that she would be happy or friendly about it though.

Quinn was just finishing cooking their breakfast—fresh trout from his river nets with a side of Amelia's biscuits, warmed by the fire, and peppermint tea with wild honey—when Elena and Roska stirred.

"Good morning, sleepy heads!" He was being overly cheerful to annoy them. Q had learned during their time in the tower that his siblings weren't morning people, and he found that irritating them when they first woke up was hilarious.

"Gods," Elena moaned, rubbing the sleep from her eyes, "will you ever not be perky in the morning?" She smiled as she took the chipped, wooden cup of steaming tea he offered her, inhaling the warm, minty scent, before taking a slow sip of the hot beverage.

"Nope," Quinn said, returning her smile and offering a second cup of tea to Roska. "I've been up for hours. I've mapped out the route we need to take, checked for any sign that the investigators have caught on to our trail, and made you this delicious feast." He gestured to the fish and biscuits, "I believe the words you're looking for are, 'Thank you, dear brother. What ever would we do without you?'"

He chuckled as Roska flicked a piece of his biscuit at him, skillfully catching it in his mouth and smiling with an obnoxious amount of pride, deliberately trying to get them riled up. At least if they were annoyed with him, they wouldn't be worried about the weight of the task that lay before them.

"How far is this witch's cottage?" Roska asked, popping the last of his honey-soaked biscuit into his mouth.

"It's about a day's hike to her fog. Then, hopefully, she'll be waiting to escort us through it so we don't have to try and force our way through that magical hells of a boundary." Quinn shuddered recalling the first time he'd ventured into that fog when he was younger, searching for the source of the river by his hut. He could still vividly recall the sounds and smells of the blazing house and the screams of his abusive foster parents as he burned them alive in their home.

"I believe she will be," Elena said. "She will sense that we're coming, and I know she'll want to help us in any way that she can."

Quinn didn't share his sister's optimism, but there was no point in voicing that. Elena knew how he felt about the witch.

"We should get going." He stood up from his log seat by the fire, dusting off his pants.

Elena rose from her spot on the floor, shifting her cloak from its previous position as a blanket to its more permanent location wrapped around her neck, closed the clasp, and shook the dirt from her hair.

Agon and Demoni—who'd spent the night sleeping curled together by the fire—returned to the shoulders of their respective humans, saying nothing, but clearly ready to go.

Roska stepped outside, presumably to relieve himself, as Elena slipped off across the river to do the same. Quinn smothered the fire and collected the last of their breakfast to eat on the way. They would reach Belladonna's fog by sunset. If they were very lucky, she'd be waiting for them. If not, Quinn hoped that the lean-to that he and Elena had used as shelter last time was still standing and would work to shelter them against the deadly cold of the frost season weather.

Their hike upstream was blissfully uneventful. Quinn was confident that he'd never used the word blissfully before, but it was the perfect word to describe the peaceful, beautiful hike through the Dark Woods. They'd eaten lunch as they walked, talked about nothing important, and teased each other endlessly. It almost felt like they were just a group of siblings on a hike rather than the products of a prophetic birth on a quest to save the entire world from a sentient black cloud hells-bent on eradicating magic and killing all magical beings.

Blissful. You sound like a pompous ass, but honestly, I don't hate it. Even Lyra's mocking tone couldn't bring him down. Quinn felt light and almost happy for the first time in more cycles than he could remember.

I don't actually think you've ever been this happy, Lyra's voice echoed in his head again.

I think you're right. I've always felt like something was missing. Like I was missing a part of myself. With Elena and Roska, though, I feel like I'm finally whole. Quinn cringed at the cheesiness of his thoughts. A solar cycle ago, he would have beat his own ass for thinking such foolish and childish things. But there he was—with the two people he was literally created and brought into the world with—and he knew that the thoughts were entirely accurate.

Q didn't like to dwell on his past too much, simply because there was no point. Thinking about all the shyt he'd been through didn't make it any easier. It did, however, tend to put him in a grouchy mood. He also didn't put much time or energy into playing the "what if...?" game. What if he'd been taken in by Amelia from the beginning? What if he'd been raised by people who truly cared about him? What if his mother had actually chosen to keep him? What if.

What if's didn't matter because his past was what made him into the strong, independent, self-reliant—arguably highly traumatized—person he was, and he genuinely liked himself. He was proud of his ability to take care of himself and those he cared about. He was proud of his home and the life he'd built for himself. He was even proud of how he handled those muxing bastard foster parents and the way he took care of his foster siblings afterward.

However, walking the woods with his blooded siblings over the last few days had been a revelation. What if he had been raised with them from the beginning? How different would their lives have been if they'd been allowed to stay together? Realistically, it didn't matter, but Q couldn't help wondering how things could have been. Not to mention, if they hadn't been separated, then Roska would never have been brainwashed by those muxing brothers. He never would have kick-started the *turmio* and the three of them wouldn't be on a most-likely-doomed quest to save magic and their own lives.

None of it really mattered because he couldn't change the past, but it was interesting to think about while they walked in companionable silence for the last stretch of the hike upstream.

"Whoa," Roska spoke up, breaking the silence and stopping in his tracks. "That... *that* is not a fog or a mist." His mouth hung open, eyes wide with amazement.

"Well, how would you describe it?" Elena asked, nudging his shoulder with her own as she brushed passed him.

"A wall. A cloud wall designed to keep anyone and everyone at bay." Roska still hadn't moved, but at least he blinked. Q was worried that his brother's eyes might pop out of his head if he stayed like that much longer.

"Yeah. That's what we said," Q said with a smirk. "A mist-fog-cloud-wall."

Quinn turned from his brother and started looking around for their previous campsite. There was a thin layer of frost covering the ground and the tree branches, making things look different from before. Q hoped that meant that no one else had seen their lean-to and it would still be waiting to house them overnight.

"What are you staring at, boy?" The clipped voice of an irritated woman came from behind Q causing him to spin around quickly, drawing his dagger in one smooth motion.

Before he knew what happened, the dagger flew from his hand and buried its blade in the half-frozen forest floor a few paces away.

"Belladonna!" Elena's squeal of excitement startled the birds that were nesting in the trees above them.

"Hello, dear," Belladonna replied, welcoming Elena into her arms in a warm, near-maternal, hug. "I'm glad to see you escaped your mother's prison. And it feels like you've got a better handle on your powers." She turned to eye Q harshly before adding, "It looks like both of you have."

She still looked at him with disdain and contempt. Quinn hated her.

No, you don't. Lyra echoed in his mind.

Fine, maybe I don't hate *her, but I definitely don't like her. I hate the way she looks at me. What the hells did I ever do to her?*

"*You* didn't do anything to me, boy," Belladonna said to him, annoyance dripping from her words. She didn't elaborate.

"Belladonna, I'd like you to meet our brother. Roska, this is Belladonna." Elena took Roska's hand and led him closer to the witch. He still hadn't moved from where he'd rooted himself upon seeing her boundary.

Q wasn't sure, but he thought Roska might be leaving frosty footprints in his wake. It was hard to tell, what with there being frost on most things already.

Belladonna nodded her head in greeting but didn't reach out to touch him until her eyes caught on Demoni, coiled around Roska's neck, flicking her tongue out at the witch.

"Hello, sweetling," Belladonna cooed, directing her words to Demoni and all but ignoring the ice dragon's human companion.

Demoni didn't say anything, but she shifted her weight to better cover Roska's jugular while giving herself a better angle to study the witch.

"You needn't be afraid of me," Belladonna said in a surprisingly soothing voice. "I'm not going to hurt you."

"You're a witch," Roska finally spoke. He said the word as though it were a curse in itself.

"Aye," Belladonna replied, her eyes shifting their focus from Demoni to Roska. "I am a witch. But I'm not the villain your Brothers made me out to be."

"They aren't my Brothers," Roska replied, his voice barely above a whisper.

"I'm sorry for what you endured at the hands of those monsters, boy." Belladonna's voice was kind. Genuinely kind. It should have made Q feel good to see her kindness extended to his brother, but he couldn't deny the wave of jealousy and rage that overwhelmed him.

"What? What is it now, boy?" Belladonna turned on him, eyebrows raised incredulously.

"Look, I appreciate that you're being nice to him and all, but what the hells? I thought you hated men. That's why you're such a—" Q started, but Elena cut him off when she stepped in front of him, holding her hands up in an effort to calm him.

"Q, you need to take a step back," she said. "You're getting a little heated."

It took him a second to understand that she was speaking literally. Q's hands were glowing a bright, warm orange, and he'd unintentionally melted the frost that had settled on the trees and forest floor around him.

Quinn took a couple of steps away from the group, inhaling deeply and trying to will himself into a more relaxed mental space.

The group watched him but didn't follow or say a word until he quelled the heat and returned to speak with Belladonna in a more level tone.

"I thought you hated all men," Q stated.

"I don't hate men. I don't trust men, but I don't hate or write off the entire male half of the human race." Belladonna replied calmly.

"Then why do you hate me?" Q threw his hands up in exasperation. He didn't really care if Belladonna liked him, but it was easier to be disliked if he knew *why* the person was so hostile towards him.

"It's not you, I told you that already," she replied simply.

Quinn glanced at his sister, hoping to find some answers or reassurance. She shrugged and shook her head. Roska held a look of utter confusion.

"Then what is it?" Quinn pressed, turning back to Belladonna. "Why are you so hostile to me, but not Elena or Roska?"

"Would you prefer I be hostile to you all?"

"No! Gods." Q could feel his anger getting the better of him again, so he paused and took a few more deep breaths before he said, "Please, just tell me what's wrong with me that you dislike me so much."

"Honestly, I'm surprised you care," Belladonna said, studying his face. She must have seen the emotions playing across his face—anger, jealousy, confusion, hurt—because she finally said, "I thought you would have figured it out when you saw her."

"Saw who?" Elena asked quietly.

"Your mother." Belladonna didn't break her eye contact with Q when she answered Elena's question.

"What does she have to do with anything?" Q had his power reined in tight, but he was worried that if she kept talking in circles and avoiding direct answers, he might lose it.

"You look so much like her. I can't look at you without seeing her." Belladonna dropped her eyes at these words. Like it physically hurt her to say them.

Quinn didn't know what to say. He just stared at her in disbelief. *What the mux?*

8

ELENA

Elena stepped up to her brother, placing a hand on his arm, feeling the heat of his fire pulsating just below the surface of his skin. Her touch brought his focus to her eyes, and she smiled gently, trying to bring him some calm and peace.

"You do look a lot like Madame LaBelle, Quinn." Elena kept her voice soft. She was worried if they pushed too much, or said the wrong thing, Q might lose control and start a forest fire.

Q showed no signs of having heard her words; his face stayed frozen in a state of confused shock. As Elena studied his features now, she could clearly see the evidence of their mother inherent in his facial structure. Her cheekbones. Her nose. Elena mentally kicked herself for not noticing the similarities when they'd first met.

"I don't mean to hold it against you," Belladonna was saying, "but I can't look at you and not see her face looking back at me. Judging me. Abandoning me." Her voice trailed off as she spoke.

Abandoning? How had their mother been involved with Belladonna to the point that the witch felt abandoned by the enchantress? Elena had always been taught that witches were near-extinct and wholly untrustworthy. Rather than question the witch

56

further, Elena decided they needed to focus on the problems at hand. They could interrogate Belladonna once they were safely within the confines of her mist. The sun was setting quickly, and they really needed to get somewhere warm.

"Belladonna," Elena said, shifting the conversation, "can you escort us through your mist? We need a place to sleep, and we could really use any advice or information you have on the *turmio*. We couldn't stop it from being released." Elena chanced a glance toward Roska, who kept his eyes downcast. "Now we have to find a way to stop it or rein it back in before it causes irreparable damage."

Belladonna said nothing, simply nodded, and turned away from them, back toward her mist. Elena took hold of Quinn's hand, squeezing his fingers to get his attention. She could feel the heat of his power licking just below the surface of his skin, warming her near-frozen palm. She squeezed a second time and watched as he blinked, his unfocused eyes becoming aware of their surroundings again, finding her face and resting there for a moment. He nodded a subtle thanks, maintaining her hold on his hand, prepared to follow in the witch's footsteps. Roska, who remained seemingly frozen in place, eyed the back of Belladonna's head suspiciously.

"Roska, please. I'm not asking you to trust her. Just trust me," Elena said, offering her other hand to him.

He hesitated for only a moment, then grasped her hand and allowed her to lead him into the mist, keeping a close, watchful eye on Belladonna.

The cottage was exactly as they'd left it. The lack of change was almost shocking. So much had happened in the last moon that Elena felt like the world should have been visibly different too. The world, however, had no interest in changing to suit her identity crisis and the emotional ride that she'd been forced to endure.

There was a fire roaring in the hearth. Castor, the moonbird and Belladonna's familiar, was resting on the back of a chair at her kitchen table. His watchful gaze followed each of them in turn as they entered the room.

Elena still held her brothers' hands, feeling the heat from Quinn's tense grasp and the frost from Roska's anxious one. It created a strange balance, a harmony, within her own body.

"Please make yourselves comfortable," Belladonna said.

Lyra wasted no time and immediately took up residence on the floor directly between the hearth and the bed. Belladonna walked over to the hearth and flipped over what appeared to be small packages made out of leaves and mud.

"What are those?" Elena asked, releasing her brothers' hands and gesturing to the items on the hearthstone. Agon slid down the back of her cloak to join Lyra by the fire. Demoni, who didn't seem comfortable or confident enough to leave Roska, remained wrapped protectively around his neck.

"These?" Belladonna asked, lifting one of the little leaf wraps gingerly with her hands. "It's fish. Wrapped in leaves, sealed with mud, to help them cook more evenly."

Quinn stirred at this announcement, showing more interest in Belladonna than he had since she compared him to their mother. "Wait, what?" he asked.

"Here," she replied, handing him one of the wraps. "They should be ready now. Elena, will you hand me a plate? Be careful when you unwrap them. They will be quite warm and not all of us have his resistance to heat." She nodded to Quinn as she handed him a plate with the leaf wrappings.

She hadn't called him "boy" like she normally did, but she hadn't called him Quinn either. Elena was perplexed. She didn't have a lot of experience with Belladonna, but it almost seemed like the witch was flustered.

Q took over unwrapping all of the fish on the plate, there were four. She'd obviously known they were coming. He inspect each fish as he unwrapped it. Clearly impressed by her leaf wraps, Quinn continued to study his, wrapping and unwrapping it several times, presumably trying to memorize the process so he could recreate it. Elena was just relieved that he had relaxed some.

Elena debated breaching the subject of their mother again. She didn't want to stir up more problems, and they'd only just gotten Quinn to calm down and focus on something else, but Belladonna's words were echoing around in Elena's mind.

Before she could voice her curiosity, Roska spoke up.

"Why would you feel abandoned by our mother?" His voice sounded rough, as though he struggled with the word *mother*. He remained standing by the door, possibly ready to flee in an instant if needed. Elena and Quinn settled into the sturdy wooden chairs at her solid oak table in the center of the room.

Belladonna looked up from the bread she was slicing on the opposite side of the table. Several emotions flashed quickly across her face before she seemed to regain control of herself and answer him.

"I knew your mother. Before she had the three of you. Before she met your father. Hells, I knew her before she was anything more than an ordinary enchantress learning her spells and skills at that damned school."

Belladonna put the knife down and sat—more like collapsed—into a chair at the table and gestured for Roska to do the same. When he didn't move right away, Belladonna's stare made it clear that she would wait for him to sit before she would continue. He finally conceded and took the empty seat between Elena and Quinn, directly opposite the witch. Elena handed him a plate and made a show of eating a large bit of the fish when he hesitated.

Belladonna didn't wait for him to eat before relaying her story.

"When I was a young witch, maybe a hundred cycles ago—deep breaths, boy, witches live a long time, it's no reason to choke on your fish—I met a cocky, sarcastic, witty girl in the woods just south of the mountain. I was new to the area, having just fled Rolam during their latest witch hunts. I didn't know about the school or the enchantresses that lived there. I hadn't met many other magical beings, aside from my family who had been slaughtered by the Brotherhood in their attempts to wipe us all out. I'd been running for days, certain that they were on my heels and I'd be dead by day's end when I tripped over her. She was collecting wild herbs in the woods, and I literally ran right into her. We both tumbled down the mountainside for a moment before smashing into a tree. She took the brunt of the impact, breaking her collarbone in the process.

"I'm fairly certain that the break is the only reason she didn't immediately attack me. I must've looked half-wild and entirely insane. She looked like a goddess. Long dark hair tied in a thick, tight braid down her back. Dirt smudged across her brow. Piercing eyes that took in every detail of my disheveled appearance. I watched her expression shift from rage and pain to one filled with pity and concern. She ignored her own injury to heal my cuts and bruises. I surprised her when I reset and healed her broken collarbone. She'd never seen a witch before. That damned school had actually been telling its students that we'd all been killed off an age ago.

"Meeting her lion was an interesting moment, but thankfully she had already taken pity on me and didn't see me as a threat. Magic or no, I wasn't in a position to take on a full-grown lion *and* an enchantress. Castor had flown ahead to find shelter for the night, so I would have been on my own. I remember how kind your mother was to me. She took me into the school, to a tower they used for grain storage, and brought me out fresh food and clean clothing. She hid me there for several days, always coming to see me and spending the nights with me. I think she was worried I'd hurt myself. I looked quite ragged, and I was utterly heartbroken. If she hadn't taken me in and shown me such kindness, I might have taken my own life, opting to save myself the heartache and rob the Brotherhood of the joys of torturing and killing me as they had with the rest of my family.

"When nearly a week had passed, your mother came to see me and took me out of the school. She said she'd found a safe place for me to live. This place," Belladonna raised her arms. "She'd even spelled the grounds to keep the witch hunters away. Together, we built this home. She used her magic to dig the well. I used mine to construct this cottage. We grew the garden together. No magic, just hard work, and love."

She faltered on the last word, took a sip of her tea, and cleared her throat before continuing.

"We spent many cycles together here. Working the land, making magic and herbal medicines that I would take down to Andover each week to sell or trade. We were very happy here for a long time. Until her ambitions got the best of her." The words were clipped with obvious anger and disappointment.

"They offered her the position of Headmistress. I was thrilled for her, at first, until she said that it would mean the end of our time together. She couldn't run the school and stay here with me, and I wouldn't be welcome in the school. Not to mention, as head-mistress, she was expected to carry a child, and I obviously couldn't give her that."

Belladonna paused. Elena wasn't sure she would continue, for several moments the witch just stared off into the darkness outside the window to the cloudless sky. She opened her mouth to ask if Belladonna knew their father when the witch spoke.

"The day she left is the day I raised my mist. As a deterrent for all trespassers, but more importantly, it served as a literal wall for your mother. She chose to leave me, so I made it impossible for her to ever return." The bitter sadness in her voice was palpable. Elena didn't know what to say. Her story was heartbreaking and made Elena dislike her mother even more.

"I'm so sorry she did that to you," Elena heard herself say.

"I told you that woman was a bitch," Q muttered, more to his fish than anyone in particular.

"Yes, boy, you're right. She is a heartless woman, and you look so much like her sometimes that I can barely stand to look at you. I realize it isn't fair, but it's hard for me to see you and not think of her betrayal."

"No, I get it," Quinn said, surprising everyone at the table. He didn't look up from his fish, but Elena could tell he was stewing in his own memories. Aggressively stabbing his food with a fork, he added, "If I had to see the face of someone who did me like that, I'd want to punch them."

Elena was thoroughly impressed by her brother's empathy. She'd never expected this sort of story about her mother, but it did make a lot of sense. She'd always known her mother preferred the company of women, but she'd needed the seed of a man to carry on her magical lineage. Elena wondered if her mother held any resentment against Elena and her brothers. Blaming them, at least in part, for the way things ended with Belladonna. It would explain a lot.

Elena felt Agon's eyes on her and shook the thoughts from her mind. She was making excuses for her mother's neglectful and terrible parenting practices. Whatever had caused her mother to be such a distant, cold-hearted, power-hungry person, it didn't excuse or even justify the way she treated her children.

9

BEATRICE

"**H**EADMISTRESS, WE HAVE NEWS from the investigators." The guard handed Beatrice three missives. It was a bit odd, as she was only expecting news from the team she'd sent after her children, but unsurprising. She had teams of investigators all over the country, looking for new enchantresses to bring into the school, keeping tabs on any potential threats, etc.

Madame LaBelle offered a curt nod to the guard, dismissing her, as she cracked the wax seal on the first message. It was from her spy at court. She was entertaining a physical relationship with the King, but she didn't trust him to keep her fully informed. She wasn't a fool. The spy stressed that there was something big happening in the castle, but hadn't been able to get definitive information as to what yet, or whether it would impact the school.

The second missive was from a team of investigators she'd sent out to the southwestern border of Waverly. There had been rumors of a magical girl helping the farmers increase their crop yields. It turned out that the girl was in fact magical, but her skills were minimal and wouldn't be worth the time and resources to train at Harbor Ridge. Madame LaBelle penned a quick response, requiring the investigators to stay with the girl for a moon and help her hone her earth magic. She might not be strong enough to train at Harbor Ridge, but that didn't mean she didn't deserve some level of training and advising before the investigators returned home.

The final missive was not what she'd been hoping for.

> We followed their trail along the river, upstream, to see the witch. She has increased her warding, and we are struggling to break through. Will send an update when we cross her boundary.

Gods, damn that stubborn woman. Beatrice had hoped, after all these cycles, Belladonna would have let it go. Yes, things hadn't gone the way either of them had wanted, but Beatrice had done what she thought was necessary. Belladonna needed to accept that and move on.

Beatrice crumpled the missive into a ball and threw it into the blazing hearth in her office.

"You can't really fault her. You are equally stubborn and haven't exactly made things easier on her. You do remember sending multiple teams of investigators out to the cottage for several moons after becoming headmistress, don't you? What were you trying to do? Drive her away? Spare your own feelings by making her leave?" Zied flicked his tail, sharing in her irritation, but to Beatrice's surprise, his annoyance was directed at her.

"What would you have had me do? We couldn't just abandon this school and all of the students. They needed us. They needed me to guide them and bring them into a stronger position of power. This," she gestured to the room they were in while implying the entire school, "is what we've been training for our whole lives. Harbor Ridge needed us. It still does." Beatrice tried to keep her tone level but found it nearly impossible to rein in all of her frustrations. They'd been having this argument for nearly twenty solar cycles. At some point, she had hoped he would let it go. It was far too late to change anything regardless. Beatrice had chosen their path and there was no going back.

"The school would have found someone else," Zied replied, his tone equal parts irate and exhausted. "You chose this place over her love. We could have been very happy there. Hells, we *were* very happy there. But you wanted more power, and you dragged me along with you. You never even asked me what I thought."

That caught Beatrice by surprise. All this time, Zied had never voiced his opinion on her taking the position of headmistress. She was shocked to realize that he was right. She hadn't talked to him about it. She hadn't even considered his feelings because she'd assumed he had the same ambitions and binding loyalty to the school that she had. Ruling the school and cultivating strong alliances with those in positions of authority throughout Waverly meant raising her own position of power and being able to protect more enchantresses. After hearing the horrific stories from Belladonna about what the witches had been put through, Beatrice was focused on keeping enchantresses from suffering the same fate. Perhaps her focus had left her blind to his feelings on the subject.

"I'm sorry," she said, her voice barely audible over the crackling fire in their hearth. "I'm sorry. I shouldn't have made any life-altering choices without consulting you. Why didn't you say anything back then?" She held his gaze, feeling his thoughts process through his mind before he responded.

"I didn't think it would make a difference. I could feel how passionately compelled you were about taking over the school. I heard you making plans with the guards and the instructors. You had made the decision the moment the words left their mouths, the instant they offered you the position. You didn't hesitate. I knew my feelings would only complicate things for you. My job, as your familiar, is to aid you. Not to create more problems for you."

Beatrice felt the sadness that weighed heavily in his mind.

"So you hid your feelings from me?" she asked. "All this time, you hid your sadness and disappointment, just to make things easier for me?"

Zied said nothing, but he opened the mental floodgates in his mind, releasing all the emotions he'd held back from her since they'd walked out of the cottage and the life they'd built with Belladonna and Castor.

If she hadn't already been seated in the sturdy chair at her desk, she would have collapsed from the weight of his unfiltered emotions. Unbidden tears sprang forth from her eyes, racing down her face without consequence as she felt all the things he'd kept from her. His sadness and grief at having left the home they'd help build. The loneliness he'd suffered through without Castor by his side.

Neither of them said a word, but their eyes stayed locked on each other for an endless moment, sharing in the sudden resurgence of grief they both felt at the loss of the ones they'd both loved more than anything.

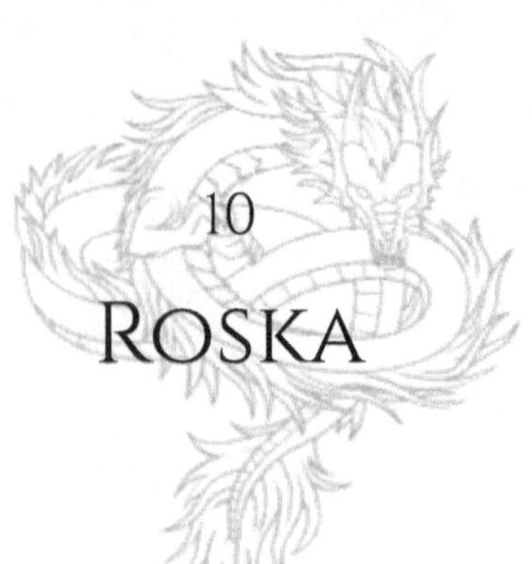

10
ROSKA

ROSKA HADN'T SAID ANYTHING the rest of the night. He'd eaten the witch's food, drank her tea, and attempted to sleep on the floor beside the bed where Elena had fallen asleep within moments of laying her head. Roska was certain he'd only gotten an hour or two of actual sleep. He'd been awake when the sun broke through the mist surrounding the cottage. Unable to force himself back to sleep, he'd taken Demoni outside to wander the clearing in the woods and ponder the story Belladonna had told them the night before.

Roska wasn't sure how much of the tale he truly believed. Elena and Quinn seemed to take her at her word, but he didn't trust the witch. Perhaps it was his bigoted upbringing, but he felt like she was hiding something from them.

"You're quite an observant creature, aren't you?"

Roska jumped, spun on his heels, and raised his hands in a defensive motion, frost at the ready to defend himself from whomever had spoken those words.

"Ah ah ah," tsked the voice. Roska turned again, trying to find the source.

"Put away your frost, and then we'll talk," it said.

"Why the hells would I do that?" Roska challenged. Cold mist swirled from the tips of his fingers, almost like smoke, as he turned toward the voice.

"Because I'm no threat to you," the voice answered calmly.

Roska felt his power rise as he tried to see who was speaking. He was standing in an empty field, a hundred paces from the cottage and at least another fifty paces from the tree line. The voice sounded close, so why couldn't he see the speaker?

"Listen to me, boy," the voice said, trying and failing to keep the irritation from its words, "if I were going to hurt you, I would have done it already, rather than making my presence known."

Can you see anything? Roska thought to Demoni, refusing to take the disembodied voice at its word.

No, Demoni answered, flickering her tongue as she tried to pinpoint its location. *But it does make a good point. Let's hear it out, but stay on guard. I'll be ready if it attacks.*

Roska didn't love the plan, but he didn't know what else to do. Slowly, he lowered his hands and pulled his frost back into the lockbox that stored his power within his chest.

"Speak then, before I change my mind." His words were clipped as he addressed the creature.

"Thank you." The voice came from directly behind him.

Roska jumped and whirled around to find a man standing before him. He had an odd, foreboding look about him. Jet black hair, ebony eyes, charcoal skin. His body seemed to draw in all the light around him, making him stand out in the most ominous way. His nose came to a sharp point, and his smile was something that Roska knew would haunt him in his nightmares for the rest of his days.

Instinctively, Roska raised his hands and called forth his power again.

"Now, now," the man said, clicking his tongue like one might when addressing an errant dog or ill-behaved child. "We promised to be civil."

"What the hells are you?" Roska demanded.

"Well that's not very nice, is it?" The man feigned offense, placing his hand on his chest as though Roska's words had physically wounded him. "*What* am I? Not *who* am I? I have a name, you know."

"Fine. What is your name?" Roska ground out, refusing to lower his hands, keeping his frost ready and waiting in case this monster lashed out.

"My name is Castor," the man said, with a flourish of his hand and a dramatic bow.

Castor...Castor... why does that sound familiar? Roska asked Demoni.

That was what the witch had called the bird in her home last night, Demoni supplied.

"Not just any old bird, dearie," the man cut in, as though he could read their thoughts, "I am a moonbird. I'm Belladonna's familiar, but I'm so much more than your average familiar. Even more powerful than you, little dragon." He pointed a sharp, talon-like finger at Demoni. "I know I look a bit frightening," Castor continued as Roska took a step away from him, "but I promise I mean no harm.

I merely wanted to chat with you about your experience with the Brotherhood and the steps you followed in the *turmio* ritual so that we might begin to deconstruct it."

Roska was at a loss for words. This man was a familiar? But he was a bird last night. Was he a shapeshifter? Or was he cursed somehow to be the witch's servant? Was he normally a bird, or was the bird form merely a punishment he was forced to endure each night as punishment for some crime he'd committed?

"So many questions." Castor smiled. "I will answer your questions if you answer mine."

Roska studied the man-bird's face. He looked like something from a fable, a creature meant as a warning to keep children from sneaking out into the forests at night. He was nearly a head taller than Roska, but he looked to weigh about the same as he did. Did the man have hollow bones, like birds do?

"Do you agree to my terms?" Castor asked, trying to keep a smirk from showing, revealing his clear amusement at Roska's mental turmoil.

"Yes, I accept your terms," Roska agreed finally.

"Splendid!" he cheered, awkwardly clapping his hands. "I'll even answer one of your questions first. I am not cursed. I was born a moonbird, alongside my witch, hatching from within the placenta that sustained us both while we grew in our mother's womb. I am a shapeshifter, so I can transform into whatever creature I desire, although I do tend to stay in my bird form because I absolutely adore flying. Oh, and yes, even as a man, my bones are hollow." His smirk returned, clearly enjoying the look of shock on Roska's face.

"Goodness me, I went and answered all of your questions. I guess that means it's my turn to ask some."

That smirk. It was the look a jackal would wear as it trapped a small rabbit. The look of a predator, cornering its prey.

"Tell me about the Brotherhood." All hint of humor or friendliness had evaporated from his voice.

Ravens were tricksters. No matter what folktale or legend, blackbirds were tricksters and bad omens. Roska had been foolish to think this moonbird would be any different.

"What do you want to know?" Roska asked, trying to keep his voice calm and maintain his control over his powers.

Castor held his gaze. "Where are they located? How many are there? What is their combat training like? What sort of weapons do they have?"

"You... you want to attack them?" Roska was shocked, although, realistically he knew he shouldn't be. Of course the familiar of a witch whose family had been massacred by the Brotherhood would seek out revenge.

Castor said nothing, letting his silence stand for his answer.

"Honestly don't know about their weapons or combat training," Roska offered, lowering his hands. He realized that Castor had spoken the truth. He wasn't a threat to Roska. He was a threat to those who had tortured and tormented Roska his entire life.

The enemy of my enemy is my friend. Roska had heard those words so many times after a beating from one of the brothers. They raised him to believe that he was their friend, but really, he was their tool. Their weapon. They were no friends of his. And Castor might not be a friend either, but they had a mutual enemy now, and Roska had no qualms about sharing what little information he had.

"I didn't get to roam the monastery, so I won't be much help if you're planning to invade or attack them there. I can tell you that there are at least two thousand Brothers living in the monastery at any given time. It's about a week's travel east of here, by horseback. I can draw you a map if you'd like."

Castor seemed almost stunned by Roska's sudden willingness to help. He tried his best to hide it, but Roska caught a glimpse of surprise in his eyes before the man-bird blinked and nodded his acceptance of the proffered map.

"I can also write out the whole ritual. I had to memorize it, so I know exactly what I did, said, and used to unleash the *turmio*." Roska started walking back toward the cottage. "I think it would be easier to do all of this back in the comfort of the house though, don't you?"

Roska couldn't help the smirk that pulling at his own lips. It probably came as a shock to Castor, but Roska had spent the last few weeks forcing himself to remember all the horrible things the Brotherhood had done to him. All the scars, both literal and metaphorical, that they'd left him with. The torture and abuse they'd put Demoni through. Hells, they cut off her muxing wings, just to punish him. They had never been his family, and they sure as shyt didn't deserve his loyalty. They'd sent him on a suicide mission, and he'd been naive enough to think that accomplishing his mission would finally earn him their trust, love, and approval.

He didn't need them. He knew what real love and trust were now that he'd finally found his siblings. He knew what true acceptance was, and he was going to fight tooth and nail to ensure that he had an entire lifetime with them.

11
QUINN

"Who is that creepy-looking guy walking with Ros-ka?" Quinn asked, glancing out the open cottage door to see his brother meandering through the frost-covered field. Q was pretty sure the man wasn't a threat—he trusted that Belladonna wouldn't allow a hostile person onto her lands—but the guy didn't look friendly. With his sharp features, ebony skin, and pitch-black hair and clothes, he looked like Death himself.

"Well that's rude," Elena mumbled as she elbowed him and took a peek outside. Q thought he saw her tense up ever-so-slightly at the sight of the man, but she didn't say anymore.

Belladonna didn't even bother turning around as she answered matter-of-factly, "That is Castor."

Quinn and Elena shared a look of suspicion and confusion. Elena's mouth hung open, and her eyebrows had shot up so high that they'd nearly disappeared into her hairline.

"I'm sorry, what?" Quinn tried to keep the mocking incredulity from his voice, but he was pretty sure he failed.

"You know Castor. My familiar." Belladonna still hadn't looked up from her books.

"Yeah, I know Castor," Q replied, slightly annoyed with her flippant attitude. "But I'm looking at a man, not a bird."

"Yes, boy. A moonbird. I'm fairly certain I already explained this all to you when you were here before." She looked up from her books now, raising an eyebrow. When Q said nothing in response, she turned her gaze to Elena. "Please tell me *you* at least learned about moonbirds in that damn school."

Elena looked from Belladonna to Q before shrugging and casting her eyes to the floor, almost as though she were ashamed of her lack of knowledge.

"Well, clearly your mother has been leaving all sorts of vital information out at that school of hers." Belladonna closed the book she had been skimming and placed her hands, one on top of the other, on the cover of the book.

"No shyt," Q replied, no longer bothering to hide his annoyance. "Are you gonna explain this or not?" He gestured out the door to Roska and the man.

"Moonbirds are shapeshifters. They can transform into any creature, so long as they've seen it in person once before." She said this as though it should have been common sense.

There was a long moment of silence while Quinn attempted to process yet another shift in his reality. Elena seemed equally shocked. Either that, or her jaw had literally unhinged, leaving her mouth hanging wide open.

"So... he can be anything? Any*one*?" Quinn finally asked, trying to grasp the weight of this news.

"Only things he's seen before. His birth form is that of the bird you've seen several times now, but he can transform into any animal or creature he's encountered before. He rarely takes this particular form. He says being a man is degrading and limiting." Belladonna chuckled, looking out the open doorway, watching her familiar casually stroll through the field with Roska. "But, yes, he could be anything or anyone he wanted, at any given time."

Q thought Belladonna looked a little smug, as she returned her focus to the books on the table, the hint of a smile playing at her lips. She clearly enjoyed springing that bit of new information on them.

"I don't know why you two look so shocked and scandalized. I told you he was a shapeshifter when you first arrived here." Belladonna shrugged, opening a new book and skimming the table of contents

"Yeah, maybe you did, but you also dropped quite a few other pieces of explosive information on us that day. Your bird didn't really rank high on my list of take-aways from our last visit," Quinn grumbled. He turned back to look out the door at the man walking with Roska. They were closer to the house now, and Q could get a better view of the man. Bird. Whatever.

He had a ferocity to him that made Q think that if he kept this shape, he would become a very unpopular—but formidable—character in Waverly's criminal underworld. Hells, he'd probably be the top gang leader in Riverayn by the end of the frost season. Waverly's capital city was beautiful, according to the merchants Q had encountered in Andover, but there was a dark side to Riverayn that bred the toughest fighters and thieves in the country.

Elena squeezed Q's shoulder before walking back to the table with Belladonna and picking up one of the books. They had been researching all morning, trying to find any reference or mention of the *turmio* so that they could start to unravel it.

So far, they'd had no luck.

No mention of *turmio*s. No mention of prophecies. No explanation as to how the King had found out about the *turmio* or the scroll Roska had seen the messenger pass off to the Brothers. They'd been staring at books for hours and still hadn't learned anything new.

"This is a waste of time," Q said, exasperation coating his words. "We're not going to find anything in these muxing books. We can't keep sitting around here waiting for this damn thing to come back and kill us all. We need to *go*. We need to *do* something."

Elena looked up from her book and rolled her eyes at him. "Well, it would go faster if you would sit down and help instead of glaring out at Roska and Castor." She paused for a moment, then it looked as though something had just clicked in her mind and she said, "Wait, Q, do you know how to read?" Her tone wasn't judgmental or condescending. Instead, she had a look of genuine curiosity, bordering on concern in her eyes.

Q considered his options. He could lie, say he never learned, and get out of having to help research. Amelia had taught him to read when he was a child. He knew how, he just never enjoyed it. For several long moments, Quinn entertained the idea, watching the concern grow in Elena's eyes. She loved books. When they'd been living in Andover with Amelia, Elena had jumped at any and all opportunities to get her hands on new books. She read everything

Amelia had in her first week—which wasn't much, considering the book merchant rarely came to their small hamlet—before quickly moving on to borrowed books from friends, townsfolk, and the town's school teacher. Her appetite for books was insatiable.

Don't be a jerk. Quinn started at Lyra's words. He thought she was asleep, curled up on a pillow by the hearth with Agon. *If you don't tell her the truth, I will.*

Quinn glared at the fox, who never even bothered to open her eyes, sighed, and said, "Yes, I know how to read. I just don't see the point. These books clearly aren't going to have any helpful information." He let out another dramatic sigh but took the empty seat beside Elena at the table and started flipping through one of the books.

"You can't know that," Elena said, returning her attention to the book in front of her. "Either way, we don't know what to do or where to go, so this is our best course of action right now."

"We don't have time for this shyt," Quinn continued to grumble.

"How do you know that, boy?" Belladonna poised the question with an incredulous eyebrow raised.

"Actually, we do have a little time," Roska said, walking into the cottage. Castor followed in behind him, shifted back into a bird, and flew over to rest on his perch by the hearth behind Belladonna.

"What are you talking about?" Elena asked. "I thought you said we'd all be dead in a few weeks and we wouldn't have time or a chance to stop the *turmio* now that it was loose in the world."

"What I said and what is actually true might not be exactly in alignment," Roska replied, a smirk playing in his eyes. "I was on a mission to destroy the world. Did you really think I wanted to give you hope that it could be stopped?"

Q stared at his brother, dumbfounded.

"You need to start explaining. Now." Elena's voice held a sharp edge. Quinn thought he saw a hint of lightning in her eyes as she threatened to unleash her stress and anxiety on Roska. Gently and ever-so-slowly—like he would if he were approaching an injured animal—Quinn placed his hand on top of Elena's. Her eyes flicked to him instantly. The rage playing in her features faltered as she saw the look of concern on his. She blinked a few times, and Q saw the lightning fade from her eyes.

"What the hells was that, El?" Q asked when he was sure she wasn't going to vaporize them all.

"I'm sorry," she replied, looking away from them both and focusing on the book open before her. "I... I don't know where that came from. I guess I'm more stressed than I realized."

"It's understandable," Roska said, taking a careful step closer to her and kneeling beside her chair. He placed his hand on her shoulder and waited until she looked down at him before he continued. "I'm sorry I didn't say anything sooner, but I didn't want to give you false hope. Talking with Castor helped me to understand more of the ritual I performed and how the *turmio* works."

"Enlighten us, then," Q snapped. His nerves were shot, and he didn't have patience for Roska's typically circular logic.

"Deep breath, *veli*," Roska said, standing up and moving to the empty chair beside Belladonna.

Q was grateful for her uncharacteristically quiet behavior. Belladonna hadn't said a word, but she seemed to be giving Roska her undivided attention, closing the book she'd been reading as her eyes followed his movements.

"Stop patronizing me and just get on with it," Quinn replied snidely.

"As you wish," Roska said with a subtle nod. "Based on our conversation, the ritual to unleash the *turmio* only set it free, but it will need time to rebuild its power before it will be capable of killing anyone."

Everyone in the room visibly relaxed at these words.

"That doesn't mean that it won't be adept at wreaking havoc," Roska continued, "but it does mean that we have time to stop it. Castor says that the *turmio* is like an infection. The cloud itself, the thing that came from the ground inside that cavern, is a weakened, incorporeal version of the true demon. It releases a noxious gas that acts like a poison, draining the power from any magical creatures who inhale it. As the power drains from the magical being, it is transferred to the *turmio*, building its strength with each new creature it infects. Thankfully, we don't think it works like a traditional virus. One magical creature cannot spread it to another magical creature. The creatures have to be infected by the source, by the *turmio* itself. So that works in our favor."

Roska paused in his explanation to take a sip of cool water, and Quinn couldn't hold his tongue.

"How the hells do you know this? Why wouldn't you tell us this weeks ago when you first agreed to help us?"

Roska lowered his cup to the table slowly. "I already told you. I didn't understand how it all worked before. Not really. I didn't want to offer false hope."

"Bullshyt. False hope would have been better than the state of utter depression and despair we've been in since that damned cavern." Elena's voice still held the same sharp tone as before, but her eyes weren't glowing as she snapped at their brother.

"You're right. I see that now. I'm sorry." Roska held her stare with what Quinn thought was a heartfelt apology.

"You determined all of this after a single conversation with Castor?" Belladonna inquired, glancing curiously over her shoulder at the moonbird.

If Quinn didn't know any better, he might have interpreted that look as something like betrayal. But that couldn't be, right? Why would she feel betrayed by her own familiar? How could Castor know things that she didn't know herself?

Maybe witches and their familiars don't share a mind like we do, Lyra offered. She still hadn't opened her eyes or lifted her head, but it was clear they had her full attention.

Maybe, he replied. Quinn would have to try and puzzle that out later. They had more important things weighing on them at the moment.

"So do you have any idea how we can stop this thing before it gets too strong and starts essentially eating people?" Quinn tried to keep his voice light, to brighten the heavy cloud of seriousness that blanketed the room, but his attempt fell flat.

"That's where it gets awkward. I need to speak to our father." Roska ignored the gasp of shock and the grunt of incredulity from Elena and Quinn respectively, turning his full attention to Belladonna. He locked eyes with her with such fierceness that it reminded Q of a time when he'd spotted a mountain lion hunting a deer in the Dark Woods.

The look on Belladonna's face matched that of the deer as well.

12

ELENA

"WHAT?" ELENA STARED AT Roska in stunned confusion.

All of the tension and anxiety that had been building within her instantly drained as she tried to process what he'd just said. She was certain she must have misheard him. Their father? They didn't even know who he was. According to their mother, he was some random farmer she'd met at a tavern and seduced for the sole purpose of reproduction—as all enchantresses did. According to the Brotherhood—although Elena wasn't sure their information was accurate—their father was a demi-god of some kind. That seemed so outlandish and farfetched that it was almost laughable. Almost.

"I know you're skeptical, *tyttö*, but he's the only one who's going to have any truly helpful information. He knows all about this because he was the one who originally uncovered the prophecy nearly an age ago." Roska's voice was irritatingly calm. As if the idea of confronting a demi-god was nothing to worry about. As if he actually believed that their father would be friendly and helpful.

"You can't be serious," Quinn said, clearly not interested in holding back or discussing the idea any further.

"I am, actually," Roska replied.

"If he really is as powerful as you say and he knew how all of this would turn out, why wouldn't he just stop it himself? Why would he mux our mother in the first place if he knew that it would kick start this shyt show?"

Elena's head snapped toward Quinn at his crass language.

"Please," she said, "don't talk about Mother that way. I know you don't like her, but that just sounds so vulgar." She shook her head, trying to shake loose the mental image of her mother being physically intimate. The idea made her shudder.

Belladonna chuckled from across the table, clearly amused by Elena's discomfort. Her laughter broke some of the tension that had been building in the room and brought them all back to focus on the problem at hand.

"I don't have all the answers to your questions, Q," Roska said, "but I think the best way to get adequate answers is to ask him yourself." He turned his gaze back to Belladonna, as though he was waiting for her to lay out a map to their father's home or something.

"I don't know what you want from me," she replied, but Elena got the idea that she wasn't being entirely truthful.

"You knew our mother before," Elena said, thinking out loud, "before she was headmistress, before she was our mother. Did you see her when she was pregnant? Did you know about us before we were born?"

Elena was starting to put the pieces of her mother's history together. The more she learned, the more she felt like her life was just a play. She was the puppet on a string that someone else was manipulating for their own sick pleasure.

"Yes, I knew her before, but I didn't speak to her for cycles after she left. I didn't see her when she was pregnant with you three, and she certainly never came to me for anything." There was a hint of bitterness in Belladonna's voice, but she didn't elaborate.

"When we first came to you, you said you were expecting us. How did you know we would come? How did you know who we were?" Quinn looked like he was trying to rein in his emotions with his fists clenched on the table. Elena could see small flames dancing just below the surface of his skin, but she was impressed with his control. He wasn't burning the table or any of the books. It was almost as if he were playing with the fire within, using it to slowly burn off some of his strong emotions.

"I recognized you," she said to Quinn, "because of your strong resemblance to your mother. Then I put the pieces together when I met and connected with your familiars."

"But how did you know about us in the first place?" Quinn pressed. "About the prophecy."

"I told you, boy. I'm well-read, and I research things."

"Did you know our father?" Elena asked quietly, staring at her hands in her lap.

Belladonna reached across the table, offering her hand to Elena. Elena immediately took the offering, squeezing her hand tightly, desperate for a safe, solid adult to lean on. Even if it was only for a moment.

"I knew him before," Belladonna replied, returning Elena's tight grasp. "Before he was your father. Before he met your mother. Hells, before I met your mother. I met Aiden while I was fleeing the witch hunters in Rolam. He wore a different face back then, of course. He sheltered me for a couple of days before sending me off in this direction. Aiden was the one who told me to seek out the enchantresses for aid."

Belladonna's eyes drifted from the table to stare out the window. Elena thought she might be lost in thoughts and old memories.

Their father had sent Belladonna here. Had he known they would need her help someday?

"What do you mean he wore a different face?" Elena asked.

At the same time, Quinn spoke. "Do you know what sort of demi-god he is?"

"Aiden's father—your grandfather—was a trickster, from what I gathered. He didn't tell me his family history, if that's what you were hoping for, but he did imply—rather heavily—that his father was the sneaky, con man of a deity. It makes sense, considering he was able to shape-shift and fool your mother. He had to be very powerful to trick her. To trick us both." Belladonna smirked.

"Do you know where we can find him?" Roska asked, bringing them back to his original question.

"No, child, I don't. Trust me, if he wants to be found, he'll make himself known. You won't be able to find him otherwise."

It was disappointing, but not altogether surprising news. Someone as powerful as Belladonna made their father sound would not be easy to find.

"Are you sure finding him is our best course of action?" Q asked Roska.

"We don't have a lot of other options," Roska said plainly. "Mother has proven she has no intention of helping, although I cannot fathom why. The Brotherhood wouldn't help us even if their lives depended on it. And by the looks of this table, you've already scoured through all of Belladonna's books and research material to no avail. I'm open to other suggestions, I just don't see any other paths before us."

Elena hated to think he was right, because it meant that the only option they had was to find someone who'd known about them since their conception and never bothered to show up for them. He clearly had no intention of being a father, and he didn't deserve to be, after what he'd left them all to suffer through. Especially her brothers. They hadn't deserved the shyt they'd been forced to live through. If this super-powerful demi-god was actually their father, he had a lot of explaining to do.

She would never understand how people could abuse children. But she couldn't comprehend the people who stood idly by, knowing the abuse was ongoing, yet do nothing to stop it. Only heartless, cruel, and selfish people would actively choose *not* to step in and protect a child from harm. *Especially* when that child was their own flesh and blood.

"So what do we do? We can't exactly sit around here, doing nothing and hoping dear old daddy decides to show up." Quinn's snark was back in full force. Elena wondered if his mind had traveled down the same resentful road that hers had.

"Go to the mountains north of Harbor Ridge. Last I heard, he was living in a crumbling tower. The remains of an old watchtower along the road to Rolam."

Elena jumped at the unexpected rough male voice that spoke up.

She jerked her head up from where she'd been studying the smooth wood of the table, stewing in her emotions. There was a man standing behind Belladonna. Elena was stunned to realize that it was Castor, in his human form.

"I'm sorry, what?" Elena tried to sound calm, but she was thoroughly thrown by the fact that the moonbird who had been perched quietly behind Belladonna was now a man, speaking directly to her.

"He's living in the ruined remains of an old watchtower. It's about a two-day hike, as the crow flies." Castor smirked at his own bad pun, before looking sorrowfully at Belladonna.

"You knew. You knew and you didn't tell me." Her voice was barely above a whisper, but the pain and heartache in her tone was palpable.

It took Elena a moment to understand what Belladonna was saying. Castor had gone off without her, found the home of their demi-god father, and kept it a secret from her. Elena's heart broke at the betrayal in Belladonna's eyes. She couldn't even begin to imagine the level of disloyalty Belladonna must have been feeling. Agon was literally incapable of keeping secrets from Elena, and vice versa.

"I'm sorry. I knew you wouldn't approve, but I also knew we would need him someday." Castor was trying to make a case for his secrecy. "As soon as those two," he nodded to Elena and Quinn, "showed up, I knew we would need to find him sooner rather than later. So I did."

Belladonna said nothing. She didn't even look at him. Instead, she rose from the table, grabbed a stack of books, and returned them to her shelves along the wall. She stood at the bookshelf, with her back to them until Castor shifted back into a moonbird and flew out of the house.

No one else said a word for the rest of the morning. Elena helped put the books away. Quinn and Roska went off to collect food from the garden to prepare for dinner. Elena thought she saw Castor watching Belladonna through the windows as he perched on the well outside, but he never came back inside. It was clear that he and Belladonna were going to have a lot to discuss once she and her brothers were asleep.

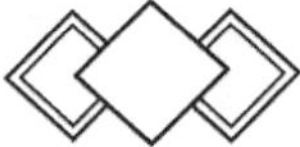

Dinner was a relatively quiet affair. Tensions were still high from their revelation-filled morning. Castor had come back into the cottage with them. Elena thought that was probably only because it had started to snow again. She desperately wanted to say something to ease the overwrought energy in the air, but she couldn't think of anything that would make any of them feel better.

She and her brothers had decided to get an early start, at first light, toward the watchtower where their father was apparently living—or possibly hiding out. Roska seemed very hopeful that the demi-god would be able to help them capture or destroy the *turmio* before it could build any real power or cause irreparable damage. Elena dearly hoped he was right. She hated to think that the world was going to suffer and magic was going to die because of them.

That was an over-simplification of the situation, of course, and not entirely accurate, as Agon was constantly pointing out to her. Still, Elena couldn't help but feel responsible for the existence of the *turmio* in their world. If she had recognized what Roska was doing in that cavern, she could have stopped him and thwarted the prophecy. Hells, if she'd never been born, then the prophecy would never have been set into motion in the first place.

You can't think like that, El, Agon chided in her mind.

I can't help it, she whined in return. *It's true. If we hadn't been born, this wouldn't be happening.*

Yes, and if you hadn't been born, YOU WOULDN'T EXIST. Is that truly what you want?

Elena glared at Agon where he lay on the pillow with Lyra and Demoni by the fire. He knew she didn't want to die, but she also didn't want to be responsible for saving the muxing world. It was too much pressure to put on one person.

But it's not all on you, Elena. You have brothers. We have a family to help and support us. Agon held her stare for a moment before glancing at his sleeping familiar-sisters. *We aren't alone, and by the looks of things, we will never have to be alone again.*

Elena looked over at her brothers, sitting beside and across from her at the table. She had brothers. It had been several weeks since that particular revelation had been unveiled and it still felt surreal.

Elena reached out and took her brothers' hands in her own, disrupting their meal and confusing them for a moment, based on the looks they both gave her.

"I know this is all scary and crazy and none of us want to be responsible for fixing this shyt." Elena smiled when Quinn raised an eyebrow at her language. He still found it amusing when she cursed. "But we are in this together. I couldn't imagine a better, more stubborn or capable pair of guys to have by my side. If we have to save the world, I'm glad you two will be the ones doing it with me."

Neither of them responded, but they both held her grasp for several moments before Quinn gave her hand a slight squeeze and released her in favor of his food.

"It will all work out," Roska said, trying to sound confident but not quite hitting the mark. "Our father will have insights and be able to help us."

Elena offered his hand a gentle squeeze and nodded. She hoped he was right, but she'd gotten her hopes up one too many times in the past, thinking someone else would be able to step in and save her—save them—from having to do the scary hero work.

Elena had a feeling things were going to get a lot harder before they got better.

Elena slept fitfully, her dreams haunting her with visions of poisonous black clouds chasing the younger students at Harbor Ridge. The screams of the terrified girls as they tried to escape but ultimately failed and were taken over by the thick, ominous weight of the clouds.

Elena woke abruptly to the sound of Castor's caws outside. The sun hadn't fully broken free of the horizon, slowly chasing away the last of the dark night sky. Agon rose from the warm fur ball he'd been curled into overnight and stretched his long body, dragging his back feet behind him as he pulled himself from the pillow to her lap. Elena scratched under his chin and tried to shake the remnants of her haunting dreams from her mind.

They planned to reach the watchtower by sunset the next day, assuming they weren't met with any impediments. Castor had offered to travel with them and show them the way, but Belladonna refused to go with them. She wouldn't explain why, but Elena got the feeling that there were some lingering hurt feelings between the witch and their father. Elena was disappointed that Belladonna wouldn't be with them, but she understood her hesitation. The witch had a complicated history with both of their parents, and Elena knew it wasn't fair of them to keep pulling Belladonna into their family issues.

Instead, they made quick work of cleaning up, packing, and eating breakfast before they headed off into Belladonna's mist just as the sun rose over the treetops. Castor chose to shift into his human form, walking with them through the mist. He spread his protective bubble with them as they traveled through the magical boundary, escorting them to their father's home.

Elena was thoroughly wrapped up in her own worries about meeting their father that she didn't notice that her brothers had stopped walking until she ran right into Q.

"Whoa!" Q stumbled forward, catching himself on a tall pine before turning back to look at her. "You ok, El?"

"Oh, shyt, yes. I'm so sorry, Q. I didn't mean to—" her words were cut off by a harsh "shush" from Castor. He motioned for them all to get low to the ground. They wouldn't be able to hide well, now that everything was covered in a fresh blanket of snow. Nevertheless, they crouched down and tried to hide behind thicker tree trunks as Castor silently transformed into his massive moonbird form and took flight.

No one said a word. They watched Castor disappear into the treetops. Their shallow breaths came out in tiny puffs of air while they anxiously awaited the moonbird's return.

Q and Lyra seemed to be having a silent conversation, then she quickly hopped off into the woods to the northwest of their location. Elena assumed Lyra was going to investigate on her own. She had never expressed much trust in Castor.

For several exceedingly painful and tense moments, the siblings knelt like frozen statues in the icy forest. Every sound put Elena further on edge. Every twig snap. Every leaf rustle. Every distant animal sound. Her lightning danced under her skin as she tried to contain in her emotions and her power. A quick glance at her brothers' hands told her that they were equally apprehensive.

Without warning, Castor landed roughly before them and was instantly frozen, burned, and electrocuted by their hair-trigger powers.

He quickly shifted back into his human form, raising his arms in self-defense. "Calm yourselves, children. It's only me." He quietly waited for the three of them to rein their respective powers back in before continuing in a hushed tone. "There is an encampment of soldiers bearing the mark of the King nearby. They're to the east of the watchtower, maybe a day's hike, and look to be heading back toward the capital. If we stick to the thicker, wilder parts of the woods and stay off the main road, we shouldn't cross paths with them. Unfortunately, it will take us longer to get to the watchtower. If we don't sleep much, it will probably only lengthen our journey by a half-day or so. You will need to keep your powers under control though. You three would light up the whole forest if you were to go off like that."

"The King has soldiers this far north? Why?" Elena's worry grew stronger with each passing moment. Riverayn was at least five days south of their location. The King rarely had soldiers so close to Harbor Ridge because their mother hated his soldiers, and he always bent over backward to keep her happy. He wouldn't have sent soldiers into the Dark Woods without Madame LaBelle's expressed permission, and she would have *never* granted such permission.

"I didn't get close enough to hear what they were doing," Castor replied curtly. "I'm not a spy or a messenger pigeon. We need to keep moving." With that, he turned away from them and started leading them farther west, away from the King's soldiers, and deeper into the Dark Woods.

They kept an almost perfectly western hike for several hours in silence. Lyra hadn't come back right away, as Castor had, but Quinn had assured her that Lyra was adept at spying and was gathering intel before returning to them. The sun was nearly directly overhead when Lyra caught up with them and shared her newfound knowledge.

"They are anticipating invading the school. They know about the *turmio* and the impact it will have on magical beings. I overheard some of the officers talking, and it seems like they plan to take over the school and hold it hostage." Lyra spoke the words matter-of-factly, but Elena could see the tension in her body, along with the smoke and heat that radiated from Lyra's tail.

"We have to warn them!" Elena cried. Madame LaBelle was a terrible mother, but that didn't mean that she—or any of the students or staff at Harbor Ridge—deserved to be killed or held hostage.

"What do you want us to do?" Quinn asked, pointedly. "Drop everything and run back to Mommy Dearest to tell her the bad guys are coming? I imagine she already knows. Plus, we can't exactly stop what we're doing here. If we don't keep going, no one will be able to stop the *turmio* and we'll all die anyway."

He was right. Rationally, she knew that, but that didn't stop her heart from racing or the growing sense of dread and nausea.

"Once we reach the watchtower, I will fly straight back to Belladonna," Castor offered. "She has a very efficient way of communicating with your mother. At least, she used to. I imagine it still works."

"Thank you," Elena said with a sigh. She hated leaving the school unprotected, but she knew her mother would have sounded alarms and increased their defenses the moment she'd learned that the *turmio* had been released. Elena just had to trust that Madame La-Belle would prioritize the well-being of her students and staff, more so than she ever had with her own children.

13

QUINN

Eqq

ELENA SEEMED TO PHYSICALLY relax some when Castor of-fered to warn Belladonna and the school. Q was grateful for the shifter's willingness to help, but he also secretly hoped that the soldiers would cause some trouble for their mother first. He didn't really want her to die, but maybe the soldiers could knock her down a few pegs. Q thought the whole country could benefit from that woman thinking a little less highly of herself.

They'd continued hiking through the woods as quietly as possible for the rest of the day. The sun was setting beyond the mountains when they finally settled on a place to rest for the night. Lyra had scouted ahead along the base of the mountain before the rest of their pack had caught up to her, and she'd found a small cave for them to hunker down in for the night. It was cold and hard, but sheltered from the increasingly heavy snowfall and would provide them with some cover from potential scouts that were likely traveling ahead of the soldiers.

"Can we risk having a fire?" Elena asked, rubbing her arms furi-ously.

"Yes, please," Demoni seconded. She'd spent the day wrapped around Roska's neck, underneath the hood of his cloak, but the reptile still looked chilled.

Quinn couldn't imagine how it must feel to be unable to heat yourself up and have to constantly rely on external heat sources. Especially as they hiked through icy woods in the frost season. He'd never really considered how the seasons might affect Lyra because she always had a warm coat when it was cold out. The heat of the growing season never seemed to bother her either. He wondered if he'd been insensitive their whole lives. Should he have been paying more attention to her needs? Should he—

Gods, shut up. Can you think of a single moment when I needed something and didn't make that known? Have I ever been that passive? Lyra's voice in his mind brought him back to the present moment.

No, of course not, he replied.

Then knock it off. We have more pressing issues. She caught his eye and directed his gaze to the smoke rising in the distance, through the trees.

Shyt, the troops were closer than he'd expected. Castor had assumed they would proceed directly toward Harbor Ridge, but based on the location of that smoke, the soldiers were taking the scenic route. Or maybe they weren't going to the school at all.

"We can't risk a fire," Quinn said, nodding to the soldier's smoke. "But we can find some decent-sized rocks along the base of the mountain. Lyra and I can heat them up. We'll have plenty of heat, but no light or smoke."

"Oh, that's brilliant," Roska said, his voice carrying a note of awe.

"Agon and I will go collect some rocks. You two start getting the cave warmed up. Quinn, do you think you could heat the floor some too? Just enough to keep it comfortable without cooking us, please."

"I make no promises," Quinn replied with a wink.

He and Lyra entered the cave first, using their respective fires to light up the space and make sure there weren't any bats or other creatures hibernating inside. Once they were sure it was clear, he channeled the heat from his palms directly into the rough stone floor. Quinn had never actually heated a floor before, so he wasn't entirely sure it would work. He was pleasantly surprised when he felt the temperature in the cave start to rise, and Demoni came to lie on the ground near him.

"That feels nice," she practically purred, stringing the "nice" out with a hiss and the flickering of her tongue.

"Just don't overheat, ok?" Quinn said. "I'd hate to have to throw you out in the snow to cool back down," he teased.

She flicked her tongue out at him, spitting a couple of her own snowflakes at his fiery hands, in response. Q took that to mean she didn't need his advice and chuckled as he continued to heat the floor.

"What's for dinner? I'm starving." Castor, who stood casually in the entrance to the cave, looked down at Quinn as though he expected Q to cook a five-course meal in the middle of the small cave.

"Cold meat and cheese, with a side of hard bread. Unless you plan on making yourself useful and start cooking something delicious without a fire," Quinn sniped.

Roska removed his pack and pulled out a couple of loaves of hard, travel-friendly bread, a small wheel of cheese, and a linen-wrapped package of dried jerky Belladonna had sent with them.

He spread the linen wrap out on the floor and took a dagger from the sheath in his boot. Quinn watched his brother slice up the bread with seamless precision from where he knelt in the middle of the cave, still working to warm the space. It was mesmerizing to see how quickly and efficiently his brother worked the blade; first slicing the bread into equal pieces for each of them, then turning his attention to the cheese wheel, making quick work of removing the wax and cutting the cheese itself into the perfect size for their newly sliced bread. Lastly, he divided up the jerky into equal shares and placed each pile of jerky next to an equally fair amount of bread and cheese for each member of their group.

Roska had managed to serve them all a fine and hearty meal and made it look "pretty"—as Elena would say—in a matter of moments. Quinn hadn't moved from his position in the center of the cave, but his eyes had grown wide as he studied his brother's skills with the dagger.

"How did you get so good with a blade?" he asked. It was Q's turn to express awe in his brother now.

"Oh, that? I worked in the kitchens a lot with the Brothers. It was the only time they let me have a sharp object, and I loved it," Roska replied with a casual shrug.

"You'll have to teach me that some time," Q said as he rose from the spot he'd been warming in the center of the cave and moved to sit beside Roska. "Want me to heat this up?" he added, gesturing to the bread and meat.

"Gods, yes," came Castor's reply before Roska could even open his mouth. "If I'm going to eat dead deer and hard bread, they should at least be warm."

Quinn rolled his eyes as Castor joined them on the floor. The sun had nearly disappeared, and along with it the light in their cave, but Quinn kept the heat and fire flowing, just below the surface of his skin. It wasn't much, but the red glow emanating from his body was enough for them to see by.

"What's taking Elena so long?"

"She should have been back a while ago," Lyra agreed.

"I'll fly out and see if I can find them. Maybe they got lost trying to find their way back here." Castor shifted back into a large black bird and hopped to the cave entrance before taking off into the night sky.

Quinn stepped outside of their cave, picked up a fallen branch, and brought it back into the cave. He dug out an old scrap of cloth and wrapped it around the end of the stick and set it on fire.

"Stay here and keep this lit. Maybe she'll be able to find us better if we have a little light to guide her." Q handed the torch to Roska and started back toward the cave entrance.

"Where are you going?" Roska asked, a hint of fear in his voice.

"I'm going to see if I can track her. Lyra should be able to sniff out her trail if I can't find their tracks. We need to get her back here quickly. It's too cold for her to stay out overnight."

"Just don't get lost. Demoni and I will stay here in case she makes her way back." Roska wrapped his cloak tighter around his neck and lifted Demoni back onto his shoulders.

Lyra bound out the cave opening and into the snow, nose searching the ground hoping to catch a whiff of Elena or Agon's scents.

It was getting dark, and it had been snowing since she'd left. Quinn tried to be optimistic, but he felt a growing sense of dread pooling in the pit of his stomach.

Where could she have gone?

14
ROSKA

THEY SEARCHED FOR HOURS. By the time Quinn, Lyra, and Castor had returned to the cave where Roska and Demoni had been anxiously waiting, the snow was up to Lyra's chest and was nearly up to Quinn's knees.

She was gone.

They'd found no sign of Elena or Agon anywhere in the woods or along the base of the mountain. It was as though they'd vanished into the darkness.

"She's a smart, strong girl," Castor said. "If they're lost in the woods, she'll find a way to keep them safe for the night."

Roska was keenly aware of the "if" in Castor's statement. *If* they were lost. No one wanted to voice the alternative. That perhaps they'd been taken.

With the King's soldiers so close, it was too much of a coincidence for Roska to believe that Elena had simply gotten lost. He thought it was far more plausible that she'd been kidnapped by the soldiers.

He didn't know exactly *why* they would take her. If they'd been this far north in search of her, or if they'd just lucked into finding her, alone and vulnerable, in the woods. It didn't really matter. All that mattered was getting her back.

"There's nothing more we can do tonight," Castor spoke again, clearly trying to comfort them but failing miserably. "You two need to get some rest. We'll start fresh in the morning. Perhaps will even find her on the way to the watchtower."

This got Quinn's attention.

"You can't seriously think we're going to abandon her and keep going to the watchtower in search of a man who never wanted anything to do with us, instead of looking for Elena. Our *sister.* She needs our help more than we need that piece of shyt demi-god father of ours." Heat radiated off of him in waves as his rage and fear mixed into a dangerous cocktail.

"Quinn." Roska stepped between his overheating brother and the moonbird shape-shifter. "Quinn, I know how you're feeling. I'm scared and worried about her too, but we can't keep blindly searching the woods when we both know it's unlikely we'll find her. I think you and I can agree that she isn't missing. She was taken. Probably by those damned soldiers. She could be halfway through the Dark Woods by now and well on the way to the capital. Or they could have taken her to Harbor Ridge. Or anywhere, really. We have no idea." Roska put his hands on Quinn's burning shoulders, pouring some of his frosty powers into his hands in an attempt to literally and metaphorically cool his brother. "We need to be smart about this."

Quinn locked eyes with Roska and held his stare for several long moments. He didn't say anything, but the heat in Quinn's skin started to fade and the literal fire in his eyes dissipated. He offered Roska a curt nod before breaking eye contact and massaging his hands as though withdrawing his flames had left them sore.

Roska turned to face Castor. "We will leave at first light. You will stay awake and alert us if anyone comes near the cave. We will go with you to our father. Gods help us, he'd better be useful." He began to turn away from the shifter, but glanced over his shoulder and added, "If anything happens to her, I will freeze the King to death with my bare hands."

He was surprised by the ferocity and coldness in his voice. He was even more surprised by the cloud of frost that followed those words as they exited his lips. But the thing that shocked him the most was the undeniable truth in the statement. Roska knew—beyond a shadow of a doubt—if Elena was hurt, he would kill the King. He wouldn't even hesitate.

The next morning, they moved quickly. No words were spoken as they tightened their cloaks and boots before throwing on their respective packs and heading back out into the knee-deep snow.

When it was clear they weren't going to make good time trudging through the snow, Quinn stopped and began digging through his enchanted pack.

"What are you looking for?" Roska finally asked as Quinn's head disappeared into the bag.

"I think Amelia packed some snowshoes in here," Quinn replied.

Snowshoes? Who was this Amelia, and why was she so prepared for everything? Roska suddenly desperately hoped that he would get to meet her someday soon. He'd heard a few stories about the infamous Amelia from Quinn and Elena over the last few weeks, and Roska secretly hoped that he would meet her and she would adopt him the way she'd adopted his brother and sister.

"Aha!" Quinn exclaimed triumphantly. He had practically crawled inside the bag, in search of these elusive snowshoes, but as he backed out of the bag, he held two pairs high above his head like trophies. He tossed a pair to Roska and showed him how to fit them onto his boots.

Castor cawed from where he'd been circling above them and turned northward. They made much better time, thanks to Amelia's snowshoes. Roska had never dealt with this sort of snow before. The Brotherhood's compound was much further south and rarely saw much snow. Even when it did snow, it rarely stuck to the ground, and it had always melted off by midday. Hiking through knee-deep snow was exhausting, but walking on top of the snow was exhilarating. If he hadn't been so worried about Elena, Roska would have probably started a snowball fight.

Castor flew down and joined them around midday, transforming into a man again, except his feet, which look unsettlingly rabbit-like.

"What the hells, man?" Quinn asked, glaring pointedly at Castor's feet.

"What?" Castor said with a shrug, "Did you have a third pair of snowshoes in your magical bag? No? I didn't think so."

Castor, with his very confusing rabbit feet, led the way as they hiked along the base of the mountain. At one point, he shifted into a mountain lion and started running and playing. He didn't stop until Lyra flicked her tail at him and nearly set him on fire. He promptly shifted into a bird and dove at her several times before shifting back into a man and walking alongside them.

Roska got the impression that Castor was trying to lighten the mood, but it wasn't going to work. Elena and Agon were missing—presumably kidnapped by the King's soldiers. Making jokes or playing wasn't going to change that.

15

QUINN

THE WATCHTOWER WAS EXACTLY as Q had imagined it: crumbling stone walls, unstable-looking, with shutter-less windows, a rotting door, and gaping holes in the roof.

"Are you sure he's here? It doesn't look like anyone has been here in a very long time." Quinn eyed the structure suspiciously.

"I'm certain," Castor replied, walking confidently up the pocked cobblestone path that lead from the main road to the watchtower's entrance. "It's nicer on the inside, I promise," he called over his shoulder, tossing a wink to the bewildered and skeptical brothers.

"It had better be," Quinn mumbled, kicking off his snowshoes and stowing them in his pack. Roska removed his as well and handed them to Q as they both followed Castor up the path to the watch-tower's rotten door.

Castor didn't bother knocking, he merely shoved the door open and gestured for the boys to lead the way. Quinn immediately called his fire into his palms and stepped cautiously into the dim room. Lyra crept in behind him, followed by Roska with Demoni around his neck. Castor flew in behind them, having shifted back into a bird.

The door slammed closed, rattling its hinges and shaking the whole tower.

Quinn froze, raising his flaming hands and channeling more power into them, filling the room with the red-orange light and heat of his fire.

The room was barren. The floor was riddled with broken rocks from the dilapidated stone staircase that spiraled upward. The only windows on the ground level were slits meant for arrows, in case of attack. It was a large space, larger than he would have expected, but Q didn't agree with Castor's assessment that it was "nicer on the inside." The inside looked like a pile of shyt. Just like the outside.

Suddenly, the room went black. Solid, oppressive, and impenetrable darkness took hold of them. Quinn couldn't see his nose on his face, despite the fact that he could still feel the heat of his fire on his hands.

Why are you here?

Quinn spun around, desperately trying to see who had spoken.

Why are you here? the voice asked again.

Quinn froze. He hadn't *heard* the question. Not with his ears, anyway. It had been asked *in his head.* It was similar to when Lyra spoke to his mind, but this felt foreign and wrong. Whoever this voice belonged to, they didn't belong inside Q's head.

He tried to force the voice out of his head and reclaim that space for himself, but the voice seemed to grow roots in the base of his brain, insistently asking the question a third time.

I'm here to speak with my father, Quinn finally answered. He didn't like giving in, but he couldn't see or hear anything else and he needed to get free to find Elena.

Why would you want to do that? The voice queried.

Because that piece of shyt left me to die and as much as I might hate him for that, magic will actually die if he can't help us save it, Quinn snapped.

What makes you think he's willing to help?

If nothing else, self-preservation seems like a safe bet. He might be a demi-god, but I can't imagine he'll be immune to the turmio, *and I doubt he has a death wish.*

There was a long pause after Quinn's response. He started to wonder if the voice had left him, abandoning him to the darkness. Just as quickly as it had appeared, the darkness vanished and Q's fire illuminated the room.

Don't be so sure, the voice added before withdrawing from Q's mind.

"What the hells was that?" Quinn turned his ire on Castor only to find the bird had shifted back into a man and was lounging on a scarlet chaise with a glass of what appeared to be blood-red wine hanging casually from his hand.

A fire roared in a hearth that had been a pile of rubbish when they'd first entered the room. The floor was no longer covered in broken bits of stone from the crumbling staircase. Instead, a luxurious rug lay under his feet. The chaise lounge wasn't the only plush item of furniture. There was another extravagant couch across from the lounge with a study cherry table between them.

Across the room—beneath a window that Quinn was certain hadn't been there a moment before—was a large, round mahogany table covered with books, and scrolls. Amongst the chaos on the table, Q noticed what appeared to be a looking glass, although it didn't resemble any looking glass he'd seen before.

"What the hells is going on here?" Quinn didn't bother containing his outrage, or his fire as he studied the room. Roska stood near the doorway, frost on his fingertips, clearly on edge as well.

"I rather thought that would be obvious," Castor replied, taking a slow sip of his wine. "Your father is a trickster, after all. The disheveled appearance was a trick. It's a very effective technique to keep unwanted visitors at bay."

Before Quinn could reply, he heard Lyra growling at something behind him. Lyra rarely ever growled—she preferred snarky comments, snapping teeth, and fire. Hearing the deep threat rumbling in the back of her throat made Q more anxious than ever. He spun on his heels to face the cause of her wrath.

The man that stood before him was nothing like what Quinn had pictured on the rare occasions that he'd thought about his father. When Q was a boy, he'd fall asleep to thoughts of who his mother might have been: what she'd looked like, how she might have held him and rocked him to sleep as a babe. When he grew a bit older, he wondered more about his father. What had the man who'd helped in his creation been like? Had he even known about Q's existence?

Q imagined his father could have been a blacksmith in a small town or a traveling merchant. For a brief period, he even imagined his father was a pirate, sailing the open seas. In these fantasies, Q dreamed that his father had fallen head over heels for a barmaid, but had been forced to leave her or risk the noose for his criminal ways.

He never once pictured his father to be an old, wrinkly, hunch-backed man with stark white hair and a beard covering half of his chest.

The old man chuckled as he took in the scene below, slowly making his way down the polished wooden stairs that wrapped along the interior of the circular room.

"My sons," he said with a smile. "It's nice to finally meet you both." His voice was gruff, not nearly as weak and frail sounding as Q would have expected from someone who looked so old.

Quinn was gobsmacked. *That* was their father? A gimpy, pathetic old man? How in the name of the Goddess had this old fool managed to trick their mother into sleeping with him?

"Firstly," the man locked eyes with Q, "you shouldn't judge someone based solely on their appearance. Secondly, we didn't do much sleeping that night, if you know what I mean." The man winked and chuckled to himself.

"Oh, gods. I don't want to think about that!" Bile rose up in the back of Q's throat. It took all of his focus to stop himself from vomiting all over the thick rug.

Castor's hearty guffaw filled the room and broke some of the awkward tension that had hung like a black cloud over them since they walked in.

"I'm sorry, my boy. I didn't mean to make you uncomfortable. I've spent the majority of the last seventeen cycles in isolation. I've forgotten my manners." He snapped his fingers and a cloud of purple smoke billowed around him. When the smoke cleared, the frail man had transformed into a strong, young man who appeared to be around his thirtieth solar cycle. His long white mane was gone, replaced by close-cropped, dark brown hair. The scraggly beard he'd had hanging nearly to his belt had vanished. In its place, the man had a well-trimmed goatee with a thin beard along his jawline. "See, Quinn, just like this room, looks can be deceiving."

16

ROSKA

"**F**ATHER?" ROSKA'S VOICE SOUNDED distant. His entire world had shifted, yet again, and he was starting to disconnect from himself. Much like he would during his "maintenance" beatings the Brothers would inflict on him regularly.

The now-young-looking man turned from Q to face Roska, a kind of pitiful sorrow filling his eyes as he took in the appearance of his second son.

"You've had such a hard life. I'm sorry for that, my son. If I could have, I would've brought you all here to stay with me the moment you were born." Their father seemed genuine, but Roska had a hard time believing his words.

"Why didn't you, then?" Roska tried but failed to keep the rage from his voice.

"It's hard to explain, and I don't think you'd accept my answer even if I told you." Their father crossed the room to a drinks cart that Roska hadn't noticed before. He gestured to the cart. "Would you boys like something to drink?"

"I don't want a muxing drink." Quinn seemed to have finally regained control of his tongue. "I want answers. I want to know why you left us in hells, separated and abused for *cycles*."

Castor shot to his feet, glaring at Quinn, and growled, "Don't you dare speak to him that way."

"Castor, please." Their father placed a hand on the shifter's shoulder and shook his head. "They have a right to be upset. They don't know the whole story."

"Why don't you enlighten us then?" Roska prompted.

"Aiden, you don't owe them anything." Castor shared a meaningful look with their father.

"They have a right to know, Castor." Aiden patted the shifter on the shoulder once, filled a glass with wine from the drink cart, and took a seat on the chaise lounge that Castor had been lazing on moments before. "If you two would like to take a seat," he gestured to the empty seats across from him, "I will try to explain things to your satisfaction."

Roska looked to Quinn. He didn't have much experience dealing with interrogations. Quinn gave a subtle nod, and they both sat down on the edge of their seats, not wanting to get too comfortable. They needed to be ready in case something went wrong.

Demoni moved from her spot around his neck, slithering down his arm, and taking up a guard position on the armrest of Roska's chair. Lyra—smoke rising faintly from the tip of her tail—came to sit between Q's feet, putting herself between their father and Quinn. Roska's frost chilled his hands, giving his fingertips a slight bluish coloring. He took a few deep breaths in an attempt to calm his nerves and rein in his power. He glanced at Quinn's hands and saw the heat from his powers had started to scorch the arms of the chair he sat in.

Quinn either didn't notice or didn't care that he was damaging their father's furniture. Roska felt driven to control his powers so he wouldn't cause any damage.

Old habits die hard, I guess, he thought to himself. The compulsion to make himself as small and unthreatening as possible still drove most of his actions. He wondered if that would ever change.

"When I first heard the prophecy," Aiden began, "I was half-drunk on a crate of fae wine, after a week of celebrating the summer solstice with those delightful—albeit quite cagey—creatures. I was still young, only a century or so at that point, and cocky. I thought I could trick them into revealing their visions to me so that I could fully understand what was to come and the role I would play."

"I take it that didn't work out so well for you," Quinn prodded.

Roska noticed the hint of flames under his brother's fingernails. "Q," Roska half-whispered, "your fingers."

"I'm fine, Ros. I've got this," he waved his fingers at Roska, "under control." Quinn turned back to their father expectantly.

"Well, it did and it didn't," the man replied, pausing to take a sip of his wine. "You see, the fae are uniquely adept at receiving and comprehending prophecies and visions from the Gods. In my arrogance, I thought as a child of Lugh I would be able to navigate their visions without issue. I was wrong. The visions bombarded my mind and left me a dribbling mess for several moons. I couldn't distinguish between what I'd seen and what was reality. Past, present, and future all merged together, and I lost my mind. I can't even tell you how long I was like that. Trapped in a mental space where time had no meaning.

"I eventually found my way back to the present, but I still couldn't comprehend what I'd seen or make heads or tails of the bits I relived in my dreams. When I stumbled—quite literally—into your mother that night, I didn't recognize her for who she was or what she would mean to me and the future of the world. I barely recognized my own reflection." He took another sip of his wine, then glanced pensively at Castor. "I suppose that could have been a result of the glamor I'd been wearing at the time." He turned back to the brothers. "You see, I have to change my look up every so often so people don't start to pick up on my seemingly endless life span."

"Wait," Roska cut in, "does that mean we are immortals too?"

"Oh, no, dear boy. I'm not immortal and neither are you. We are considerably harder to kill, but we most certainly can die."

Roska didn't know how to respond to that. He hadn't really considered what it meant to have a demi-god as a father. Aside from granting him previously-mythical powers, he realized that it also potentially enabled him to outlive the Brothers. He smiled to himself, imagining the day he would dance on their graves.

"This pleases you?" Aiden observed. "I'm glad to hear it! Most people get excited for a moment, then realize that they're going to outlive everyone they love, they tend to get very depressed. Brooding and whining about everything."

Roska didn't even hesitate in his response. "I only love two people and, according to you, they will be living indefinitely with me."

Roska was fairly certain he heard Quinn's neck crack with the speed at which his brother turned his head to face him. Roska hadn't vocalized the feelings he'd developed for his siblings. He'd realized it moons ago when they first met in the cavern and they'd shown him kindness for the first time in his life. He loved them. His biggest regret was that he hadn't gotten a chance to tell Elena before she'd been taken.

"Elena!" he shouted. Somehow in their life-altering meeting with their father, they'd forgotten Elena was the reason they'd come here in the first place.

"What about her?" Aiden asked, clearly thrown by the sudden change of topic.

"She's missing. Which you might have known if you'd taken a more serious interest in your children, you shyt." Quinn's rage was beginning to bubble over, and his chair was paying the price. Roska felt slightly guilty for the damage Q was causing, but he couldn't fault his brother for the anger he felt. Roska wholeheartedly agreed with him. If their father had taken a more active role—or any role at all—in their lives, things would have turned out very differently and Elena wouldn't have been taken to begin with.

"Is she missing or was she taken?" Aiden asked the question like he knew the answer.

Roska stared at their father. Stunned for a moment by the all-knowing air about his inquiry.

"You knew she'd be taken, didn't you?" When he finally spoke, the tension in Roska's voice was matched by the ice in his veins and the frosty mist radiating off his hands. "How the hells could you *knowingly* let this happen? She could be killed!"

"I guarantee you," Quinn bit out, "if she is killed, I will come back here and see just how "hard to kill" you really are."

Roska blanched at Q's words, but seeing the look of sheer rage boiling just below the surface of his brother's face, Roska knew Quinn meant every word. Not for the first time, Roska prayed Elena would be safe. For her sake as well as Q's.

17
AIDEN

AIDEN STUDIED HIS BOYS as they sat across from him, threatening to murder him. He beamed with pride. These boys, who had only known each other for a few moons after meeting under exceptionally challenging conditions, were working together and excelling.

Yes, he'd known Elena would be taken, but he hadn't known exactly when or where. He wouldn't have been able to stop it from happening, even if he'd known the exact moment that she'd be kidnapped. She was on the path they needed her to be on in order to save magic.

But how could he explain all of this to the boys in a way that they would understand and accept?

You can't, dumbass. They're gonna hate you no matter what you say, Aleerah answered snarkily. His faithful—if not a little condescending—wolf-like familiar lounged at the top of the stairs, judging him.

Come now. Is that level of harshness really necessary? Aiden replied.

I've found honesty to be the best policy. Especially when dealing with dumbasses. She had always felt like it was her job to keep him grounded, so he didn't get "too full of himself," as she often said. He heard her cackling laugh in his mind.

"What the hells are you smiling about?" Quinn rose from his chair and took an aggressive step toward Aiden. Lyra, his quick-witted fox, was standing before her human, smoke unfurling rapidly from the tip of her tail as she bared her teeth at Aiden.

Castor rose to meet Quinn's advance, but Aiden placed a hand on his friend's arm to deter him.

"I'm sorry," Aiden said quickly, trying to defuse the situation. "I didn't mean to offend you. I'm not smiling about Elena being taken, I promise you. I can also promise that she is exactly where she's supposed to be. As are you," he added with a pointed look at both of his sons.

His *sons*. He never would have pictured himself as a father before, but with his children before him now, he couldn't have imagined a different life.

Come the mux on. Aleerah's contempt was palpable. Aiden wondered if the boys could feel her disdain as it flooded the tower. *You can't reminisce about fatherhood or brag to yourself about how amazing your kids are. You had nothing to do with their upbringing. They are who they are, in spite of you.*

The truth of her words grated on him. He hadn't been an active father because he knew that they needed to grow up stronger than he could have taught them to be himself. He and Aleerah had had this same argument since the triplet's conception. Not that it mattered anymore. The prophecy was in motion now. There was nothing left to do but point them in the right direction and hope for the best.

"Elena is on a separate mission, but she will be there with you at the end, to stop the *turmio* and help right the world. You don't need to worry about her." He tried to sound comforting, but the rising temperature in the room and the flames in Quinn's eyes told Aiden that his words failed to hit their mark.

"You slimy, useless, piece of shyt." Quinn slowly raised his flaming hand and pointed directly at Aiden's chest. "You don't get to act all high and mighty after leaving us to suffer for *cycles*. If we didn't need your help to stop this damned prophecy, I would burn you to ash right now."

Quinn lowered his hand, took a deep breath, and spoke again. "We didn't come here to connect with you. We've done just fine for the last sixteen cycles. We don't need a father. What we need is a magical wizard demi-god to help us recapture the *turmio* before anyone gets killed."

Even though he knew Quinn's feelings were valid and justified, Aiden couldn't help feeling discarded by his son's bitter words.

It was Castor's turn to comfort Aiden as he laid a cool, black hand—with uniquely talon-like fingernails—on Aiden's knee. It was time to get to work. Aiden would have time to dwell on his life choices later. His children needed him, and it was time he finally stepped up to the challenge.

18
QUINN

QUINN'S FIRE PULSED UNDER his skin, hidden behind the sleeves of his fur-lined woolen coat. Lyra's tail was still smoking. The room would have been an oven, if not for the balance of frosty temperatures pouring from Roska's hands and Demoni's opened mouth.

If he took a moment to navigate his feelings, Q would have realized that most of his hostility wasn't actually directed at their father. He was worried about Elena, and it seemed as though Aiden had no intention of helping them rescue her. Which meant they'd wasted a full day traveling in the wrong direction. Elena was headed south, toward Riverayn, and they'd gone in the opposite direction to find their useless father.

Q took a deep breath, recalling his fire as best he could, and spoke in a tight voice. "If you aren't going to help us save her because you say she's where she's supposed to be, then what the hells are we supposed to do?"

"Exactly what we came here to do," Castor answered. "We are here to find a way to recapture the *turmio*. Your father is the most skilled wizard I've ever met. If anyone can help you end this before it gets out of hand, it's him."

Aiden said nothing, but Quinn thought he saw a touch of nerves flash across their father's face. Quinn studied the man for a long moment. He wasn't at all what Quinn had expected when they had decided to find their father, but meeting Madame LaBelle had been equally eye-opening. It was just further proof that someone's birth parents didn't shape who that person would grow to be.

Madame LaBelle and Aiden had given Q his physical qualities and his fiery magic, but they didn't make him into the strong, independent, protective guy he'd become. Hells, they had nothing to do with his character, his loyalty. Those were a direct result of Amelia's compassion and Quinn's desire to protect those he cared about from having to endure the things he'd been forced to go through.

Lyra glanced over her shoulder at Q. She sensed the change in his mood and seemed startled by it. Quinn knew she'd understand his thought process, she experienced it with him, but it caused a sudden shift in his mood, and he knew that would be jarring for her.

"Fine," Q said, addressing Castor, but locking eyes with Aiden. "How do we stop the *turmio* and save magic?"

"Well, that is an excellent question, isn't it?" Aiden replied. His attempt at a smile fell flat. Q didn't know or trust this man, and it was going to take more than a few friendly smiles and half-ass attempts at jokes for him to earn Q's trust.

"Yeah," Quinn said dryly. "That's why I asked it."

"I hate to disappoint you boys—" Aiden started.

"Too late," Quinn cut in.

"Quinn, give him a minute." Roska's frost had started to thaw, although Q could still see the cool mist drifting slowly away from his brother's fingertips.

Quinn conceded, taking his seat again, and motioned for Aiden to continue.

"You see, like I mentioned, the prophecy got jumbled in my mind, along with about a hundred other prophecies and visions of the past and possible futures. I can't give you a step-by-step guide to defeating the *turmio* because I honestly don't know how." Aiden's eyes flicked from Roska's icy blue stare to Q's fiery glare.

He rose from his lounge and motioned for them to follow him over to the table under the window. Quinn reluctantly complied, Lyra and Roska quick on his heels. "You see this?" Aiden said, handing Q a tattered bit of parchment. "This is the original written record of the prophecy."

Quinn looked down at the abused document in his hands. "How can you tell? There aren't any words here? Just faded markings and maybe an old drawing. Hells, I've seen children make more logical drawings in the sand. With sticks."

Aiden chuckled at Q's observation, which just irritated Quinn more.

Stop trying to bond with me, asshole. That window closed a long *time ago.*

Maybe he's one of those "better late than never" types of people? Lyra offered.

Maybe she was right, but Quinn definitely wasn't that type of person. Better late than never only applied if you were welcome any time. As far as Q was concerned, the window to being a parent to someone closed quickly. Especially if you're some kinda immortal demi-god. Aiden had all the time in the muxing world. He chose to waste that time not being there for his kids. Q felt no obligation to give the man a second chance now.

"Yes, it's a bit worn, but with a bit of magic and a great deal of patience, I was able to extract these original words from the page." Aiden took the page from Quinn and handed a second, more legible, piece of parchment to him. "See, here? This is the part you've heard before. About the Dragon's teeth and the allies masked as foe." He turned to Roska and said, "That bit was about you, you know."

"Wait, how do you know that we've heard it before?" Suspicions prickled in the back of Q's mind.

"What? Oh, um…" Aiden seemed genuinely thrown by Quinn's question, and it was clear that their father was struggling to come up with a convincing answer.

"Because he's been spying on you since your conception." The condescending female voice startled them all.

Quinn had barely reined in his powers but was wound so tight that a flare sprang from his fingertips and singed the rug.

"Aleerah!" Aiden admonished. With a wave of his hand, the flames were extinguished and the rug appeared undamaged. "You startled them. Can't you see they're already stressed without you sneaking up on them like that?"

Quinn stared open-mouthed at the creature before him. She appeared to be some kind of wolf, but she was the size of a small horse. Her fur was a brilliant cinnamon brown, but her eyes were what captured Quinn's attention. They were two different colors. One was a clear blue, like the sky on a sunny, growing season day. The other was the color of the deepest sea. Or, at least the color that Q imagined the sea to be. The depths of blue and teal that filled her eye drew him in. He imagined a person could drown in that color if they weren't careful.

Lyra's growl dragged Quinn out of his enchantment and brought him back to the present. Lyra had positioned herself between the massive wolf and Q. He didn't stop her, but Quinn knew that if it came to violence, Lyra wouldn't survive. One snap of those enormous teeth and they'd both be dead.

"Easy, girl." Q tried to soothe Lyra's frayed nerves, but he didn't have much luck. The wolf, Aleerah, was a massive and imposing force. Nothing Quinn could say or do would calm Lyra when she felt *this* threatened by another creature. Lyra's tail was on fire, poised straight up behind her, prepared to strike.

Aleerah didn't move. She held Lyra's stare but kept her magical eyes passive and non-threatening. Quinn's breath was trapped in his lungs as he waited to see how things would shake out. Roska and Demoni stood frozen beside him.

There was something in Aleerah's eyes that made Quinn think of home. Their comfortable hut in the woods. Their room at Amelia's. Any time they'd woken up with Elena and Agon nearby. A feeling of warmth and contentment washed over him, and he saw the tension leave Lyra's defensive pose. She lowered her tail, extinguishing her flame, and took a seat at his feet.

Aleerah offered a subtle nod to Lyra, before turning her attention back to the brothers.

"As I was saying," she went on as though nothing had happened, "your father has been watching all three of you since your conception. With the aid of that looking glass."

Quinn looked over his shoulder at the odd, purple-tinted looking glass he'd seen when he'd first noticed the table.

"How does it work?" Roska asked.

"It's actually quite brilliant," Aiden began, rushing around the table to pick up the looking glass. He offered it to Roska and looked like he was about to dive into a lengthy explanation of the tool and how it worked, but was thankfully cut off by the oversized wolf.

"It's magic. That's enough of an explanation for now. We have more pressing issues."

Q was starting to like the massive beast. She didn't put up with Aiden's arrogance. Quinn really appreciated her directness.

"Can we use it to see where Elena is being held?" Quinn asked, directing his question to the wolf and all but ignoring his father.

"I'm sorry, Quinn," Aleerah replied, eyes downcast. "I'm afraid it can't. We tried to check in on you all last night and looked for her once we realized she was no longer with you. Something is shielding her from the magic in the looking glass. We cannot see her."

Mux. Quinn hated that things were never easy. He wasn't surprised, but just once, he wanted things to be simple.

19

ROSKA

ROSKA LOOKED FROM QUINN'S disappointed face to their father's jittery hands, before settling on the dire wolf's sad eyes.

A dire wolf. He never thought he'd see one in person. He'd read about them in the Brotherhood's library—on the rare occasion that Brother Liam was in charge of his lessons. The books had made it sound as though dire wolves had died out ages ago, yet here she was. Aleerah was a thing of beauty. More than that though, she was a wonder. A thing that shouldn't exist. Just like himself.

"I'm sorry we can't help you rescue Elena." Aleerah sat before them, head lowered in disappointment or shame, Roska wasn't sure. "Unfortunately, Aiden is right. Elena is on the path she needs to be on to save magic and the world. Don't worry, sweet boys. You will see your sister again soon. The prophecy guarantees it."

The tightness that had been restricting Roska's ability to breathe lightened some at her words. It wasn't a huge comfort, because Roska knew Elena would face quite an intense trial at the hands of the King and his soldiers, but he trusted that the gods weren't through with them yet. He would see Elena again soon, and then he'd be able to tell her how much she meant to him and how grateful he was to have her in his life.

"Ok, well, if you can't help us save her, and you can't show us where she is or if she's ok, how do we know you can even help us with the *turmio*?" Roska's skepticism was growing, despite his boundless desire to connect with their father. He'd dreamed about getting to know his family since the first day the Brothers had told him they existed. Meeting their mother had turned out to be a massive disappointment, but he hadn't expected much from that interaction. The Brothers might have spent the first sixteen cycles of his life trying to brainwash him against magic, but it seemed they had actually been right about their mother.

Still, spending time with Q and Elena had changed Roska's whole world. He hoped—possibly foolishly—that he might find a similar connection with their father.

"Well, you see..." Aiden began. He gently placed the looking glass back on the table, wringing his hands and casting a nervous look up to Aleerah before he continued. "I'm actually the one who trapped it in the first place. Not alone, obviously. I had some help." Aiden plastered an overzealous smile on his face as he held Roska's gaze. "I'm confident that with the help of you three and your magnificent familiars, we will be able to recapture the beast before he regains his corporeal form."

"Say that again," Q demanded, glaring harshly at their father.

"I, um, I was part of the group of wizards, witches, and enchantresses who trapped the *turmio* in that cavern ages ago." Aiden's smile faltered and a nervous look consumed his face. He spoke so slowly that Roska started to wonder if the act of speaking was somehow painful for him. He'd heard stories during his time with the Brothers of magical spells and curses that could make it physically impossible for someone to speak about a subject. According to the Brotherhood, it was a way to keep the non-magical community from having access to magical powers or the knowledge of all the backroom deals the magical beings used to maintain their power and control over the country.

"It was quite a long time ago, you see, and my mind has been a jumbled mess for the majority of the time since that night. I think I can probably remember how we did it before." Aiden was trying to sound hopeful. Roska could see it in the way he offered them a weak smile. Unfortunately, Aiden wasn't as practiced at lying as his sons were at reading people.

"You've got to be muxing kidding me." Quinn's exasperated tone surprised Roska. He'd expected Q to explode in a fiery rage and burn down the tower. Instead, Q seemed to deflate. Roska watched his brother take a few steps backward and collapse into a waiting chair. "This can't be happening. You were supposed to be able to help. *You* were supposed to be the solution."

Quinn looked so defeated. Roska had never seen him this way. Even when they were captured and tied up outside their campsite by the creek that first night, Quinn had been a spitfire, picking fights and hurling insults like he wasn't scared at all. Looking at him now, Roska worried that his brother might finally have broken under all the pressure that had been building for the better part of the last solar cycle.

"I know this isn't what you wanted to hear," Aleerah began.

"But I promise, we *can* help you. We will stop the *turmio*," Aiden added, finishing her thought.

"How can you promise that?" Quinn asked dejectedly.

"I'm confident that we can figure it out with this." Aiden picked up the parchment he'd started showing them before Aleerah had made her grand entrance. "This has the full prophecy. Accurately translated, so it's basically a map of what to do and where to go."

Roska couldn't believe what he was hearing. A map? To guide them through these trials and help them undo the mess he'd made? It almost sounded too good to be true.

"What's the catch?" Q asked.

"There's no catch," Aiden replied. "Well, not really. I mean, the prophecy states that one of you will 'fall' but that could mean any-thing really." He quickly glanced away from Quinn's hard stare and started shuffling the papers on his cluttered table.

"One of us will 'fall'?" Roska asked. "Like literally fall down? Or like one of us will die?"

"We can't be certain," Aleerah said. "Regardless, we need to do everything we can to stop this damned thing or we will all die. Along with countless other magical creatures."

Roska knew she was right, but he couldn't fight the desire to be selfish and protect his siblings. He'd only just gotten to know them, and he had so much more to learn from and about them. He refused to let any of them die. He would find another way. There *had* to be another way.

Roska and Aiden spent the next few hours pouring over Aiden's books and going over the ritual Roska had completed to release the *turmio*. Aiden theorized that with enough knowledge of how Roska unleashed the beast, along with his "complete" version of the prophecy, and his rough memory—Roska was being generous with that description—of how he had helped to trap the creature all those cycles before, they might be able to piece together how to trap it again.

The sun was setting behind the mountain outside the window they'd been working at all day. They still had no new information or answers.

Castor had flown off as soon as it was clear they were going to be researching the rest of the day. Quinn had disappeared with Lyra and Aleerah outside sometime around their lunch break. Just like at Belladonna's, Quinn was short-tempered and quick to lash out the longer he'd been forced to sit still and research. Aleerah recommended that Quinn and Lyra go with her to hunt for dinner. Roska thought Q might have actually jumped for joy if he hadn't been harboring so much resentment toward their father.

Roska understood Q's feelings, but he also knew that this might be their only chance to get to know the man who'd sired them. He wasn't going to miss the opportunity.

"Aiden," Roska began slowly, "can you tell me anything about your father? I would love to know more about our bloodline. I'm very curious to know what flows in my veins."

Aiden looked up from the book he'd been researching, scratched the well-trimmed hair along his jawline, and gave Roska a pensive look. His father was quiet for a long time, studying him to the point that Roska started to worry that the question might have been considered rude and he'd somehow managed to offend the demi-god. Roska was seconds away from retracting his question when Aiden sighed and nodded.

"Aye, I suppose knowing one's history does help see one's path more clearly." Aiden rose from his chair and walked over the to drink cart. "Would you like anything? I have every manner of wine imaginable. And whatever I don't have, I can typically conjure without any trouble."

Roska thought his words were a tad boastful, but he also imagined they were true. Their father was the son of a God. Roska found it hard to believe that there was anything beyond his reach.

You're giving this man too much credit, Demoni hissed in Roska's mind. *He's a demi-god, but he's not a hero, and he's not infallible.*

Demoni was more inclined to side with Quinn when it came to passing judgment on their father. Aiden had watched them suffer, cycle after cycle, and never once stepped in to help or protect them. As far as Demoni was concerned, Aiden was as much of a father as a stud horse was to a newborn foal.

"I wouldn't mind some coffee, if that's something you can conjure," Roska said to Aiden. Much to his surprise, his father nodded, picked up an empty wine glass, and snapped his fingers. In a flash of purple smoke, the wine glass transformed into a steaming mug of delicious-smelling coffee.

"Milk? Cream?" Aiden offered.

Roska was too stunned to speak, merely shaking his head and accepting the proffered mug. He took a slow, cautious sip and was blown away by the flavor. It was unlike any he'd ever had before—which really wasn't saying much since the stuff they had at the monastery was more acid than actual flavor. There were hints of cinnamon and chocolate in the piping hot mug of warmth with only a touch of the acidity he'd had to suffer through at the monastery.

Roska couldn't contain the moan of pleasure that escaped his lips.

"Good, yeah?" Aiden chuckled. He poured himself another glass of wine and returned to the table. "All right, so you wish to know about my father, your grandsire? Where should I start..." He took a sip of his wine and said, "I suppose the logical thing would be to start at the beginning. My mother was the fifth daughter of a farmer in a town that no longer exists in a country that has long since been swallowed up by other countries over the ages. Her father, my grandsire, was not a kind man, and he resented his wife and daughters. He'd wanted a son, but his wife continued to bear him daughters.

"One day, after a particularly vicious fight with her father, my mom pack her few belongings and ran away. Towns were few and far between back then, but she knew that if she stayed in her father's home, she wouldn't survive another cycle. The way she told me the story, she met my father on the side of a creek. He looked like he'd been beaten and robbed. Covered in cuts and bruises, his left eye swollen shut, blood soaking his shirt. My mother took pity on him, dragged him from the creek to the cover of the trees, and treated his wounds. She spent days taking care of him in the woods, hunting for them, keeping him warm at night, and dressing his wounds. One night, he revealed the truth about himself to her. He was Lugh, he'd told her, Trickster God of the North and a magically powerful man. He explained that his injuries were the result of a battle with his brother, the God of War, and he thanked her for offering him aid in his time of need.

"He asked her what he could do to repay her kindness, and she simply said that she wanted love. She asked him to grant her the love she'd never experienced in her home but knew was possible. My father, being the trickster that he was, used her desperate desire to be loved against her, sharing her bed for the night, and disappearing before she woke. Leaving her to carry and raise me on her own.

"My mother never once complained about the burden she'd been left to bear all alone. Even on her deathbed, she looked at me with such unfathomable love, telling me that he had given her everything she'd ever wanted. I suppose there was a poetry to his efforts. She wanted to feel the love of a family, the love a parent feels for their child, and he'd given her that. Still, it seemed like a rather shytty way to do it, if you ask me." Aiden shrugged, sipping his wine and studying Roska's expression. Roska got the impression his father was trying to read how he would react to the story about his grandsire and grandmother.

Roska took a sip of his own beverage to hide his face while he contemplated all that he'd just learned.

"Have you ever met him?" Roska asked, breaking the heavy silence that had descended on the room.

"Once. About a hundred cycles ago." Aiden's eyes flicked from Roska's face to the fire in the hearth. "He wasn't what I'd expected. He remembered my mother and spoke of her fondly. I punched him in the nose."

Roska choked on his coffee, spitting half of it out across the table. "You what?!"

"Well, he abandoned my mother, pregnant and unmarried, in an unforgiving landscape. Leaving her to fend for herself and raise me entirely on her own. And I wasn't an easy child. That woman was a saint, and she deserved better than he'd given her." Aiden shrugged, but Roska could see the rage boiling just below the surface in his father's eyes. "I told him so, right before I broke his perfect muxing nose."

"I... I can't believe you punched a god. And lived to tell about it!" Roska stared at his father, in awe of his brashness. "Q would love that story. He might realize that he's more like you than he wants to believe."

"Oh, aye, Quinn has definitely inherited my fiery temper, although he's taken it to a much more literal level." Aiden chuckled. He looked at Roska, and Roska could see a hint of that fire still burning behind his father's eyes. "You all seem to have inherited bits of my personality, for better or worse. But I can't take credit for the strength of character you each have. The three of you are the absolute best thing I've ever helped bring about in this world. I hope someday I can convince you all of that."

20
BEATRICE

"Headmistress." An urgent knock on the office door roused Beatrice from her memories, forcing her attention to the here-and-now.

"Come in."

Marsali rushed into the room, arms filled with dozens of missives and a look of terror in her eyes.

"Apologies, Headmistress," she muttered, clearly trying to maintain control of her emotions but failing completely. "It's happening. Investigators from all over Waverly have been writing to us in various stages of panic. Their magics aren't working. Either not as they should, or not at all. And many of our younger students have fallen ill. The infirmary is overfilled with young girls who are weak, and their familiars seem to be fading away."

Marsali's eyes filled with tears as she looked to Beatrice for a solution. Unfortunately, the headmistress had nothing to offer. This was the work of the *turmio*, and there wasn't anything she could do to stop it or save the students. Their only hope was the triplets. Beatrice had tried to protect them. First by separating them, then by locking them away in that damned tower. But none of it mattered. This was all fated to happen, and she couldn't do a thing to save them. To save anyone.

Beatrice rose from her chair, took the missives from Marsali, and placed them in a pile on her desk. Then she took the girl's hands in her own, holding her gaze and taking dramatic deep breaths, encouraging Marsali to copy her actions.

"You're right," Beatrice said plainly. "This is the result of the *turmio*. There's nothing we can do to stop what's happening to magic. It is all acting according to prophecy. The only thing we can do is make the girls as comfortable as possible and pray to the Mother that Elena and her brothers are able to recapture that damned beast before things become irreversible."

Beatrice released Marsali's hands and wiped the tears from the girl's face. "We need to focus on what we can control and put our energies towards protecting this school and her inhabitants. The *turmio* is attacking the young and less-skilled first, which means we have a little time before it starts to affect those of us with more power and control over our magic. We need to take advantage of this while we can. Goddess knows the magept will be quick to attack and try to take from us the moment they realize we've been weakened."

"But why, Headmistress? Why would they want to hurt us? We've been nothing but kind to them all these years." Marsali was distraught. Beatrice felt guilty for the truth she was about to reveal to her, but it was necessary.

"They don't see it that way." Beatrice dropped her hands and looked out the window, toward the town at the edge of the Dark Woods. "They see us as the enemy. Power-crazed, child-stealing, selfish monsters who sit up in our tower, judging them and using them to suit our needs. It's not entirely inaccurate, although it is a rather narrow viewpoint. We have always prioritized magic and the well-being of magical creatures. The magept feel slighted. Maybe they're right to feel that way, but their anger toward us is misplaced. If anything, they should be upset with the King and Queen. It's not our fault that the King has given so much of his time, energy, and funding to us."

Even as she said it, Beatrice knew she was wrong. The King loved her. At least, he thought he did. Beatrice wasn't sure that man knew what love really was. Regardless, he'd taken to attempting to woe her through massive gifts of gold and precious gems to fund the school's expeditions and searches for more enchantresses throughout Waverly. Beatrice never outright asked for these gifts, but she never denied or discouraged them either. She had a sense that he'd raised the taxes on his citizens numerous times to pay for the lavish gifts he bestowed on her. Perhaps she should have been more prudent, maintained a more balanced relationship with the King. Maybe then the magept of Waverly wouldn't resent the magical community as much.

Of course, it was far too late for that now.

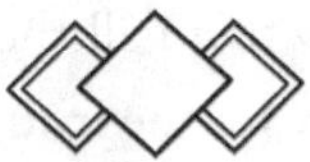

Beatrice, with Zied striding powerfully at her side, took time that morning to visit with the sick young girls in the infirmary. She wanted to offer them hope and comfort, but there was none to be had. There was nothing she or any of the skilled healers could do that would ease the girls in their suffering. Nevertheless, as Headmistress, it was her job to project confidence and calm. Beatrice made a point to stop by each child's bedside and offer a prayer to the Mother Goddess for their protection and speedy recovery.

She silently prayed for their quick and painless release from this hells.

Marsali hadn't been exaggerating when she said the children's familiars were fading away. It looked as though the creatures were slowly disappearing from the world. Beatrice wasn't entirely sure what would happen once the familiars faded completely, but she knew for a fact—having witnessed it herself many solar cycles ago—that once the familiar died, the enchantress would soon follow.

Beatrice hated that the children were suffering so, but she also knew that most of them, if not all, would perish before the triplets would be able to stop the *turmio*. It had only been a matter of weeks before the first child had fallen ill. Beatrice knew that these children would likely never see the next moon.

Not for the first time, she cursed herself. For her hubris. For her selfishness. For her downright stupidity. If she hadn't been so damned arrogant, thinking she was the center of this prophecy, believing that she could shape it to suit her desires, none of this would have happened. These children wouldn't be dying.

Thinking like that won't help these girls now. Zied nudged her thigh as she moved on to the next cot. The girl in the bed couldn't be more than eight, her familiar—a wolfhound pup—curled on her chest as they both struggled to take a full breath. The simple act of breathing was so exhausting, the girl looked as though she'd welcome death.

Nothing will help these girls now, Beatrice replied flatly. She knelt beside the cot, placing one hand on the young girl's brow while laying her other hand on the pup's head.

She whispered the same prayer while also casting a spell to ease the child's lungs and help her to breathe a little easier. It was the magical equivalent of sticking one's finger in the hole of a dam, but it was the best she could do all things considered.

The girl weakly offered her thanks, closed her eyes, and drifted off to an uneasy sleep.

Beatrice stayed by the girl's side a moment longer, whispering another prayer to the Mother Goddess. "Please," she said, her voice barely audible, "protect these girls. Keep them safe, ease their suffering, and hasten my children. We won't survive like this much longer."

She smoothed the hair on the girl's head, gently patted the pup, and rose to visit the next girl.

21
QUINN

CROUCHED LOW IN THE snow, hidden behind the under-brush, Quinn notched an arrow, taking aim at the small herd of deer meandering fifty paces ahead through the winter forest. It was dusk, the sun finally setting on what had felt like the longest day of Q's life. Aleerah was to the north of the herd, and Lyra had positioned herself to the south. They only needed one deer to feed them all, but Q was always overly thoughtful when hunting deer. He never liked to pick the does, if he could avoid it, because he hated the idea of leaving a babe without its mother. And he never wanted to kill off the young bucks. Which left him hunting the older males. He tried to pick the "middle-aged" stags, ones who were likely past their reproducing prime, but who weren't leaders of the herd, so the rest of the deer weren't left without their metaphorical rudder.

Rationally, Quinn knew he put way too much thought into pick-ing out which deer to kill and eat, but he respected these creatures and their right to live. He never took the decision to end a life—any life—lightly. This animal would die so the rest of them could con-tinue to survive. It was a sacrifice the animal had no say in, but

Quinn was compelled to be as reverent as possible. These creatures deserved that much, at least.

He lined up his shot, took a deep breath, thanked the Mother Goddess for this meal, exhaled, and let loose his shot. His arrow hit its mark, as they always did, right behind the deer's shoulder, directly through the heart. The stag dropped, instantly dead. The herd took off in different directions, disappearing into the darkness.

Aleerah crept forward, sniffed the felled deer, and nodded her appreciation to Quinn. "That was an excellent shot."

"He's gotten very good at kill shots. It's more impressive when he's hunting rabbits." Lyra hopped through the thick snow over to Aleerah and their dinner.

"Thanks, I think," Quinn replied. He didn't know how to take their compliments. He'd just taken a life, and they were commending him for it.

"You didn't kill it for fun, Q," Lyra spoke, reading his mind. "You aren't that kind of hunter. You kill to survive. Nothing more."

"Let's get this back to the tower." Quinn shrugged off her words. He knelt before the deer, placed a hand on its side, and offered it a quiet thanks for its sacrifice as well as an apology for being the one to end its life.

He repositioned himself to hoist the body across his shoulders, but Aleerah stepped in, nosing the body up and tossing it into the air, skillfully catching it across her back. She adjusted it slightly and turned back toward the tower. Quinn shared an impressed glance with Lyra before following behind the massive wolf, now carrying at least two hundred and fifty pounds of dead weight.

They hadn't ventured too far from the tower; they hadn't needed to. Their little hunting trip had taken much longer than it actually needed to because Quinn had needed to get out of that place and away from his father for a while.

In just one day, his entire world had flipped on its head, and Q had no idea how to process it all. Elena was gone. Supposedly she was fine, but he found it hard to believe that Elena could be kidnapped by the man who wanted to kill off magic, and yet Elena would remain unharmed. Q believed his father when he said they would see her again and she wouldn't be killed, but he also knew that she would not be returning to them unscathed.

You have to trust that she will take care of herself, Lyra attempted to comfort him. *She's been through hells already, and she's always come out on top. There's no reason to think this will be any different.*

She's never been kidnapped by an entire army before, Quinn pointed out.

True, but they've never dealt with an electric weasel and a pissed off enchantress with anger management issues, Lyra countered.

She doesn't have anger management issues! Quinn tossed Lyra a glare as they exited the woods, following Aleerah onto the main road that would take them back to the watchtower.

Oh, you're right, Lyra conceded. *That's you.*

Despite himself, Quinn let out a low chuckle. He'd known she was baiting him, and he'd walked right into it anyway. He couldn't help it; he did have anger issues. Justifiable, considering his upbringing, but it got him in some... fiery situations more often than not.

"I know you're worried about her," Aleerah said, "but I promise you that things will work out as they are meant to and you will see her again before the frost thaws."

"Well, considering the frost only started to stick to the ground a week ago, that doesn't give me a lot of comfort," Quinn snapped, although his words didn't carry the same angry bite they'd had earlier in the day. He hated to admit it, but Q was slowly accepting that this was their path, and Elena's path had taken her away for a while.

Quinn had never considered himself a very religious man. Amelia had taught him about all the gods and goddesses of their world, but he rarely paid them much attention. He would thank the Mother for a successful hunt or on the rare occasion when he grew vegetables in his garden, but otherwise, he didn't put much faith in fate or destiny.

However, ever since he'd stumbled upon Elena on the side of the road all those moons ago, he'd started to wonder how much of his life was truly his own. He sometimes imagined that his life wasn't his at all. That he was merely a puppet being controlled by some unseen higher power, pulling his strings and making him do the things they wanted, regardless of his own desires.

It was a bleak outlook, but it felt more and more accurate with each passing day.

Aleerah shrugged the stag off at the entrance of the watchtower, just inside the room where Quinn could see Roska and Aiden still hunched over the books.

"I'll take care of this thing if you can bring me a cooking spit and a butcher's knife," Quinn said to Aleerah as he repositioned the stag to get a better angle with his knife.

"No need!" Aiden snapped his finger and, in a puff of purple smoke, the deer was skinned, cleaned, butchered, and a large chunk of it hung from the spit now positioned across the hearth.

"What the mux?" Quinn exclaimed, jumping away from the slowly dissipating cloud of smoke. "What did you do that for?"

"I thought I was helping," Aiden replied, eyes wide with surprise and worry etched in his features.

"You didn't need to do that. I'm perfectly capable of handling my own kills." The rage was back in Q's voice.

"Take a breath, *veli*. He was only trying to help." Roska stepped in between Quinn and Aiden. Q glared at his brother. Did he honestly think Aiden needed to be protected, shielded from Quinn?

You do kinda have murder eyes right now, Lyra piped in.

Mux off.

Quinn took three dramatic deep breaths, holding Roska's stare the whole time. He would never have admitted it out loud, but taking a few deep breaths did actually help soothe Quinn's raw nerves. A little.

"I'm sorry," Aiden said. He stepped out from behind Roska, hands raised in surrender. "I didn't mean to offend you, Quinn. I was truly just trying to help. I can snap my fingers again and undo it all, if you'd prefer."

"No, that would be stupid." Quinn tried to keep the aggressive bite from his tone. He mostly succeeded.

"Well, this day has been far more exciting than I could have imagined." Aleerah's snark was a close match to Lyra's. Quinn wondered for a moment if familiars could inherit personality traits from their parents' familiars.

"What happened to the hide?" Q asked Aiden, trying his best to keep his voice calm.

"Oh, it's right here," Aiden snapped his fingers again, and in another flash of purple smoke, the hide lay on the floor in front of Q. Cleaned, prepped, and ready to be used in their clothing.

"Great. Thanks," Quinn mumbled, picking it up, grabbing his pack and Roska's cloak, then he turned and disappeared outside again.

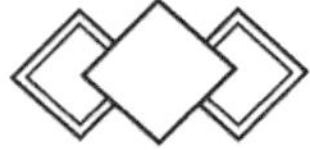

The sound of flapping wings, then footsteps crunching in the snow that covered the cobblestone pathway broke the night's silence.

"Gods, you're grumpy today."

Mux everything, Quinn thought.

"Why the hells did you come back?" Q snapped at Castor. Quinn took a seat on a broken stone fence that ran along the edge of the main road.

"Belladonna isn't home, so I thought I'd come see how things were progressing over here. It looks like everything is going well." Castor smirked, eyeing Quinn's supplies with bemused curiosity.

"Yeah, buddy, everything muxing perfect over here. Now, fly home and wait for your witch." Quinn tossed his pack on the ground before him, laid his brother's cloak across his lap, and started lining up the hide along the inside of it.

"I take it Daddy Aiden isn't living up to your expectations." Castor took an unwelcome seat beside Quinn on the snow-covered stones.

"I *really* don't want to have this conversation with you." Quinn took yet another deep breath. "Look, if you're going to insist on staying, at least make yourself useful. Go find some dry wood. I need a fire to see what I'm doing here."

"Can't you just..." Castor waved his hands around wildly, wiggling his fingers.

"Ha. Ha." Quinn raised one of his hands, wiggled his fingers, and watched the flames dance along his fingertips. "I can start a fire this way, but I can't exactly sew while my hands are on fire, can I?"

"You could try," Castor suggested, still wiggling his fingers in Q's face.

"I could also see what happens when a moonbird catches on fire." Quinn glared at Castor as the flames grew larger on his hand.

"You're no fun." Castor sighed, but he got up and wandered along the edge of the wood, collecting what little dry wood was available. He made a small stack and stepped back as Quinn turned his flames on the wood. Within moments, they had a small fire burning comfortably at their feet. It wasn't very bright, but it offered enough light for Quinn to get started adding the hide to Roska's cloak.

With Lyra inside, Quinn had an instant relay of any major breakthroughs they might have in their research to recapture the *turmio*. Castor sat silently beside Q, studying the stars and mostly ignoring Quinn entirely.

As much as he disliked the shifter, Quinn found himself grateful for the company. Not because Castor was such an insightful conversationalist, but because his quiet presence gave Quinn the option to be alone with his thoughts or have someone to talk things through with.

They sat in companionable silence for an hour or so, until the wood burned to ash and their breath became clearly visible, even without the benefit of the flame's light. Quinn had started packing up and was about to head inside when Castor spoke.

"You can't know what it was like for him. Watching the three of you, in separate hells, and knowing he couldn't step in to help you—no matter how badly he wanted to. It would have changed your fates and the fate of the world." Castor's voice was barely above a whisper, but his words shook Quinn as though they'd been shouted. "He spent the first ten cycles of your life, drinking himself into a stupor so he physically wouldn't be able to save you. I lost count of how many times he *forced me* to barricade him in the tower, just to stop him from running off to kill those demon-spawn foster parents of yours. Or the times Aleerah and I had to chase him down and bring him back here before he reached the monastery to rescue

Roska. He loves the three of you so much. It has been killing him every moment of every day since your conception. Knowing the hard road you'd be forced to take, and knowing that he couldn't save you from it without risking the lives of every single magical being in this world." Castor locked Quinn in a hard stare. "He has hated himself every single second of every single day for the last sixteen solar cycles. He might deserve your rage, but he also deserves your trust."

Quinn felt something cold and wet run down his cheek. He raised a hand to touch his face and found a stream of quiet tears making their way down his filthy, heartbroken face. The tears had come, unwanted and unnoticed.

Castor didn't say another word. He rose from his seat on the stone wall, jumped into the air, and shifted smoothly into his moonbird form. Quinn stood in the deafening silence of the snowy night, watching the silhouette of the shifter disappear in the moonlit sky.

22

BELLADONNA

BELLADONNA HAD LEFT HER house within an hour of Castor disappearing into the mist with the siblings. She was irritated and highly motivated to finally have the conversation with Beatrice that she'd been avoiding—or ignoring—for the last twenty cycles or so. She hadn't even given herself time to process the fact that Castor had been keeping such life-altering secrets from her for at least a dozen cycles, probably more.

Belladonna hadn't even realized such a thing was possible. It felt like a violation of their entire relationship. Their connection was unlike that between enchantress and familiar in that witches and their familiars were more autonomous. She'd never considered that their level of independence would mean that Castor—her life partner and best friend—would have secrets of his own. She'd certainly never kept anything from him. Belladonna was more hurt than she would have admitted to him, even though she was certain he felt her betrayal the moment he'd mentioned Aiden.

She hadn't thought of that man in nearly sixteen cycles, and she had been quite happy with that fact. She was proud of her ability to block him from her memory. completely scrubbing his presence and

156

the profound impact he'd had on her from her mind. To find out that Castor had been in communication with that lunatic? Not just in communication with, but *friends* with him? Belladonna hadn't felt that level of painful betrayal since Beatrice had left.

Rather than dwell on her feelings about Aiden, Belladonna had hastily packed a bag of clothes and travel-friendly food, added a few extra layers of deterrents to her mist, and headed out into the woods to confront the woman who'd broken her heart all those cycles ago. Belladonna was confident that this meeting would begin badly, possibly a little violently. She hoped that they'd finally be able to talk and she could offer Beatrice some support against the looming threats that Belladonna knew would be circling the school in the coming days. Once the magept realized that the enchantresses were losing their powers, they would seize the opportunity to remove Madame LaBelle from her seat of power.

Belladonna was especially concerned about the Royal Family. While living in her cottage in the woods had kept her isolated, Belladonna had still managed to keep a finger on the pulse of Waverly's politics. The King was sleeping with Beatrice, which drove Belladonna to a rage she rarely let herself acknowledge. Surely he would jump at the chance to take the head enchantress' power and authority for himself when he realized her powers had diminished and she was no longer a threat. The *turmio* would be the death of them, undoubtedly. It was just a question of whether that damned poison would kill them or if the Royal Family and their thirst for power would take them out first.

The journey to Harbor Ridge only took about a day and a half during the planting and growing seasons, but with the frost season taking over, the seemingly endless snowfall made the trip take twice as long. Belladonna had stayed as close to the creek as possible, making her way from her cottage and clearing to the main road that would take her to the school.

She'd spent the first night in Quinn's hut. She hadn't asked permission, but she decided it was a fair trade since she'd housed the siblings for a few nights. Plus, she left him a couple of magical surprises that she was sure would make up for any annoyance or violation he might have felt at her sleeping in his home uninvited.

And honestly, what was he going to do? Come back and pout? Burn something? She chuckled to herself. That boy had some serious—albeit justified—anger issues. She'd left his hut at first light and was nearly to the main road when she heard a strange noise. Or, rather, a cacophony of strange noises.

Men shouting. Metal on metal. The whinny and wicker of at least a dozen horses, likely more.

What the mux is going on?

Belladonna crouched low, hiding as best she could in the underbrush, casting a few subtle spells to hide her from the soldiers who had made camp along the roadside. She cringed as she took in the immense damage they'd inflicted on the forest. Demolished saplings that had just settled in for the frost season. Branches from her fir and cypress trees had been brutally hacked away to make room for their monstrous tents. Then she caught the whiff of smoked meat. Not just deer, but rabbit, fish, and even the distinct aroma of fawn meat. These arrogant, selfish monsters had killed a fawn in *her* forest!

Before she had consciously made the choice, Belladonna felt her magic flow through her like lava overflowing its mountainous boundaries. Just as she was about to unleash the full force of her fury on the soldiers, she heard something that instantly froze her in place.

"But sir," a soldier said, "what if she awakens? That weasel of hers nearly took out an entire platoon when we captured them."

Weasel?

"Calm yourself, Jamieson," came the curt reply. "The Brotherhood guaranteed that one dose from the poison arrow would keep that girl," he literally spat on the ground at the word, "and her familiar unconscious and compliant long enough for us to reach Riverayn without incident."

Those muxing bastards! Not only did they abuse Roska throughout his entire life and unleashed the one thing that could quite possibly kill all the magical creatures in the world, but now they had kidnapped Elena and poisoned her and Agon! Belladonna was tempted to let her magics loose, using the power of the forest to capture all of these heartless men. She could easily use the roots from these gorgeous, magical trees to bury each and every one of these soldiers alive.

Belladonna desperately wanted to free Elena from their clutches. While she wasn't related to the siblings by blood, she felt a love and kinship toward them that compelled her to protect them and fight for them when needed.

Unbidden and unwelcome, a memory rushed into Belladonna's mind, knocking her to her knees and incapacitating her with its demands to be remembered. Darkness flooded her vision as the memory took hold and pulled her under.

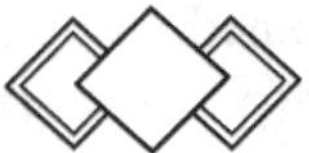

Some fifty cycles ago, when she was still happily living with Beatrice in their cottage. It had been a quiet day, like most. Belladonna had been working in the garden, clearing out the dead plants from the previous season and planning which seedlings would go where when a strange old man had stumbled into their clearing. These were peaceful times. As such, they didn't have any protective wardings or spells to deter visitors around their home.

Immediately, Belladonna had rushed to his aid, sending Castor to fetch Beatrice and Zied, who had gone hunting in the woods. The man was disheveled, haggard, and covered in hundreds of small scratches, as though he'd fallen through a dozen blackberry bushes to get to them. Belladonna gently wrapped the man's arm across her shoulders and helped him to stand, guiding him to their home and a comfortable seat by the fire. She'd just finished pouring him a fresh cup of tea when Beatrice returned, out of breath and flushed.

"What happened?" Beatrice practically shouted, rushing over to Belladonna and taking the witch's face in her hands. She studied

Belladonna's features for a moment, then quickly ran her hands down Belladonna's arms, presumably checking for injuries.

"I'm fine," Belladonna said firmly, taking Beatrice's hands in her own and squeezing them to emphasize her point. Still holding tightly to Bea's hands, Belladonna turned to Castor, "What the hells did you tell her?"

Castor shrugged, as much as a moonbird can shrug, "I said there was a strange man in the clearing and you needed her to hurry up."

"He made it sound more dire than that," Zied added, flicking his tail in annoyance and glaring at Castor who sat on his perch by the hearth.

"I'm sorry, love," Belladonna said to Bea. "I didn't mean for him to scare you. I just meant for him to bring you home so you could help me heal and care for our guest." She pointed at the old man in the chair, quietly sipping his tea and trying to act like he wasn't hanging on every word they were saying.

Bea turned to face the man, scrutinizing his appearance and barely concealing a look of disgust. "Why are you here?" she asked harshly.

"Bea," Belladonna chastised quietly, "that's rude. He's clearly been through something. He needs our healing and patience."

"One moment," Beatrice said to the man, sharing a pointed look with Zied and practically dragging Belladonna outside. "How can you be so calm? That man showed up here, in the middle of the woods, our *home*. You of all people should be more wary of men."

"I'm not a child, Bea, and I'd appreciate it if you'd stop treating me as though I am." Belladonna ripped her hand from Beatrice's. "I'm fully aware that men are untrustworthy and can be indescribably cruel. I still have nightmares remembering the things those muxing Brothers did to my family. But that doesn't mean that I should become like them, turning any male into a suspect and treating them with the same cruelty that my family was forced to endure."

The icy rage in Belladonna manifested in a layer of frost encircling her feet in the otherwise brilliant green forest clearing.

"You're right, love," Beatrice said, gently taking Belladonna's hands in her own again. "I'm sorry I snapped at you. I was just so worried. I can't bear the thought of anyone—especially some man—hurting you."

"I know, and I understand that Bea, but you have to learn to trust my judgment." Belladonna allowed Beatrice to tuck some of her leafy green hair behind her ear, leaning into her lover's hand and locking eyes with Beatrice. "I know what a hostile man looks like, the energy and aura that radiates off a man with less than honorable intentions. This man, this poor, battered old man, has the aura of someone in desperate need of a safe place to rest."

"I don't like it," Beatrice stated bluntly, "but I trust your judgment. If you say he's not here to hurt us, then I believe it."

The strange man stayed with them for days—eating their food, drinking their tea—never saying a word. The first day, he'd mumbled incoherently in his sleep, but he gave them no information as to who he was or why he was there.

By lunch on the fourth day, Beatrice pulled Belladonna aside in the garden, looking so anxious that she might peel her own skin off.

"This cannot continue. He cannot stay here. We can take him to Andover. There's an inn there, and the owner seems nice enough—for a man. Let's just take him there and be done with this."

"Bea, we can't just abandon this man. The Mother sent him here for a reason. We are meant to help him." Belladonna wasn't a particularly religious woman, but she knew that things like this didn't just happen. There was a cosmic reason for this man's appearance, and she was determined to find out what it was.

"Well, we need to do something different, godsdammit. Maybe we should enchant his tea. Get him to open up and tell us what the hells he's doing here." Beatrice was anxious. She hated the unexplained. It would have made Belladonna chuckle if not for the threat in Beatrice's words.

"No," Belladonna said firmly, tightening her grip on Bea's hand. "We do not spell people without their consent unless it is in defense of ourselves or others."

It was easily the most frustrating argument that they always seemed to have. Beatrice was taught that magic was her right and she had the freedom to use it whenever and however she saw fit. Belladonna knew better. Just because a person had the power to control someone's mind, belief or actions didn't mean that they should. That was one of the basic tenets of witch practice. Harm none. Consent was required in order to perform magic on anyone unless you were protecting yourself or the lives of innocents.

"Bells, come on. You can't be serious here! That man barely has the mental capacity to stand upright. We can't get consent from that fool." The strain in Beatrice's face betrayed her calm tone.

"If we can't get consent, then we can't perform magic on him. I'm not having this discussion with you, Beatrice. We will not spell that man just to make things easier for you." Belladonna ground out the words through gritted teeth. She was sick of this same fight. It was the only one they ever seemed to have.

"Well we can't keep going like this—" Their argument was cut short by an animalistic roar so deep Belladonna could feel the vibrations of the sound rattling within her chest.

They both turned to face the source of the sound; spells and enchantments already building in their hands, prepared to defend themselves from whatever beast had created the noise. That's when they first saw Aleerah. Bloody, scarred, and wild-eyed, the dire wolf charged into their clearing, although Belladonna wasn't sure the beast knew where she was. Her warm brown fur was matted and thick with blood, and she appeared to be limping.

Just as the dire wolf made it to the center of the clearing, the man came rushing out of the cottage, looking more spry than Belladonna had ever seen him. The wolf collapsed in a crumpled heap beside their well, and the old man rushed to her side. Belladonna couldn't understand his words, but she could feel the magic flowing from him, into the animal.

"Holy Mother," Beatrice exhaled the words in a whisper. "She's his familiar. Mux. The old fool has a familiar? How did we miss that?"

"I don't think he wanted us to know," Belladonna replied in an equally hushed tone.

23

ROSKA

Once Quinn came back in from the cold, the three of them ate dinner in silence. Roska wanted to tell Q about the breakthrough he and Aiden had found while researching the history of the *turmio*. He wanted to tell his brother that they had a plan for stopping it, recapturing the demon before it got too strong and started killing, but he knew his brother wasn't in the right headspace to hear what Roska was going to say.

Lyra had warned them off telling him as soon as they'd started vocalizing their plan. She'd hushed them—actually hushed both Roska and Aiden—told them not to discuss it when she was within earshot, then she disappeared upstairs with Demoni and Aleerah.

Roska felt a strong sense of respect for her. She knew that their plan was going to be risky—the type of risky that Q would refuse to even entertain—so she'd taken herself out of it. If she didn't know the plan, then Q couldn't know it and Roska could do what needed to be done.

If he was being completely honest with himself, Roska didn't want this to be the plan either, but according to Aiden and their research, it was the only way.

Roska hoped that he would get to see Elena once more before it all came to an end.

The next morning, they had an incredibly awkward breakfast of oats, eggs, and more of Aiden's magical coffee. The weighty silence was broken when Lyra snapped and said, "This is stupid. We are all adults here. Yes, bad shyt happened. Yes, you have every right to be pissed about it, but come the mux *on*, Q. We need to get past this. Assuming you want to save the whole damn world and get our sister back. That is what you want, isn't it?"

Quinn glared at her but said nothing.

"Of course that's what you want," Lyra continued, walking over to sit directly in front of him in the chair he'd scorched the day before. "So get over yourself long enough to make that happen. You can hate the man forever—if you really think that will be productive—but right now we need to get our priorities straight."

Roska couldn't help but admire the way she spoke to Q. Roska himself would never have taken such a forceful tone with his brother, but Lyra and Q had a very different relationship and it clearly worked well for them.

Q still didn't speak, but Roska could see some of his brother's rage get bottled back up and forced down deep inside Q's internal lockbox. It was an unhealthy habit that the siblings had all developed in an attempt to cope with their respective hellsish upbringings.

Q gave Lyra a curt nod, offered a weak smile to Roska, and turned back to the last of his oatmeal. He still didn't speak, but he finally seemed willing to listen, and that was enough for now.

Roska accepted his brother's concession and dove into the plan that he and Aiden had begun to formulate the night before. "We know that Elena has been taken by the King's soldiers, presumably to Riverayn. We don't really know why they took her, although I suspect it was an attempt to cripple Mother and make her submit to the King. I guess he never noticed that she doesn't seem to place her own children above the well-being of Harbor Ridge. Kidnapping her daughter won't have the effect I think he was hoping for." Roska hated thinking that way about their mother, but she'd made it fairly clear when she'd locked them away in that tower that her loyalty was to the school first. If the King was hoping to use Elena as a pawn to get Madame LaBelle to submit to his rule, he was going to be sorely disappointed and Elena would pay the price for it.

Q's carefully bottled rage seemed to be surfacing again. Roska watched smoke rise from the table under Q's hand, and the metal spoon he'd been using began to wilt.

"How are we going to rescue her?" Quinn asked through gritted teeth. It was clear he was desperately trying to contain his fiery mood.

"We aren't," Aiden answered bluntly.

It was the wrong thing to say.

Quinn rounded on their father, rising so quickly from his seat that the chair flipped over and slid across the floor. Flames flicked across Quinn's fingers, dancing up his arms and in his eyes. Lyra positioned herself between Q and Aiden again, as Roska called his ice into his palms, prepared to extinguish any fires his brother started.

"What did you say?" Quinn's gravelly voice sent chills up Roska's spine. His brother was balancing on a knife's edge, and he was ready to jump off, taking their father into a fiery hells with him.

Roska stepped into Q's field of view, hands raised in surrender although it would only take a quick glance for his brother to see the frosty air pouring from Roska's hands. He needed Q to calm down, ideally willingly, but Roska was prepared to cool his brother off himself if need be.

Aiden raised his hands as well and spoke in a softer tone when he answered Quinn's question. "We aren't going to rescue her because she's going to rescue herself." Aiden pointed to the books open on the desk below the window. "The prophecy states that she will free herself from her captors and meet you back in the cavern where this all began."

"And we're just supposed to take your word for it? Trust you? I don't think so." The heat was steadily rising in the room. Roska felt sweat dripping down his spine, even as he watched the ice form on his fingertips.

"Quinn," Roska said in the most soothing voice he could muster, "we don't have another option. The *turmio* grows stronger every day. If we try to rescue El, we will waste precious time. By the time we got to her, freed her, and made it back to the mountains, the *turmio* would be too strong. We won't be able to overpower it, and we will all die. We can't risk the fate of the world to save her." Roska lowered his hands, locking eyes with his brother. "I know how cruel it sounds, but we have to trust that Elena is strong enough to take care of herself. We can't put the fate of the world and the lives of all magical beings at risk to save her. We have to think of the greater good."

Roska studied his brother with pleading, desperate eyes. He knew that he was asking Quinn to do the impossible. Seemingly abandon their sister to her fate, in the hopes that she would survive and liberate herself, while the two of them headed off in the opposite direction to save the world.

He hated that they were in this position at all, and Roska felt an immense sense of guilt at their predicament. If he hadn't unleashed the *turmio* in the first place, none of this would be happening. It was a guilt that he had to wrestle with every single day. If they failed to stop the *turmio* or if Elena didn't survive her captivity, he would never forgive himself.

On the bright side, if we fail to stop the turmio *we'll all die and the guilt will just disappear.* Demoni had a dark sense of humor, but she wasn't wrong. They had a matter of days to recapture the *turmio* before it became too powerful and annihilated them all.

Quinn seemed to deflate, the heat instantly dissipated, and his flames disappeared into his skin. He sank heavily down to the floor, as though his internal fire had melted his bones instead of the tower. Roska was stunned. Q looked up at him, eyes blinking back tears as he wordlessly begged for a solution to their problems.

Roska lowered his hands and knelt before his brother. "We have a plan. We will fix all of this. She will be ok."

Truthfully, Roska wasn't sure that any of those words were true, but he hated seeing Q look so defeated.

They were triplets, sure, but Quinn had always taken the lead and felt more like an older brother to Roska. Elena felt like his older sister, and the middle sibling, based on how often she played mediator between the brothers. Roska wasn't sure how much longer they could carry on without her.

24
QUINN

Q HAD SLEPT FITFULLY in the tower night before. Then he'd nearly turned the watchtower into an oven, roasting all of them alive. Quinn gazed sightlessly into his bowl of oatmeal. His fist gripped a metal spoon as though it were a lifeline, and he would drift out to sea if he released it.

He didn't want to be strong or reliable anymore. He didn't give a damn about the rest of the world. He *needed* to rescue Elena. She was the only person who truly saw him and didn't judge him for his actions. She was his family, the first blood relation he'd ever known, and she'd already been through too much because he hadn't been there to save her. Now he was letting her down all over again.

You are not letting her down, Lyra said, interrupting his thoughts. *She was kidnapped, and that isn't anyone's fault but the muxing assholes who took her. But she's strong. She will take care of herself, just like she has in the past. She didn't need us to rescue her then and she doesn't need us to save her now.*

Lyra made good points, but as Q righted his chair and attempted to melt his spoon back into its original shape, he didn't give a damn about logic or rational thinking. He just wanted his sister back.

Roska was still talking to him, explaining some shyt they'd learned or researched or whatever, but Quinn wasn't listening. He was too busy stewing in his own self-pity and trying to keep his rage under control to pay attention to his brother's long-winded explanation. Q knew he should be listening because the chances were very good that the plan Aiden had talked Roska into—Q was certain that muxing man was pulling all the strings again—would be dangerous and likely deadly, but he just couldn't focus.

When the spoon had been melted back into a rough idea of how it used to be, Quinn sank roughly into the chair he'd burned, leaned his head back, and closed his eyes. If he couldn't go off to save her, then he just wanted to sleep until all of this was over.

Q awoke suddenly to the sound of slamming books and loud voices.

Lyra nudged his knee with her warm nose. "We need to get moving," she said gently. She knew how he was feeling, all the stress that weighed him down as though a physical boulder had settled firmly on his chest. It was probably her idea to let him sleep while Roska and Aiden prepared for their journey.

Quinn sat forward in the chair, rubbing the sleep from his eyes and roughing his hand through his hair, desperately trying to wake himself up. He rose from the chair, stretching his back and taking pleasure in the popping sound that his spine made as he twisted.

He ruffled Lyra's hair, scratching behind her ears as a thank you for letting him rest, then turned to his brother. Roska was filling his pack with various foods and travel cookware that Quinn was certain had been conjured by their father.

"What is the point of packing these things?" he asked incredulously. "If you can just snap your fingers and make them appear, why do we need to lug all this shyt around with us?"

Roska glared at Q and opened his mouth—presumably to lecture him on rudeness—but Aiden spoke first.

"It's not a bad question," he replied. "I can conjure all of this easily here because this is my home, and I've placed hundreds of wards, protections, and amplifiers throughout this tower and the surrounding lands. Once we get out of range, my powers will be lessened, and I won't want to waste my energy on conjuring a pot or some carrots."

"You're telling me that when we leave this place, you're gonna be useless?" Quinn couldn't believe it. Their father, the *demi-god*, was only powerful when he hid in his tower forever. Mux everything.

"Not useless," Aiden corrected coolly. "Just less useful. The recovery time between using my powers will be longer. Don't worry, laddie. I'll be plenty useful when it comes to quelling that damned *turmio.*" He winked confidently at Quinn.

Quinn rolled his eyes, turning his back on their father and collecting his own pack. He loaded the bag with carrots, potatoes, four new waterskins, a seemingly endless pile of dried meat, and three bundles of dried wood. He begrudgingly conceded to their father's suggestion to bring their own wood into the forest since dry wood was harder to come by in the frost season. Quinn found himself in awe of Amelia's bag. The magic that made it capable of carrying so many things, without feeling heavy or slowing him down was amazing. It also made him miss her terribly. He couldn't help but wonder if he would ever see her again.

"I think we can make it as far as Belladonna's before the sun sets tomorrow." Aiden's voice brought Q back to the task at hand.

"Do you think that wise?" Aleerah asked cautiously.

"What? Of course! It's been dozens of cycles. I'm certain she doesn't hate me anymore," Aiden replied, a sly grin spreading across his face. Aleerah held his stare firmly. "All right, I'm fairly confident that she won't try to kill me this time."

Aleerah made a noise that Quinn interpreted as the dire wolf's version of a scoff.

"She tried to kill you?" Roska couldn't have hidden the confusion in his voice if he'd tried.

"Not surprising, honestly," Quinn chuckled to himself. "I mean, I get the impulse."

He'd half expected their father to get mad at this comment, and maybe he would have if Aleerah hadn't started laughing so hard that she was literally rolling on the floor. The sound startled them all at first, but when Lyra barked a laugh in return, everyone seemed to relax. The tension that had been building all morning seemed to ease a bit. Quinn was still anxious with worry for Elena, but he had to trust that she would take care of herself and meet them at the cave. She was strong, and she wasn't really alone. Agon was with her, and

Q knew that the two of them were unstoppable. She would be ok. She had to be.

They moved at a much slower pace than Quinn was comfortable with, but they'd agreed to stay off the main roads in case there were more soldiers lurking about. Not to mention the never-ending snow that fell from the bleak expanse of gray above them. They made it to Belladonna's just as the sun was setting beyond the mountains on the third day. Quinn had been anxious about having to contend with the fog without Belladonna or Castor there to guide them through, but it seemed that their father had a similar immunity to the fog's powers. Aiden shared his immunity with the brothers, making their journey through the powerful fog entirely uneventful. Q never would have said so, but he was surprisingly grateful for Aiden's company as they passed through the fog without incident.

Castor flew out to greet them once they stepped into the clearing. He smoothly transformed from his massive black bird form into the familiar form of the deep ebony man. He shook hands with Aiden, offering a nod to the brothers, and scratching Aleerah and Lyra under their respective chins. Demoni was wrapped tightly around Roska's neck, using his heat to maintain her own. Castor offered her a quick nod, which she returned with a small puff of icy breath.

"Belladonna isn't here," Castor announced to no one in particular. "By the looks of things, she packed a bag and left almost as soon as you three left that day."

"Where would she go?" Roska asked, concern laced through his words.

"Not sure, truthfully. She never likes to go anywhere." Castor shrugged. Q was a little surprised by the lack of concern in Castor's voice. "I would know if she were in danger," the shifter said as if he'd read Q's thoughts. "I can sense that she's south of here. Not too far, so if there is trouble, I'll be able to reach her quickly. I imagine she's still mad at me, so I'm giving her space. For now."

"Will she mind if we stay here tonight?" Roska asked.

"Not likely. But if she gets upset then she should have been here to tell us no, right?" Castor tossed a cocky grin over his shoulder as he headed away from them, back toward the cottage.

Quinn hesitated for only a moment. He decided that if the situation were reversed, the witch wouldn't pause for a moment before crashing into his home and using it as a rest spot for the night. Especially with the ever-thickening snow falling all around them.

They made themselves at home in the cottage. Lyra nosed some fresh logs into the hearth, then flicked her tail to start the fire. The men dropped their snow-covered packs by the door and hung their cloaks by the hearth in the hopes of the fire drying out their clothes before they left in the morning.

Castor started a pot of tea for them as Quinn and Roska sat at the table by the fire, peeling off their snow-soaked boots and placing them beside the fire as well.

"So, why did the witch try to kill you?" Quinn asked when the silence between them became unbearable.

"Oh! I love this story!" Castor chimed in gleefully.

"Shut it, you. You were no help back then," Aiden chided, shaking snow from his hair onto the shifter. He took a seat facing Quinn and added, "That is a rather complicated tale. Are you sure you want to hear it?"

"Have you ever known me to ask a question that I didn't intend to hear the answer to? From what I hear, you'd been stalking us with your magic mirror for cycles. I think you already know the answer to that question and you're just stalling." Quinn kept his tone as neutral as possible, but inside he was still struggling to talk to this man without lashing out.

"Fair enough," Aiden nodded, leaning back in his chair and scratching the rough hair on his chin. "I guess it all started when I was staying with your mother and Belladonna in this very cottage some fifty cycles ago. You see, I was still struggling with my mind after my encounter with the fae, and it had left me broken and lost. I managed to find myself in this clearing—entirely by accident, mind you—one bright morning... at least I think it was morning..." Aiden's mind seemed to trail off, along with his sentence.

When it was clear that Aiden was lost in his memories and wasn't going to finish the story, Castor jumped in. "I'll skip all the boring details and get right to the fun parts. He stayed with us for several days, never saying a word, causing exhausting tension between Belladonna and Beatrice until Aleerah burst into the clearing nearly a week later.

"We hadn't realized he was anything other than human until he started talking to this massive beast," Castor waved his hand at Aleerah where she lay by the door, "and she responded. It was shocking, to say the least. He was the first man any of us had ever seen that had magic. Belladonna didn't know how to react, but your mother immediately went on the defensive, throwing up wards to create a protective barrier between us and them. Belladonna wasn't sure that attacking was the right move until Aiden turned on us. He screamed like a wild animal and started hurling fireballs at us. Beatrice's magic was very effective at blocking his attacks, but it took all of her energy and focus to maintain, so she wasn't able to fight back.

"When one of his fireballs nearly broke Beatrice's defenses, Belladonna snapped. She turned the forest against Aiden and Aleerah, lashing out with roots and using the tree branches to whip them and drive them away."

To Quinn's surprise, Aleerah chuckled at this point in the retelling. Roska and Quinn both stared at her, confused by her reaction.

"See this scar here?" She used her tail to point to a long slash across her muzzle. "That damn witch got me. That had never happened before. Or since."

Quinn wasn't sure, but he thought he heard a hint of pride in her voice. He couldn't tell if it was directed at herself for not having been scarred more or at Belladonna for managing to leave a mark.

"It was an unexpected turn of events, I will say," Aiden piped in again. "I'd never seen a woman so full of rage. It seems that by threatening to hurt the one she loved, I'd unleashed some sort of murderous fury within Belladonna. I'm not sure she even knew she had it in her until that day."

"Oh, no," Castor said. "She definitely knew. She'd spent ages trying to ignore that side of herself. Ever since the first wave of witch hunts in Rolam. But that's not my story to tell."

"So what happened next?" Roska asked.

"We fled," Aiden said with a shrug. "When a woman looks at you with that kind of violence in her eyes, you don't stick around to try and talk her out of it. You get the hells out of her way."

Quinn couldn't help but admire the way Belladonna had handled that situation. Gods knew if Q was ever put in a situation like that again, where he was forced to kill to protect the ones he loved, he wouldn't hesitate for a second.

And the way things had been going lately, Quinn was pretty sure that sentiment would be tested again. Sooner rather than later.

25

AIDEN

AIDEN HADN'T BEEN THRILLED to share that story with the boys, but it was all true and they deserved transparency from him, at the very least. After all they'd been through and all the men who had betrayed their respective trusts, Aiden had vowed long ago that—if he ever got to meet them—he would never lie to his children.

So far, so good.

While he hadn't told a lie, he *had* left out some key information about the plan he and Roska had devised when they'd explained their intentions to Quinn the night before. Roska and Lyra both agreed that Q wouldn't approve of their plan, and Aiden didn't want to contradict them. He was still in a very precarious situation, trying to build trust and connect with his children while also saving the world. He agreed that Q would be infuriated at what they needed to do to contain the *turmio*, but Aiden was also fairly confident that Q could be reasoned with and made to understand the necessity of their actions. But keeping it from Quinn was easier and Aiden had never been one to take the harder path when a simpler route was presented.

Coward. Aleerah was outside, patrolling the clearing in case the soldiers decided to brave Belladonna's mist. It was unlikely, but she was obstinate and refused to accept his flawless logic.

Well, that's needlessly rude. Aiden looked at his boys where they lay, sharing Belladonna's bed and sleeping *mostly* soundly—although he was pretty sure he'd heard Roska whimper in his sleep once or twice.

Rude, but true. You would rather lie to your son than face the truth of what you're asking your other son to do.

I am not *lying to anyone.* Aiden didn't really mean to snap at her, but he was feeling quite sensitive about the choices he was making. Having her call him out on the questionability of them was upsetting.

Call it what you want, you are intentionally misleading him because you are a coward. Afraid of your own child. Aleerah wasn't being malicious, Aiden reminded himself, she was just pointing out things he wanted to ignore. She was always good at that. He resented her endlessly for it. *You know I'm right*, she continued. *You just don't want him to dislike you. Guess what? He already does. Might as well be honest with him.*

Gods, you're in a mood tonight. Aiden had a high tolerance for Aleerah's cranky attitude most nights, but watching his sons sleeping before him—as opposed to through his looking glass after four or five bottles of wine—shifted his perspective on things and lowered his patience for her snide remarks.

I'm simply pointing out important things that you seem more than happy to ignore. This isn't something you can put off forever. He will find out. Sooner rather than later. And he will be fuming that you both kept it from him. He felt Aleerah take a deep breath before she continued. *I'm not trying to upset you. I'm just trying to make you see that it will be so much worse for* him *if you don't tell him until it's too late.*

Aiden knew she was right. No point admitting it though, because then she'd be insufferable. He couldn't tell Q. Not yet. He couldn't bear the hatred he would see on his son's face when their plan finally fell into place.

"Where does Belladonna keep her herbs and supplies?" Aiden whispered to Castor, choosing not to respond to Aleerah at all.

"In that cupboard," he replied with a nod. "What are you looking for?" He rose from the chair he'd been lounging in, crossed the room, and opened the cupboard.

"Licorice or blood root, wormwood, and ivy for the binding spell. Also angelica and nettle for the banishing spell. I had the rest in my tower, but I haven't done a lot of binding or banishing over the last dozen cycles or so, and my supplies have run out."

Castor started pulling jars and mesh sachets from the cupboard, laying them out on the table for Aiden's perusal.

"Looks like she has everything but the nettle," Castor said, placing a small, blue, glass jar of dried wormwood onto the table. "But that should be easy enough to find in the woods tonight. How much do you need? I'll fly out and get some so we can start drying it out."

"It will actually be better fresh, not dried. I'll go with you. We're going to need a lot." Aiden rose from his chair, grabbed a woven basket from the counter near Belladonna's indoor water pump, and knelt before Lyra as she lay beside the stones surrounding the hearth. "If anything happens, alert Aleerah and we'll be back in a blink. I don't expect anything to, but just in case."

Lyra nodded, then laid her head back on her paws and watched him walk out the door with Castor.

Aiden wasn't entirely sure how many nettles they would need. It really depended on how strong the *turmio* had gotten already and how much stronger it would be by the time they made it to the cavern and completed the ritual.

When they'd exited the cottage, Castor had shifted back into his moonbird form and taken flight. He circled overhead, diving suddenly, and returned with claws full of nettle. Aiden was grateful for his shifter friend because it meant that he didn't have to touch the irritating herb as much himself. He'd conjured a thick leather glove for himself, carrying the basket in one hand and carefully collecting the stinging nettle with his protected hand.

Stinging nettle was aptly named, leaving welts and blisters on skin. Aiden had an unpleasant experience with it in his younger years. The memory came creeping back to him as he wandered carefully through the trees, ever cautious of the near-caustic nettle. He'd been a young lad, maybe halfway through his first century, when he'd come across a group of nymphs bathing in a river. In his arrogance, Aiden had immediately assumed that the lasses would want to bed a demi-god and had liberated himself of his clothing before jumping into the river beside them—uninvited.

At the time, Aiden hadn't known that nymphs had the power to control their namesake plants, so when a lovely, lithe young nymph invited him to lay with her on the riverside, he'd been all too eager to comply. He hadn't taken any notice of what the other nymphs had chuckled. Aiden thought he caught her name in the chuckles and half-whispered jokes.

Netti.

He hadn't thought anything of it.

Foolish young Aiden stretched out beside Netti, being sure to show off the muscles he'd inherited from his trickster father. He flashed her his most winning grin, which she returned with an enchanting smile. Aiden knew now that her smile had in fact been literally enchanting, making him so enthralled with her that he missed the fact that she was calling forth her namesake.

Just as he'd leaned in to kiss her, she'd sprung her trap. Nettle covered him like a blanket. Every inch of his *very* exposed skin was instantly irritated. Welts and blisters formed in moments and the itching, burning sensation consumed his entire body.

Aiden shook his head, trying to rid himself of the devastatingly embarrassing memories.

Ah, those were the good ol' days, Aleerah laughed in his mind.

You're heartless, Aiden chuckled in response. *I couldn't walk for days. Couldn't sit for over a week!*

I remember! It was glorious. Aiden could hear her bark of laughter from across the clearing. She had truly loved that moment in their shared history. It was probably in the top five most embarrassing moments of his life—or at least of his first hundred solar cycles—and she had been over the damn moon about the whole thing. Aiden couldn't help laughing about it as he walked through the forest now though. He'd definitely learned his lesson that day: never approach a female naked unless *expressly* invited.

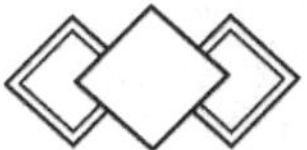

After about an hour of wandering, collecting, and skillfully avoiding burning himself with the plant, Aiden and Castor had nearly filled the basket to the brim with stinging nettle.

"If this isn't enough to banish that parasitic demon back to the hells he sprung loose from, then we're all muxed." Aiden eyed the basket with more pride than was warranted, considering Castor had brought in at least three times the number of plants he'd plucked himself.

"We could all be muxed regardless. This plan of yours is incredibly reckless and a bit suicidal, don't you think?" Castor asked after shifting back into his human form.

"Maybe," Aiden conceded. "But doing nothing means certain death, so here we are."

26

BELLADONNA

I T WAS DARK WHEN Belladonna opened her eyes. A fresh blanket of snow covered her, making her nearly invisible from the road. It was a wonder she hadn't frozen to death. As she shook the remnents of the taxing flashback from her mind, Belladonna realized that she was covered in needles and branches. She glanced up at the fir trees that towered above her where she lay on the forest floor. The trees had protected her, creating a barrier between her and the snow that was still falling. Belladonna rose from the cocoon of evergreen needles, brushing the snow from her hair and face. She turned to the trees around her, placing her bare hand on each tree in turn and sending them a message of gratitude through the warmth of the contact.

"Thank you all for your kind generosity," she whispered to the trees.

Shaking the last of the snow off her cloak, Belladonna studied the area around her. The clearing the soldiers had created was now empty. It seems they packed up and moved on while she was unconscious. Damn that demi-god and his vexing memories. She'd buried her previous encounter with him intentionally, and now he was forcing himself back into her mind and her present without her consent.

Just like a man, she thought grimly. *Always showing up when they're not wanted and wreaking havoc before disappearing and leaving the women to deal with the mess.*

Not unlike the men who had massacred the forest for a night's sleep before packing up and moving on as though nothing had happened. They were on the main road to Riverayn now which meant that they wouldn't need to murder her forests any further, she hoped.

Belladonna stood rooted to the soil, debating her options. She could chase after Elena and Agon, fight off the battalion of soldiers who were now holding her hostage—in a drug-induced state, by the sound of it. She could head off to find the boys, make sure the soldiers hadn't hurt them in their attempts to capture Elena. Or she could continue on as planned. Go to Harbor Ridge, confront that arrogant headmistress of theirs and warn her about the hells she helped to unleash on the world. Not to mention the impending assault the King's soldiers would likely rain down on the school now that the *turmio* was released and magic was fading.

If only Beatrice hadn't been so damned headstrong. If she had chosen to stay with Belladonna, living a peaceful simple life in their cottage in the woods, none of this would have happened. The triplets would never have been conceived and the whole damned prophecy could have been averted.

Belladonna's shoulders drooped. She didn't really wish the triplets had never been born. Within mere moments of meeting

Elena and Quinn in the woods that day so many moons ago, she knew she would love them as her own until her dying breath. She'd felt the same fierce love for Roska the instant she'd seen him step foot within her clearing. They might have been Bea's offspring, but Belladonna loved them as though they were her own children.

And she needed to have some words with their mother.

27

ROSKA

"**W**HY DIDN'T YOU KILL anything bigger?" Roska asked, munching on the last bite of the rabbit Q had shot for them earlier in the evening. Sitting around the fire, the boys ate their meal and tried to distract themselves from the fact that Elena was missing, they still had no idea why she'd been taken, what was happening to her, and they were running out of time to stop the *turmio* before it caused permanent damage.

They'd spent the night at Belladonna's and awoken with the sun. After a quick breakfast, they'd headed off into the Dark Woods again, toward the Dragon's Teeth and back to where all of this had begun just a couple of moons ago.

"Sick of rabbit already?" Q smirked.

Roska tried not to be jealous of his brother, but Quinn moved through the forest with practiced ease. Not only was he comfortable, confident, and capable in the middle of the woods, he was equally self-assured amongst strangers in a new town. Hells, Q never seemed out of his element because *every* element was his.

"Well, that deer back in the tower was delicious. Less stringy and more filling," Roska replied coolly.

"Yeah," Q said, "but what the hells would we do with it all? It's not like we have a way to store all the meat, bones, and hide. Deer is delicious, I agree with you there, Ros, but it's also a *lot* of meat, and we don't exactly have a travel-size root cellar with us."

His tone wasn't condescending or patronizing, but Roska still felt like an idiot for not seeing the obvious truth in Q's simple statement. Of course he couldn't kill bigger game. They had no means to preserve or transport so much meat. It would be senseless and cruel to kill such a magnificent creature for just one meal and leave the rest of the body to rot in the woods.

"If you're over rabbit, we could try fishing next time we find a stream. I could teach you to fish, too. It's really easy. No need to aim or anything." Quinn added the last comment with a wink as he nudged Roska's shoulder.

"Gods, you're never going to let me live that down, are you?" Roska asked, feeling his cheeks heat up as he remembered the first—and only—time he'd let Q try to teach him to shoot a bow and he nearly shot Elena in the leg.

"Not likely," Q chuckled.

"She was fine! It didn't even break the skin." Roska's cheeks were on fire as he used a small knife to cut off another piece of rabbit.

"She was, but it was hilarious," Quinn laughed. "I've never seen her move so fast!"

Aiden snickered behind his wine goblet. Roska wasn't entirely sure when their father had conjured the glass. Either the drink or the goblet itself was enchanted because it never ran out of wine. He'd take a sip and the glass would magically refill itself.

For a moment, Roska wanted to ask their father why he didn't conjure food for them, instead of Quinn having to hunt, prep, and cook their meal, but Roska realized that it was because Q loved those things. Their father had unintentionally upset—bordering on enraged—Q when he'd used magic on the deer in the tower. Aiden was giving Q the space to do the things that he loved without any magical interference. It was kind when Roska thought about it.

"I would like fish," Demoni spoke up from her curled position beside their fire. This was their first frost season outside of the shelter of the House of Healing Light, and she wasn't happy about it. Her cold-blooded nature made the snow and ice exceptionally hazardous. Since unleashing his powers, Roska had noticed that his own body temperature seemed to be slightly lower, which made it even harder for Demoni to use his warmth to keep her body at a comfortable temperature.

"Well, if Ros doesn't want to learn, I'm sure there's a way I can teach you to fish too," Quinn offered.

"I want to learn," Roska replied indignantly. He wanted to be self-sufficient, if only so that he could help out more. He often felt like he was a burden more than an asset to his siblings, and he hated that feeling. Roska desperately wanted to be a useful member of their team, their family.

"Great! Tomorrow, we'll be traveling along the river and I can teach you there. We can skip Nexton since we know where we're going this time. I recommend skipping Fàidh too. Unless you wanna see what this freezing weather does to an old man's—"

Q's words were cut off by the sharp snap of Lyra's jaws. Roska knew where his brother's sentence had been going though, and he was perfectly happy to skip the naked old man.

Aiden hadn't spoken much since they'd left Belladonna's. Roska studied him from across the fire. The demi-god sat on the forest floor, leaning back against an old fir tree, staring up into the snow-covered limbs of the evergreen. Roska had a sinking feeling that their father was being especially quiet because he was nervous. While they hadn't known the man for very long, it was still unsettling to see their father as anything other than cool, calm, and cocky. Looking at Aiden, with his endless wine goblet, the strain of nerves etched across his face, Roska began to feel his own nerves fray as well.

They had a plan. It would work, but it was going to be hard and dangerous. The prophecy said "one must fall" and Roska knew what that meant now. He just had to make it through the next couple of days, and then he would put to rights all the things he'd thrown asunder in his foolish quest to make the Brotherhood proud of him.

As they settled down for the night, preparing to camp under the cover of the forest canopy, the snow began falling more heavily. The sight of the frosty showers added to Roska's concerns about Demoni. He didn't know what would happen to Demoni if their fire went out and the stones Quinn warmed for her lost their heat before the sun rose. Just as Roska was about to voice his concerns,

Lyra laid down beside Demoni by the fire, covering the ice dragon with her fiery tail.

"I can keep the heat flowing in my tail all night, if you need it," Lyra said to Demoni.

Demoni said nothing, but nodded her glittering teal head and burrowed further under the orange and white fur of Lyra's tail. Roska could see the snow melting around them as they lay there, forming a near-perfect circle of thawed forest floor, surrounded by ankle-deep snow.

Roska couldn't speak. Emotion tightened his throat as he looked from Lyra to Quinn. Gratitude for their unending kindness made it impossible for him to form words. He felt the cold sting of tears as they filled his eyes. Roska quickly blinked them away and offered his own nod to Quinn.

Q and Lyra had both become very accommodating when it came to Demoni's need for heat. It was physically uncomfortable for everyone involved when Quinn touched Demoni for an extended period of time. After their first night under the stars, Q had started heating up stones in his fiery hands and placing them in Roska's pack for Demoni to travel on.

Even after spending moons with them, Roska still struggled to accept help or kindness from his siblings. He said a nightly prayer of thanks to the Mother Goddess for reconnecting him with his family. Not only for reuniting them, but giving him such a kind and unconditionally loving pair of siblings. Roska had spent the first sixteen cycles of his life being told—multiple times a day—that he was unworthy. Unworthy of love. Unworthy of kindness. Unworthy of the air he breathed. It was a lot for Roska to try and unpack and reset his mind as he realized that the Brothers were wrong.

Roska pulled his cloak tight around his body as he laid back against the snowy ground. He couldn't imagine a life without his siblings. He knew what was coming, but he prayed to the Mother Goddess for an alternative solution. He wasn't ready to lose them yet.

28

QUINN

Q UINN HAD HOPED THEY'D be able to skip out on another night in that less-than-charming inn in Nexton. He thought they'd all be perfectly comfortable spending yet another night under the stars.

He'd been out-voted.

Aiden volunteered to get them a room at the inn, while Roska and Demoni thawed by the massive hearth in the dining hall and Quinn went to the bar to order some dinner for them all. Lyra and Aleerah opted to stay outside, keeping watch and enjoying the frosty weather.

Q tried not to be annoyed with how quickly Lyra had bonded with Aleerah. He knew it was good for her to have another canine friend, but he was still jealous. How could she be so friendly with the familiar of their father who abandoned them?

He knew holding a grudge against their father wasn't productive, but Q couldn't help it. He just kept imagining how much better—and less bloody—his childhood could have been if his father had chosen to step up.

He tried to remind himself, based on what Castor had said, that it wasn't that simple. Aiden wanted to take care of them, supposedly, but he couldn't because it would have muxed up their role in the prophecy. On their hike through the woods from Belladonna's, Quinn found himself wondering if the whole prophecy could have been averted if their damned parents had given two shyts and taken better care of their muxing children.

Ultimately though, none of that mattered. They couldn't change the past, and they had a massive shyt show ahead of them. Dwelling on what could have been wouldn't do him any good. He needed to focus on the problems before them.

He returned to their table with two full tankards of ale and sat down hard in the chair beside his brother, back to the wall, facing the door.

"Here, drink this." He shoved a full mug toward his brother, sloshing some of the ale onto the scarred tabletop.

Roska eyed the drink suspiciously. "What is this?"

"It's ale. It will warm you up, I promise. They're bringing out some beef stew in a few." Q nodded to the kitchen behind the bar and took a swig of his drink. It wasn't as good as the brew that Amelia made, but it was decent.

Roska studied the dark amber liquid for a moment longer before carefully picking up his tankard and taking a tentative sip. Quinn tried to contain his laughter as his brother grimaced and nearly spat the ale onto the floor.

"Don't like it?" Q asked, hiding his laughter behind his tankard.

Roska shook his head, too busy gagging to respond. The food arrived just in time and Q watched in amusement as his brother shoveled a far-too-hot spoonful of stew into his mouth.

"Be careful, love," the young waitress warned a few seconds too late.

"Yeah, I'm not sure that's the best way to get the taste of ale out of your mouth, bro," Quinn smirked at his brother, who was sitting with his mouth wide open, trying to cool his freshly burned tongue. Q slowly stirred his stew, blowing gently on the top of the steaming bowl.

"You ok, darlin'? Canna git ye some wa'er?" The waitress patted Roska gently on the back, but Q watched as his brother flinched as though she'd slapped him. The girl—who couldn't have been much older than them—jerked her hand back quickly and glanced to Quinn with a look of confusion laced with fear in her eyes.

"I think water would be great, thanks," Quinn said to the nervous girl, and she disappeared into the crowd, making a beeline for the bar. She returned just as quickly with two large tankards of water, placed them on the table, and left without a word.

Quinn said nothing, but he kept a watchful eye on his brother for the remainder of their meal. He understood his brother's reaction to being touched. Q could vividly remember the way he reacted the first time Amelia had tried to hug him. He'd screamed bloody murder and started swinging his fists, kicking out at her and demanding she leave him alone. He could see the hurt in her face so clearly, even now. She'd been upset by his reaction to her touch, for sure, but underneath that feeling of hurt, he'd seen a look of simmering anger.

It had taken him several moons to realize that her anger hadn't been directed at him. She'd been pissed at Q's former foster parents and the fact that his time with them had left him so afraid of any physical contact.

While he might not know exactly what his brother had gone through, Quinn knew it would take some time for Ros to feel comfortable with anyone touching him. He would show his brother the same patience that Amelia had shown him.

Aiden was waiting for them in their room upstairs when Roska and Quinn finished their meal. Demoni had coiled herself up Roska's forearm, hiding under his sleeve once she had absorbed the warmth she'd been lacking out in the snow.

"I got the biggest room I could," Aiden told them as they walked in, "and then I conjured these beds." He gestured to three cots that lined the wall. "They originally had one large bed in this space. While I'm in favor of family bonding, that seemed a bit much. Even for me."

Quinn felt a little heart sick. The last time he'd been here, he'd shared a bed with Elena. He hadn't known she was his sister yet, which had made things awkward, but they'd bonded that night. *Gods, I miss her.*

"Thank you, Father," Roska said, walking over to the bed closest to the fireplace. He took his cloak off and laid it across the foot of the cot.

"Yeah," Quinn added quietly. "Thanks." He wasn't thrilled about sharing a room with their father, but they didn't have a lot of other options.

"I assume Aleerah is spending the night outside," Aiden said to no one in particular as he sat on the edge of the cot under the window.

"Yeah, she and Lyra were enjoying the snow too much to come in for dinner," Quinn answered.

"I'm not surprised." Aiden stretched his arms overhead, releasing several loud cracks in his arms and back. "She is made for this sort of weather. That thick coat of hers will protect her from the frost better than anything."

"Lyra's the same way," Quinn added, absentmindedly. He didn't really want to make small talk, but Elena and Amelia would have been disappointed with him if he didn't at least try to connect with his father. He didn't want to hear the lectures they'd have for him if Roska ratted him out later for being rude to Aiden. Better to suck it up and play nice. For now.

"I think they're both out of their minds," Roska said with a small smile. "It's too damn cold out there."

"You do see the irony in that, right?" Quinn poked at his brother. "You, FrostBorn, are uncomfortable with the cold."

Roska flicked his fingers at Quinn, causing some snowflakes to fly into Q's face. "Irony, maybe, but I imagine I'll be much happier in the growing season than you and your thick-furred firefox, Flame-Born."

Quinn could only shrug with a smile as he wiped the snow from his eyelashes. The growing season was definitely not his favorite. It was too damn hot all the time.

"I knew it," Roska gloated.

"Yes, you all have an interesting balance to strike between the Mother Goddess and your own powers." Aiden looked at his sons, and Q almost thought he saw a hint of nostalgia in their father's eyes.

"I wonder which season is Elena's favorite." Roska stretched out in his cot, leaning his back against the wall.

"She seemed really happy in the harvest season," Quinn offered, mimicking his brother's pose in his own cot. "Although that could just be because she'd finally gotten out from under our mother's oppressive thumb."

"No, you're right," Aiden said. "She always seemed to thrive in the harvest seasons. The planting seasons are good for her too, but the storms tend to make her more volatile, and her powers become unpredictable."

Quinn stared at Aiden, mouth hanging wide.

"How do you know that?" Roska asked.

"Aleerah told you, I've been watching the three of you since your conception." Aiden tried to sound casual, but Quinn could tell he wasn't comfortable with the awkward silence his words had created. "I just wanted to feel connected to you all. That's all."

Quinn didn't know what to say. He couldn't think of anything nice or even polite to say in response to their father's admission, and he knew Elena wouldn't want him to be cruel. Thankfully, Roska knew exactly how to respond.

"I understand why you didn't want to interfere in our paths, in order to protect the future and the intended outcome of the prophecy, but you have to know that spying on us all this time was disturbing. You had to know that if we ever found out, it wouldn't go over well." Ros summed up Quinn's sentiments perfectly. "You're not an idiot," he added.

"I weighed my options," Aiden replied. He shifted his position on his cot to better face the two of them. "I could have ignored your existence. Acted like I didn't know anything about your lives or the paths you would be forced to take. But that would have been taking the easy way out." He paused to look them both in the eye, one at a time. "You have to know that the hardest thing a parent can experience is to see their child in pain and not be able to do anything about it. I knew the three of you would have to face seemingly insurmountable obstacles and suffer undeniable pain and torment. I *knew* it was coming, and as much as I wanted to shield you from it, I knew that I couldn't." He dropped his gaze, wringing his hands in his lap. Quinn thought he saw a sheen of tears in their father's eyes. "I knew the hells you would face," Aiden's voice cracked. He swallowed hard before continuing, never lifting his eyes from his lap. "I knew you would survive and that I couldn't help you. But I also knew that I couldn't let you suffer alone. You didn't know I was there, but I watched every second of your lives, and I suffered right along with you." Quinn could see that his father was openly crying now, the tears falling silently into Aiden's tightly clenched hands.

"The worst pain a parent can feel is watching their child suffer and knowing they are powerless to stop it."

29

ROSKA

ROSKA'S DREAMS HAD BEEN plagued with his absolute worst memories. Beatings he'd taken. Nights he had spent praying for death. Pleading with the Mother Goddess to free him and Demoni from the hells they were living in. In his dreams, however, Roska had been watching himself from afar. Almost as though he'd been experiencing his father's viewpoint, rather than reliving the moments. He woke drenched in sweat, hours before sunrise. Rather than risk revisiting more traumatic memories, Roska had laid in his cot, listening to the comforting sounds of his brother and father breathing deeply, and watching the sky from their small window fade from the darkest blue to the gentle lavender of a new day.

Roska was stewing in his darker memories when Quinn started to stir. Roska sat up and stretched in his bed, popping the sore joints in his shoulders and rolling his neck from side to side. He wasn't going to be very pleasant to be around today if he didn't get his head right. Roska needed to get his mind away from those memories. Lock them away until things were calm and he could truly deal with them.

That is the worst idea you've ever had and you know it. Demoni jumped into his lap, demanding his attention by digging her sharp little claws into the meat of his thighs. *Bottling things up is how we ended up creating an uncontrollable snowstorm in the middle of that school.*

Perhaps, but we don't really have the time to process all this right now, Roska countered.

We really won't have time for it if you start a blizzard in the middle of that cavern this time. I'm not saying you need to resolve all your issues right this second. Just do what Elena said. Feel your feelings, acknowledge them, and let them go. Of course she would quote Elena. How could Roska reasonably argue with someone whose bottled up emotions had resulted in the unintentional murder of four rapists?

Roska had been shocked when Elena had told him that story. Not because she'd killed those men; they'd deserved it and so much more. No, what had surprised him was how calm she'd been when she spoke. They'd been locked in the tower at Harbor Ridge, talking about how to control their powers and understanding what triggered their magic. Roska could vividly picture the lightning dancing in her eyes as she told her story. She'd been in complete control of her magic, even as she revisited such a traumatic memory. It was awe-inspiring. Roska wasn't sure he would ever have that sort of control over his own powers, but he knew Demoni—quoting Elena—was right. Bottling up his trauma and ignoring it wouldn't help anyone.

Quinn wasn't quite up yet, and Aiden showed no signs of movement, so Roska sat back in his bed, resting his spine against the wall. Demoni remained in his lap, although she'd released her sharp grip on his legs. He leaned his head against the stone wall and closed his eyes. With his hands laying palms up on either side of his legs, Roska took several deep breaths. With each breath, he recalled one of the memories that had plagued his sleep. He held the images in his mind as he inhaled, held his breath for a count of five, focusing on the feelings he'd felt in each memory, then exhaled the memory away. Acknowledging the experience, recognizing the hurt that it caused and the power it gave him, and letting it go.

Roska had just finished letting go of the last nightmarish memory when Quinn spoke up.

"I know you're the FrostBorn and all, but that doesn't mean you have to sleep in a bed full of snow, Ros." Q eyed Roska's bed with a mixture of amusement and concern.

Roska looked down at his hands to see that he had unintentionally filled his cot with a layer of snow. He'd processed his feelings as best he could, but he'd still lost control. Mildly, but still.

His face must have shown his distress because Quinn quickly added, "No worries, man! It's a magical bed anyway. I'm sure demi-god Dad can clean that with a snap."

As if on cue, Aiden snapped his fingers, causing the snow to vanish, without even opening his eyes.

"How long will it take us to get to the Dragon's Teeth from here?" Roska asked, eager to change the subject.

"Well, I would've thought we'd be there by now, but this damn snowstorm is really slowing us down." Quinn rose from his cot, stretching his back and rubbing the sleep from his eyes. "When Elena and I came through here before, we made it to the base of the mountains in a day. At the rate we're going, it will take at least twice that long. There aren't any forests to hide our trail here, but we also can't risk the main road. We'll have to travel along the river more today, and keep low. The grass is high, or it was in the harvest season. It will disguise us some, but we'll need to move slowly to avoid attracting unwanted attention."

"Then we'd better get moving." It was the first thing Aiden had said all morning, as he hopped up—surprisingly spry for a centuries-old demi-god.

Roska stood from his cot, walked over to the hearth, and slipped his feet into his now-dry boots. Quinn followed suit, then handed Roska his pack and cloak before donning his own. Aiden snapped his fingers and the cots vanished, replaced by the large wood and straw bed that must have initially filled the room.

Roska took one last glance around the room, grateful for the night of peace and bonding he'd been granted with his father and brother. He hated to leave knowing that he would likely never have an experience like that again.

They had just finished eating breakfast in the dining hall and were getting up to leave when Quinn suddenly shook his head and motioned for them to remain seated. He leaned in closer, beckoning them to do the same, and spoke.

"We can't leave. Not yet. Lyra just told me there's a troop of soldiers coming up the main road through town. We won't be able to sneak out without catching their notice, so we need to hang back here for a bit. Give those muxing bastards a chance to get in and out without seeing us." Quinn's voice was harsh and immediately brought an icy chill to Roska's gut. The soldiers were here. Why?

"Do you think they followed us?" Roska asked, his voice a hushed whisper. His back was to the door. He desperately wanted to turn so that he might see the soldiers as they came in, but he didn't think that would do well in their attempts to remain inconspicuous.

"I can't be sure, but I hope not." Q tossed a quick glance over his shoulder toward the door just as the soldiers pushed into the room, bringing a rush of icy wind and snow with them.

Aiden leaned back in his chair, stretching casually. From his vantage point, Roska knew Aiden had the best view of the soldiers as they made their way across the dining hall heading straight for the bar. He offered the brothers a quiet play-by-play of what the soldiers were doing. Roska took a sip of his mostly empty teacup, listening intently to his father's words, attempting to track the soldiers in his mind.

"Just three, right now," Aiden told them, "but they look like officers. Their battalion will likely be making or breaking camp close by. If we're lucky, these three are just here for a fresh cuppa and will be on their merry way soon."

Subtly, Aiden passed his hand over the teapot on their table and Roska saw a wisp of steam begin to rise anew from the spout. Roska tried to hide his wonderment as he slowly lifted the formerly empty pot and refilled his cup, then his brother's, with the fresh morning brew.

"Not to get off-topic here, but why the hells did we pay for a pot of tea if you could just wave your hand and fill a pot for free? We could have saved our coin." Quinn muttered under his breath, more talking to his steaming cup than their father.

"Apologies, son," Aiden replied without taking his eyes off the officers. "I didn't think you'd approve of stiffing this fine establishment out of their potential earnings."

Quinn said nothing, but Roska thought he saw his brother smirk behind his teacup.

"Cannae git ye anythin' else, lads?" A young waitress seemed to appear out of nowhere behind him, causing Roska to start, spilling tea all over his lap. "Oh ach, sorry, dear. I didna mean ta startle ye." She rushed to clean the spilled tea with her bar towel, wiping it across the table, before kneeling to gently dab the tea from his trousers.

Roska froze, unable to even blink as the girl carefully attempted to clean the hot tea from his lap. He locked eyes with Quinn over the top of the girl's fiery red hair, unsure what to do and utterly terrified to move a muscle. Much to his surprise—and dismay—Q was struggling to stifle his laughter as he watched the scene unfold. The heat rose in Roska's cheeks and neck as the girl finished cleaning the tea and rose from his side. Roska noticed her gaze locked on his lap, and quickly covered his embarrassment with his hands, casting a pleading look to Q in the hopes that his brother would offer a reprieve and save him from death by humiliation.

"No worries, miss," Aiden said, dragging the girl's eyes from Roska's entirely unintentional and utterly disastrous bodily reaction to her physical attentions. "Accidents happen. Could we get another plate of biscuits?" he added, without taking his eyes off the table where the officers had taken up residence.

"Aye, o' course, sir." The girl offered a quick nod, casting one last glance and a wink at Roska before turning on her heel and bounding off through the crowd, back to the kitchens.

Roska slammed his head onto the table, splashing more tea and wishing he could disappear completely.

Quinn let loose the weak grip he'd had on his laughter, bursting into loud cackles and slapping Roska on the back as though he'd won some sort of prize. "Gods, that was the best thing I've seen in weeks," he said between fits of laughter.

"I'm so glad you enjoyed the show." Roska didn't bother lifting his head from the worn—and slightly sticky—table.

"Come on now, don't be mad." Quinn took a deep breath, attempting to contain in his pleasure at Roska's expense. "It's not a big deal. So you got a little... excited when a pretty girl knelt before you. Who hasn't?" Roska felt Q's hand on his shoulder, trying to gently rouse him into an upright position, but Roska refused to move. If he could have melted all the way through the floor, he would have happily.

"That's actually how I met your mother." Aiden's lips lifted in a half-smile.

Roska shot upright, blanching at their father's words. Q stared, mouth agape, at Aiden as though he couldn't quite comprehend what the man had just said.

"Here you go, lad," came a female voice. Roska looked at the woman, suddenly very grateful for her presence. He was a little taken aback to realize that the woman who spoke wasn't the same young waitress as before. Roska couldn't decide if the feeling that settled in his stomach was one of relief or disappointment.

It didn't matter anyway. It's not like he was ever going to see that girl again.

"Thank you, Miss," Aiden said. He'd never once taken his eyes off the officers. It was equal parts impressive and relief-inducing. At least his father hadn't actually *seen* what had unfolded between him and the pretty red-haired girl.

"If ye need anythin' else, jus' holler," the woman added with a smile. Then she sauntered off to the next table, clearly oblivious to what had taken place with the last waitress.

They sat in awkward silence for several moments before Aiden informed them that the officers were finally leaving. Roska remained at the table with his father and brother for a while longer, waiting for the all-clear from Lyra to let them know it was safe to leave the inn without being seen by the soldiers.

As they shouldered their packs and walked out the door, Roska couldn't help but look back over his shoulder, unconsciously seeking out the fiery waitress who had had such an unexpected effect on him.

He caught the flash of her brilliant red hair out of the corner of his eye. He stopped in his tracks, turning to watch her work behind the bar for a few seconds, trying to commit her visage to memory. The way her curls pulled free of the braid she'd attempted to contain them in. The freckles that decorated her face like the night sky's constellations. The palest blue that filled her eyes. She was a vision he hoped he'd never forget but knew he'd probably never see again.

30

BEATRICE

BEATRICE TOOK A LONG, desperate, and un-Headmistress-like swig of her wine. Staring out the south-facing window of her office, she had an unobstructed view of the cemetery.

The cemetery.

One moon ago, Harbor Ridge hadn't even possessed a cemetery. Now the plot of previously fallow and snow-covered farmland was dotted with nearly a dozen headstones. Girls as young as four, who had come to the school so that they might have a safe haven to learn and practice their crafts, were gone. They'd fallen ill the quickest, their familiars fading within days of their arrival in the infirmary. Each child passed mere hours after the loss of their familiar. One simply cannot survive without one's soul.

Beatrice had finally finished responding to all of the missives from her investigators in the field, recalling each and every one back to the school for protection. Many had started arriving already. They'd taken up residence in the barracks with the guards, although Beatrice had been informed that they were rapidly running out of beds.

The older girls, those who were encroaching on or just entering womanhood were starting to feel the effects of the *turmio*. They weren't sick yet, but their magics were becoming unreliable. Beatrice had been forced to explain to the girls what was happening in the world—at least, a minimal explanation, no need to tell them they were all going to die soon—and discourage the girls from practicing. The girls weren't happy with these new rules, but they'd heard the rumors and seen the school's new cemetery, so they accepted the restrictions without a fight.

Beatrice had spent the last few days working with the guards to design the most effective defense system that wouldn't require magic to maintain it. It had proven to be quite the challenge, but once they recruited some of the top Magineering students and their instructors, they managed to design a very impressive and magic-free system of walls, catapults, canons, archery towers, and various other defensive structures. Based on the drawings and schematics the magineers had shown the headmistress for final approval, it looked like the medieval structures she'd studied during her time as a student. With some more refined improvements, of course.

The magineers assured her that—assuming their own magics didn't fail them—they could have the structures in place by the end of the week. Beatrice prayed that they were right. She'd gotten several reports over the last few days, as well as first-hand accounts from those returning from the field, that the soldiers from Riverayn were making their way to Harbor Ridge.

Her arrogant mind wanted to believe that the King was sending these soldiers to protect her and the school, but her realistic nature told her that wasn't likely to be the case. It was far more conceivable to think that the capital knew something was off with magic and saw it as an opportunity to seize power for themselves.

Beatrice scoffed at the mere idea. The hubris involved in thinking that a battalion—or even the entire army—could come and claim Harbor Ridge for the Crown was laughable under any other circumstances. It made her wonder if the King might not be quite as enthralled with her as she once believed. Unleashing the *turmio* would be a very efficient way to expunge the magical creatures from Waverly. Hells, it would be the only way the magept could gain the upper hand and take control of the school.

She tried to imagine the King hatching such a nefarious plot, but it didn't seem like something he was capable of. He wasn't a weak man, but he wasn't terribly ambitious either. He wanted direct access to the seas, rather than relying on river trade, but otherwise, he wasn't interested in magic as a power source. Perhaps it was because he considered her to be his ally and didn't feel the need to control her. Perhaps it was because he was a damned fool and didn't think beyond his next sexual release. Regardless, this sort of long-game plan wasn't something he would have concocted. Not alone anyway.

Beatrice turned to look out the eastern window, watching the rocks float through the air as the magineers directed the guards and older students to build the main wall that would encircle the school. Along the wall, there would be towers for the archers to stand guard, catapults, vats filled with boiling tar, oil, or water, and a large collection of smaller boulders that could be dropped onto invading soldiers if they attempted to breach the wall. In less than a week, they'd managed to encircle half the school.

One of the benefits of running the only school for enchantresses in the country was that every enchantress in Waverly felt loyal to the school. Several of the women had worked themselves to the point of exhaustion the first day. Beatrice had stepped in on the second day, enforcing breaks and limiting the number of hours each enchantress could work at a time. She appreciated their commitment, but—as she told the women at the start of the second day—they couldn't help anyone if they worked themselves into an early grave.

It would all get done, she had told them, but the whole point of this defense system was to keep them all alive.

A curt knock at the door forced her to take her attention off her mounting list of concerns.

"Come in," she said.

"Pardon the intrusion, Headmistress, but there's a woman here to see you." The guard cast a nervous look over her shoulder as she closed the door behind her.

"Who is it, Imogen?" Beatrice asked, her tone indicating that she was not in the mood for foolishness. Zied lifted his head from his paws. His ears suddenly perked up as he sniffed the air.

"Ma'am, she... well, she claims to know you, and she seems very strange. I'm not sure how she made it inside the school. She just walked right up to us and demanded to see you. I'm sorry, Headmistress." Imogen shook her head, as though she were trying to shake loose a thought that had been caught in her mind. "I'm not even sure why I entertained her demands and interrupted you. A thousand apologies, Headmistress."

The guard looked thoroughly confused, but Beatrice felt a growing sense of dread as she realized who it was on the other side of her door.

"Gods damn that witch."

31

BELLADONNA

"Come now, Bea. Is that really how you greet an old, dear friend?" Belladonna leaned against the doorframe, casually studying the room that Beatrice had left her for. She tried to contain the rage she felt, passing it off as mere disdain, but she wasn't confident that she'd achieved her goal.

The guard stared at her in shock. It was obvious that no one ever walked into the Headmistress' office without some sort of formal invitation. Yet here she was, a witch—and a filthy one at that since she hadn't bothered to get cleaned up before barging into Beatrice's fancy office—welcoming herself into a space that was so clearly not meant for her.

"You can't just—" the guard started, but Beatrice cut her off.

"You're dismissed, Imogen. I'll handle it from here."

After another dozen or so apologies, the flustered guard rushed from the office, careful not to slam the door in her haste to escape the mounting tension in the room. Then they were alone. For the first time in over twenty cycles.

"What are you doing here?" Beatrice practically hissed at her.

Zied didn't seem to share Beatrice's animosity toward Belladonna. He immediately rose from the giant pillow he'd been resting on and rubbed his massive, furry head against her legs, demanding affection as only a lion could—meaning he nearly knocked her to the ground in his efforts to show his love for her.

Belladonna dropped to her knees, rather than get entirely trampled by the lion, burying her hands in his fur and scratched behind his ears like she recalled him loving.

"Hello, Beautiful," Belladonna cooed. "I've missed you so much." She promptly wrapped her arms around his thick neck and buried her face in his mane. Zied responded with a resounding purr that filled the room, rubbing his face against hers and carefully licking the tears she hadn't meant to shed from her cheeks.

"Belladonna, why are you here?" Beatrice asked again. Her voice still firm, but Belladonna thought she heard her voice waver ever-so-slightly. Bea wasn't as emotionally hardened as she wanted people to believe.

Belladonna looked up at her from her position on the floor. Zied had practically climbed into her lap, and Belladonna knew she wouldn't be moving from that spot for a while.

"We need to talk, and I didn't think you'd respond to a letter." Belladonna tried to lighten the mood with a friendly smile, but Beatrice just stared at her. The hurt and confusion that Belladonna felt at seeing Bea again was perfectly mirrored in Beatrice's eyes and body language. This wasn't an encounter either of them were prepared to have, yet it was unavoidable.

"I met your children," Belladonna said, attempting a different tactic.

"Are they ok?" Beatrice's body language instantly switched from defensive self-preservation to anxious, her knuckles turning white as she clenched her fists at her sides.

"They are strong. So much stronger than I ever would have imagined." Belladonna wanted to reach a hand out—offer physical comfort to the woman she'd loved for so many years—but she wasn't confident that Beatrice would be open to such affections. Belladonna knew that she wouldn't be able to handle Bea's rejection yet again. Instead, she stroked Zied's mane and tried to focus on the reason she'd come here in the first place. "They went off with Castor to find their father."

"They did *what*?" Beatrice's voice hit an octave Belladonna hadn't known her capable of.

"Yes, apparently that bloody fool has been living in a crumbling watchtower in the mountains north of here. At the border. The children went to see him in the hopes that he would be able to help them stop the *turmio*." Belladonna watched Beatrice's face, hoping to gauge her reaction to the news.

"I can't believe he's been here this whole time. That muxing bastard. Tricked me into having his children and then sat back to watch the disasters that would arise as a result." Beatrice began pacing now, fuming with unspent frustration.

"I'm not sure you can put all the blame on him," Belladonna said calmly. "After all, you knew what you were getting into when you went out to get impregnated. It was one of the excuses you used when you left me."

Belladonna didn't want to be cruel, but she wasn't going to sug-arcoat shyt either. Bea had made her choice long ago and now they were all having to deal with the fallout.

"How dare you! I didn't want to leave you. I tried to bring you *with* me," Beatrice snapped.

"Oh yes, that would have gone over swimmingly with your coun-sel of self-righteous enchantresses. You know they all looked down on me as a witch, deemed me unworthy." Belladonna couldn't bear to look at Beatrice anymore. Turning her attention back to the lion whose head consumed her lap. "Not to mention I'm literally incapable of giving you children. Which is apparently the most im-portant job for an enchantress around here."

"That's not fair," Beatrice whispered, kneeling down beside her. Belladonna didn't look up, but from the corner of her eye, she saw Bea reach out, almost touching her arm before recoiling and step-ping away. As though physical distance would ease the debilitating pain in their respective hearts.

"It doesn't matter," Belladonna said quickly. They needed to change the subject or she would definitely end up crying. More. Besides, this wasn't why she'd come. "I wanted to warn you about the soldiers. There was an entire garrison on the road through the Dark Woods. Demolishing the saplings and wreaking all sorts of havoc, I might add. But I overheard two of the officers talking about a girl whose electric weasel nearly took out an entire platoon."

"Elena," Beatrice gasped.

"Yes, I think so. From the sounds of it, they were taking her to Riverayn."

"Why?" All of the color seemed to drain from Beatrice's face. "What could they want with her?"

"Have you upset the King lately?" Belladonna asked, trying to keep the scorn from her tone.

"That old fool?" Beatrice scoffed. "No. The only thing I could do to upset that idiot would be to stop letting him come around. Besides," she added with a dismissive wave of her hand, "he's not clever enough to plot against me. He thinks he's in love with me."

Belladonna tried not to bristle at the callousness of Beatrice's words. Why should she care if her former lover had found someone new to warm her bed? She'd known about Bea's affair with the King. It was the most poorly kept secret in Waverly. Still, it irked Belladonna more than she liked to hear Beatrice talk about her lover. Even if she was blunt and emotionless about it.

"Well, these were definitely his soldiers. If not him, then who else would be so cavalier as to kidnap your only known child?" Belladonna really didn't want to be having this conversation. Part of her wished she'd never even come here. Being this close to the woman she loved and not being able to touch her was a special kind of torture.

"There really is no other person who would be stupid enough to try this." Beatrice glared out the window, in the direction of Riverayn.

32

QUINN

Two days. Two muxing days. They should have reached the cave by now. Instead, they had been stuck in this damned inn for *two days*. Between the endless snow and the army of soldiers that set up camp just outside of town, Quinn wasn't sure they'd ever make it to the mountains.

Lyra and Aleerah were stealthily stalking the soldiers; tracking them and trying to overhear their plans. Unfortunately, that meant that Quinn, Roska, and Aiden were staying in Nexton a while longer. Lyra kept him updated with the intel she'd overheard, but Quinn couldn't shake the restless feeling. He was essentially stuck in the inn, drinking too much tea and battling his inner turmoil at the idea of not being able to rescue Elena.

The only high point to their otherwise stifling stagnation was watching Ros try to interact with that pretty waitress. After that first morning with the "lap incident," Roska had become obsessed—no, Aiden called it "enamored"—with the girl. He always managed to find her in the crowded dining hall, watching her move around the room with practiced ease. Q had to agree. She was cute, but he didn't see the point in getting wrapped up in any sort of relationship with the girl considering they had bigger things to focus on.

Aiden, however, kept encouraging Roska. Offering tips on how to approach her, and constantly waving her over to the table—which is why Q had been drinking too much tea. Q thought it was nice enough, but a waste of time. Although he couldn't deny the change he'd seen in his brother over the last two days. Roska was slowly coming out of his shell, gaining confidence. He didn't even flinch when the waitress put her hand on his shoulder the last time she'd swung by their table.

Still, Q knew that they needed to get moving. The soldiers had made camp just outside of town, blocking their road to the mountains. He'd attempted to scout a path around them, but Q was starting to think they'd brought the entire muxing army. There was no getting around the soldiers unless they wanted to travel a week in the wrong direction. Based on what Lyra and Aleerah had overheard, the soldiers would likely be moving on in another day. Maybe two.

Which meant more sitting around, trying to ignore the growing sense of doom that was slowly driving him to insanity.

We will get there. Lyra tried to comfort him while keeping watch on the officers having lunch in their tent at the border between their campsite and the town.

Yes, but will we get there in time? Quinn replied, anxiety causing his tone to be clipped and irritated.

We'll get there when we get there, she snapped back. *We can't leave now without being detected, so we will leave when we can. Getting snippy and rude with me won't change anything.*

Q picked up his chipped teacup and took an irritated sip of the bitter liquid.

"Why can't we order ale? Just once I want to take a drink and not cringe at the disgusting flavor in my mouth." Quinn glared at Aiden, who simply took a sip of his own tea and shrugged.

"Ale fogs the mind. It's fine when you're in a safe place, looking to relax and unwind. But we aren't in a safe space." Aiden subtly nodded to the soldiers three tables over. "We need to keep our heads. Tea, especially this delightful blend of black tea and honey, will keep us alert and hydrated. Have a biscuit, son." He slid the plate of sweet treats over to Quinn. Q continued to glare at their father, refusing a biscuit and desperately wishing he was anywhere else.

"I'm worried about her too," Roska said suddenly. Q had assumed his brother was so enthralled by the waitress to even notice his mood. "But I have to have faith that the Mother Goddess didn't bring us together only to tear Elena away from us so suddenly."

Roska took one of the biscuits, snapped it in two, and held the larger piece to Q. Begrudgingly, Q took the proffered treat, dipping it into his tea and grunting a quick thanks.

"I guess I'm just not as pious as you. I'm used to good things being ripped from my grasp without warning." Quinn didn't bother hiding his bitterness.

"We will see her again. It has been prophesied. You said Lyra overheard the soldiers are planning to move on tomorrow, yes? Then we will be able to get back on the trail tomorrow as well." Roska placed his hand gingerly on Q's arm. "She is strong. She will make it to the cave, and we will recapture the *turmio*. Then we can all come back here and have as much ale as you can stand."

Quinn couldn't help but smile at Roska's boundless optimism.

"You are annoyingly confident. Just like her," he quipped.

"One of us has to be." Ros smirked, squeezing his hold on Q's arm before releasing him, taking a sip of his own tea, and grimacing. "Besides, ale can't possibly be much worse than this." He eyed his cup suspiciously, placing it back on the table and surreptitiously gazing around the room until he found his waitress again.

Q watched his brother's eyes light up as the girl moved about the dining hall.

"You know, Ros, you could just talk to her. I promise it won't be that bad. Hells, you might even learn her name!" Quinn snickered as Roska's face turned almost as red as his waitress's hair.

"I already know her name," he said in a reverent whisper.

"You do? When did you talk to her? Why didn't you tell me?" Quinn sat forward in his chair. He was suddenly far more invested in this development than he wanted to admit.

"I haven't. I overheard the innkeeper call her Brigit. Just as stunning and majestic as the goddess who shares her name." Roska's voice had taken on a dreamy note, never taking his eyes off the girl.

"Yeah, this is progressing from affectionate to creepy very quickly." Q looked over to the girl, catching her attention with the wave of his hand. "You need to talk to her. If you keep going like this, you're going to turn into one of those creepy stalker types that I had to throw out of Amelia's once or twice for leering at Elena."

Roska frantically turned to face him. Quinn couldn't help the bubble of laughter that escaped. This was going to be hilarious or awful. Maybe both.

33

ROSKA

"**G**ODS, NO," ROSKA WHISPERED.

A wide, cheshire grin split across Q's face as he watched Roska search for a place to hide. Aiden leaned back in his chair, stoic as always.

"Wha cannae git ye, lad?" the waitress asked, addressing Quinn, but Roska could feel the heat of her gaze on his skin. She might be talking to Q, but she was looking at Roska. He didn't look up to face her. Roska knew that the girl was glaring at him, annoyed and uncomfortable with his constant leering. He'd tried to stop, he really had, but something about her drew him in. Roska felt utterly helpless. His eyes sought her out, whether he wanted them to or not.

"Actually, my brother was just telling me that he thought you were the prettiest girl he'd ever seen." Quinn nudged Roska, trying to force him to look up.

"Is tha so?" she pivoted to face Roska. He felt the wind on his back as she tossed her wild curls over her shoulder.

Gods help me. Roska seemed physically incapable of looking the girl in the face, but he also didn't want to seem rude. He struggled to look at her, his gaze settled on her neck, rather than her stunning, crystal blue eyes. He caught the scent of her in the air. Wood smoke—from the kitchen ovens—and the yeasty warm smell of fresh-baked bread. His mouth nearly watered at the bouquet of delicious scents that surrounded her.

Say something, you idiot. Say literally anything, Roska begged and pleaded with his own mind.

Demoni, sensing his anguish, tightened her grip around his forearm where she had wrapped herself the moment Q had called the waitress over.

Just look up and smile at her, she offered.

I can't! She thinks I'm creepy and weird for staring at her all the time. Roska continued to avoid the waitress's eyes as he tried to come up with something to say. *She probably hates me and wishes we would just leave.*

"Yeah, he wanted to ask your name, but he's a bit shy," Quinn continued talking to the girl as though Roska wasn't sitting right next to him, making a complete fool of himself.

"I'm Brigit," she said softly, maneuvering her face to lock eyes with Roska. She held his stare, and he realized that she wasn't glaring at him at all. She was smiling, possibly even blushing.

"Brigit," Roska finally spoke. Her name was a quiet melody on his tongue. A song of peace and inner calm that rang throughout his body as she studied him. Roska studied her in return, the flecks of gold in her eyes, the soft curve of her slightly parted lips, the constellation of freckles covering her nose and cheeks. "You're a goddess."

Brigit's cheeks flushed bright red immediately, and Roska was overwhelmed with feelings of shame and fear. He'd said it out loud. He hadn't meant to, and now he'd embarrassed and offended her. *Mux everything*.

Roska looked away, to hide his own embarrassment and give Brigit an opportunity to escape their awkward interaction.

He nearly jumped out of his skin when she gently placed her hand on his shoulder, bringing his attention back to her deity-like face. She was smiling as she said, "Thank ye, love."

He might have passed out right then and there, but he knew Quinn would never let him live it down. Although, that probably didn't matter much, since Roska didn't expect to live to see the end of the frost season anyway.

The world around them faded away as he basked in the glorious light of her goddess-like presence. The warmth of Brigit's hand on his shoulder seemed to spread through his body, awakening and enlivening parts of him that he thought had died many cycles ago. He was drawn into the stillness he found in her eyes and the comfort she gave him in the simplicity of her smile.

Across the dining hall, someone dropped a plate in the kitchens causing an explosion of cheers and clapping from the dining hall patrons. The sudden burst of noise shattered their perfect moment of serenity and forced them back into the reality of the world.

Shaking his head, clearing the fog from his mind, Roska glanced away from Brigit to his brother. Q was watching them studiously, although Roska couldn't tell if he was assessing their interaction or merely waiting to see how Roska would react to her touch.

Roska had surprised himself by his reaction to her. The overwhelming sense of peace she brought to him with her simple touch and the gentleness of her smile astounded him. He never wanted to leave her side. Based on her hand still firmly resting on his shoulder, she felt the same.

Why would she want to be with a soulless monster like you? Roska flinched as the voice of Brother Lucian echoed in his mind. Brother Lucian had taken a special pride in breaking Roska's spirits, relishing the days when Roska was in his charge during his shifts in the armory. He constantly reminded Roska of his worth—or lack thereof—and was quick to beat him down—literally—at the slightest perceived provocation.

Roska cast his eyes to his lap, hoping to hide his shame from Brigit. No need to let her see just how damaged he was. Whether she noticed the shift in his mood or not was unclear because she was called over to another table before Roska attempted to look up again.

"Well that was interesting," Quinn prodded quietly, leaning in closer to Roska to keep their conversation from being overheard. "What the mux was that about?"

"I don't know what you're talking about," Roska said a little too quickly. He picked up his neglected tea and purposefully refused to look around the room, denying his eyes their demands to seek out Brigit again.

"You two looked like you were about to make a baby right here on the table, then all of a sudden you shut down. What the hells, bro?" Quinn's words were crass, but his tone was filled with concern.

Roska didn't respond, keeping his attention focused on the tea before him.

You can't let the Brothers and their lies get to you, Demoni said, tightening her grip on his arm ever-so-slightly.

How do you propose I do that? Roska snapped at her.

He hadn't meant to sound so harsh, but he couldn't help it. He'd determined over the last few moons that "rational" wasn't a trait that any of the triplets had inherited. The more time he spent with Aiden, the more he started to wonder if any member of their family had developed rational thinking.

"He was wrong." Aiden spoke calmly but with a tight firmness in his voice that made Roska think he was fighting back some strong emotions. Roska turned his attention from his tea to their father, watching a series of emotions play across the man's face.

"Who? Me? I'm never wrong." Quinn smiled smugly.

"No. Brother Lucian." Aiden directed his words to Roska, his jaw clenching before he spoke again. "I know he told you that you aren't deserving of love. I know he convinced you that you are a monster. He was wrong. You are a remarkable young man, and you deserve all the love and kindness this world has to offer."

His father's words surprised him. It was still jarring to know that someone else had witnessed those moments in his life. Roska flashed back to his nightmares from their first night in the inn. He desperately wanted to believe their father, but Roska felt confident that it would take more than the kindness of a pretty girl and some nice words from their otherwise absent father to undo the cycles of mental and physical abuse he'd endured at the hands of his caretakers.

None of them spoke for the rest of the meal. Roska didn't seek Brigit out again. He spent the remainder of their time in the dining hall fighting flashbacks and accidentally freezing the tea in his cup.

34

BEATRICE

EATRICE HADN'T THOUGHT THERE was anything left in the world that could surprise her. Yet here she was, practically hiding in her office for the last two days, avoiding Belladonna and all the feelings her arrival had unearthed.

How the hells was Beatrice supposed to prepare for war when that witch was right down the hall reminding her of all the things she'd left behind?

Beatrice had barely slept since Belladonna's arrival. Her dreams were filled with old memories of their cottage in the woods, mixed with visions of what could have been. It left her restless and exhausted. She needed to focus.

All of her investigators had returned to the school, which meant the guards' quarters were filled to capacity, and they had expanded to fill the empty beds left by the children now resting eternally in the cemetery. It was morbid, but they didn't have any other options.

The wall fully encircled the school—highly impressive progress had been made once the investigators volunteered to help hurry the process along. They were now focused on making it taller and thicker.

The last of the investigators had arrived the night before, bringing with them the latest intel on the army's location. It seemed that the army was trying to flank them, splitting into two massive forces and attempting to approach from the north and southeast. Harbor Ridge was well protected by the mountains it resided within, making it near impossible to surround the school, but now that they'd built the wall and its accompanying towers, Beatrice felt confident that the soldiers wouldn't be able to breach the school. At least, not until magic fully failed them.

All of these things weighed heavily on her, but the one thing that pulled her attention the most was that damned witch. Belladonna had been helping out with the wall, reinforcing it by calling on the forest around them to strengthen the wall and erase the road that typically led through the Dark Woods.

Castor had shown up later in the afternoon on the same day that Belladonna had arrived. When Beatrice had noticed some tension and frigidity between them, she'd been tempted to ask Belladonna about it, but she quickly reminded herself that it was not her place and none of her business.

"It could be our business," Zied had quickly put in. "We could still have them. You just have to apologize and ask for her to come back."

"*I* have to apologize?" Beatrice had snapped at him. "For what? For doing the right thing? For fulfilling my duty—*our* duty—to the world and protecting magic? I've done nothing to apologize for. If she wanted to be with me, she could have come with us all those cycles ago. She chose to stay in the woods. Alone."

Zied hadn't spoken to her since.

Beatrice tried to convince herself that he was being unreasonable, expecting her to apologize as though she'd been the one who'd made the mistake. All her life, Beatrice had been raised to prioritize her obligation to magic and Harbor Ridge over anything and everything else. Enchantresses weren't supposed to fall in love specifically to avoid situations like this. It made things more complicated than they needed to be.

Beatrice was the headmistress. The Headmistress's life was the school. She'd tried to invite Belladonna to join her in that life, but she had refused. If anyone should apologize, it's that stubborn witch.

There was a knock at the door.

"Headmistress?"

"Come in." Beatrice looked up from the pile of papers and books on her desk. "What is it, Marsali?"

"We've lost another one, Headmistress." Marsali didn't even bother trying to hide the tears that streamed down her cheeks. Her eyes were bloodshot and swollen, likely from another endless night of heartbreak watching over the ever-growing number of patients in the infirmary.

Beatrice had tried to convince Marsali to take a night off from the devastation of it all, to take a small respite, but she'd refused, insisting that the girls deserved to have someone by their side at the end. Marsali wasn't the only woman who'd taken up the role of death doula. Nearly all the enchantresses who weren't helping fortify their defenses were taking shifts in the infirmary. It was an unspoken agreement: these children couldn't be saved, but they didn't have to die scared and alone either.

"That makes it an even twenty now. Gods, when will this end." Beatrice spoke aloud, but she was mostly talking to herself. She pushed her hands roughly through her typically flawless hair. Beatrice knew she likely looked as rough as Marsali. The lack of sleep and the unbearable weight of the losses they'd experienced with no end in sight was wearing her thin. Beatrice—trying to ignore the tightness in her throat and the tears that threatened—focused her attention on the heartbroken woman before her.

"We've also brought in three more girls to the infirmary. Based on the degradation of their familiars, they won't last the week." Marsali scrubbed a hand across her raw cheeks, hopelessly wiping away the tears that continued to pool in her eyes and overflow her lashes.

Beatrice rose and rounded her desk, taking the young woman in her arms in a rare—but entirely warranted—moment of compassion and maternal care. Gently rubbing her back, Marsali sagged into Beatrice's arms, letting the headmistress carry her weight for a few moments while she released the last vestige of self-control, giving over to her anguish.

After a few moments, Marsali seemed to regain her composure, straightening her back and disconnecting from Beatrice. She cast her eyes to her boots, trying to hide her embarrassment at having broken down, but Beatrice gingerly placed a finger under the young woman's chin, guiding her face back up.

"You have been doing an amazing job, caring for and comforting our girls. I don't know what we would do without you. You have every right to feel heartbroken, and no one would begrudge you if you took a day or two to take care of yourself. We can't constantly pour all of our energies into others. It will be the death of you, dear." Beatrice said the words firmly, but not unkindly. She wanted to impress upon Marsali the need for self-preservation and self-care. "Take a couple of days away from the infirmary. No, I'm not debating or discussing this. Take two days and focus on taking care of yourself. If you insist on helping around the school, then you may work in the kitchens. The cooks always need extra hands."

Beatrice offered this last bit as a small concession, as she knew that Marsali would certainly refuse to do nothing for two days, and she also knew that the girl loved to bake. This was the best solution for everyone. At least, she hoped.

Marsali consented to the change in her duties, offered Beatrice a kind, tired smile, and departed.

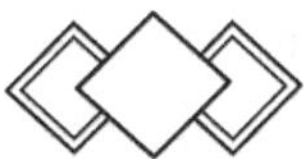

"You can't avoid me forever."

Damn. Beatrice turned around, slowly and deliberately, to face the witch.

"What are you doing in here? No one but myself and my personal guards is allowed in my private quarters." Beatrice had been cleansing her face and reapplying her glamours, as was her nightly routine when Belladonna had let herself into her sacred space.

"Oh? Is that so? Because I can smell the stench of that pompous King of yours all over this 'sacred space.'" Belladonna sneered, casually reading Beatrice's mind and throwing her own thoughts back at her. "I didn't realize he meant so much to you that he was allowed in your sanctum sanctorum." Belladonna roamed casually around the room, as though she'd been there a hundred times. As though she belonged there as much as Beatrice.

Beatrice hated how much she loved having Belladonna in her space. How natural it felt to be alone in this room with her. She'd desperately wanted Belladonna to leave. Leave this room. Leave the school. Walk back out of her life again and never return.

I feel like it needs to be clarified that we *walked out last time, not* them. They *didn't want us to leave. I didn't want us to leave. You were the only one who wanted to go.* Zied didn't bother lifting his head as he corrected her reminiscence.

I did what needed to be done. I did my duty. As all enchantresses should. That had become her mantra any time they attempted to have this conversation. It was exhausting.

Beatrice tried to remind herself of her duty and responsibilities now, as she watched Belladonna glide around the room. She seemed to barely touch the floor. Her dark skin in sharp contrast to the stark white curtains and sheets that attempted to make the room more cozy.

Beatrice had never bothered with decor, seeing the room as merely a place to rest and recharge before rising at dawn again to tackle the day's work. Watching her former lover inspecting the room now, she wished she'd taken the time to make the space more inviting.

She also hated herself for even thinking such things.

Yes, enchantresses often sought the comforts of other women in the halls of Harbor Ridge. It wasn't scandalous or even frowned upon. But the Headmistress was meant to be a beacon of virtue. Creating life and spreading knowledge. Love was not something a headmistress could afford. It took too much of her time and attention. The headmistress' life was one of romantic solitude and utter devotion to the prosperity of her staff and pupils.

"I can hear your mind racing from here, Bea. Just talk to me." Belladonna sat on the edge of the headmistress' bed, back straight as a sapling. The witch's eyes were trained on Beatrice as though she was the center of Belladonna's universe.

"You were. For a long time." Belladonna smiled softly, reading Beatrice's mind yet again.

"You have to stop doing that." Beatrice sighed, resigning herself to having *this* conversation.

"You have to stop trying to control everything," Belladonna countered.

"In case you haven't noticed, maintaining control is literally my job." Beatrice motioned vaguely to the school around them.

"Perhaps," Belladonna said simply, offering a nod in concession. "But that doesn't mean that you have to control everything about everyone all the time. Honestly, Bea, that's entirely impossible, and you will drive yourself to an early grave trying."

Beatrice flinched reflexively, glancing in the direction of the cemetery that now marked the land just beyond her field of view.

"Shyt, I'm sorry, Bea." Belladonna rose quickly, crossing the room in a moment and cautiously placing her warm hands on Beatrice's shoulders. "I didn't mean to upset you. I spoke without thinking."

Beatrice felt the burn of tears in her eyes. She was so tempted to just let go. Give herself over to the grief and take comfort in Belladonna's embrace. Like she had so many times before, all those cycles ago. It would be so easy. Like slipping back into an old, well-loved dress.

But she shouldn't. She couldn't. The Headmistress could not show weakness. It was her job to be strong for everyone. To take care of their needs.

"But who takes care of you, Bea?" Belladonna's question was kind, lacking in judgment, and so quiet Beatrice might have missed it entirely if she hadn't been staring so intently at Belladonna's soft, plush lips.

Beatrice flicked her eyes over Belladonna's face, studying the woman before her for the first time since her arrival. Time had changed her some, but it had not been unkind to her. There were tiny creases along the sides of Belladonna's eyes, making her appear even more intelligent. Small slivers of silver streaked through her exquisite evergreen locks. The most intriguing part of her, though, was her eyes. They'd always been a direct line to Belladonna's soul. When angry or irritable, they shone an icy, clear blue. When she was anxious, they held a hint of sea green, betraying the nausea she was likely feeling. When she was feeling amorous, her eyes practically glowed vibrant verdant. At this moment, Belladonna's eyes were the soothing blue of the sky just before dusk. Deep. Majestic. Calm.

Beatrice couldn't help but feel a pang of jealousy. Despite the tension between them, Belladonna was entirely at peace. The last time Beatrice felt that sort of calm was the last morning she'd woken up in their shared bed in the cottage. The morning the counsel had shown up and offered her the position of Headmistress.

Belladonna slid her hands up Beatrice's shoulders, gently taking the headmistress's face in her hands and stroking her thumbs soothingly over Beatrice's cheeks. Back and forth. The tenderness of Bella's repetitive motion elicited an almost meditative feeling within Beatrice. Closing her eyes, she felt herself lean into the witch's touch.

"You can talk to me, Bea," Belladonna whispered, her words a warm breath on Beatrice's cheek. "Please."

It was the please that finally broke her. The desperate, pleading voice, begging to be let in. Offering to lighten the weight Beatrice had been forced to carry alone all this time.

She couldn't help herself. Beatrice collapsed at the feet of the only woman she'd ever loved, tears falling endlessly.

"I don't know what to do," she managed between unwelcome sobs.

Belladonna sat on the floor with her, taking Beatrice into her arms and holding her as tightly as she could without causing pain.

Beatrice wasn't sure how long they sat on the floor like that. Her crying like a child while Belladonna rubbed her back and whispered sweet, reassuring things in her ear. When she finally regained her composure, Beatrice looked up to find the window was completely dark. It had been dusk when Belladonna had first entered the room.

Beatrice sat back slowly, not quite ready to disconnect from Belladonna entirely, but also needing to stretch her back and neck. Slowly, with the cautious air of a newborn fawn stepping into the sun for the first time, Beatrice reached a hand out to take Belladonna's. Without a breath of hesitation, the witch took the proffered hand and gave it a gentle, reassuring squeeze.

No words were said, as they sat on the hard, cold stone floor of the bedroom, watching each other and waiting to see who would make the next move. Beatrice knew they were in a precarious situation, and—as much as she loathed to admit it—she had no idea what the right course of action was.

All she knew was that Belladonna was the deep breath of cool, fresh air that she desperately needed. Especially with what was to come.

She hadn't meant to, but Beatrice found herself staring at Belladonna's lips once more. The lips that had brought her so much pleasure and comfort over the cycles. The lips that haunted her dreams. The lips she desperately yearned to press against her own.

Belladonna seemed to notice Beatrice's fixation, reflexively licking her lips. The quick dart of her pink tongue drew Beatrice in closer, like a moth to flame.

"I've missed you so much," Beatrice heard herself say. She hadn't meant to say anything, certainly not such a powerful admission of longing.

"You could have had me any time. I'm not the one who left." Belladonna's voice was husky, as though the words physically pained her.

"No. You didn't." Beatrice agreed. "But you didn't come after me either."

"I didn't think you wanted me to." Belladonna lifted a hand, wiping something from her cheek.

Beatrice tore her eyes from Belladonna's lips to see that her beloved witch was crying. Refusing to let go of the woman's hand, Beatrice used her free hand to wipe away another tear as it made its way down Belladonna's round cheek.

"I never stopped wanting you," Beatrice said simply. Placing her hand at the base of Belladonna's neck, she gently pulled the witch's face closer.

It was an invitation. A gentle request that could easily be rejected if Belladonna no longer shared her affections.

For the longest moment of her life, Beatrice stilled, waiting to see how Belladonna would respond.

Then, with a speed she hadn't thought the witch capable of, Belladonna's lips crashed fervently against her own.

35

ELENA

ELENA HAD NO IDEA how long she'd been unconscious or where she was. The only thing Elena knew for certain was that she was alone. Utterly and completely alone. Her brothers were gone, but more than that, Agon was missing. She could still feel him, but he felt far away. He was locked away somewhere dark, cold, and small. A cage, maybe? Elena couldn't be certain, and she couldn't reach him. She'd tried communicating with him through their shared mind, but either he was unconscious and unable to respond, or he was too far away to hear her.

"Mother, you can't possibly be serious." Elena heard a young man's muffled voice through the darkness. She crawled along the cold, hard floor of the oppressively dark room, trying to find a door or a way out. She moved toward the sound of the posh voice, her movements slow and cautious.

"I don't know what you're talking about, Niko," came an equally posh older female voice in response.

"You kidnapped a girl! You have to see that you've taken this too far. It's one thing to harbor resentments and anger toward Father and his philandering ways, but to kidnap a girl who had literally *nothing* to do with it is lunacy." The man's voice was harsh and tense, but Elena could still hear a hint of consternation in his words.

"Nothing?" the woman shrieked. "You think that little witch has nothing to do with this? Her *mother*," she spat the word out as though it left a foul taste in her mouth, "is the reason your father has strayed so far. That woman has bewitched him with that abhorrent magic of hers. Then she sent her foolish child to try and stop my *turmio*. After I spent so many solar cycles collecting all the necessary ingredients and tools needed to cleanse the world of her and her filth."

She triggered the turmio? Elena's breath caught in her chest as she realized just who's conversation she was overhearing. She sat back on her heels, staring blindly at the stone wall separating herself from her captors. They'd been wrong. So very wrong. The King hadn't unleashed the *turmio* to liberate himself from their mother. The Queen had.

When she was a girl, Elena had often heard the older girls share stories of the vindictive acts they had unleashed on arrogant magept men who had tried to take what they wanted from the enchantresses. The phrase "Hells hath no fury like a woman betrayed" was tossed around often, as the girls chuckled and replayed their exploits to their peers. Clearly, the phrase applied to magept women as well.

"So what's your plan then? Ransom her back to the headmistress? Use the money you receive to flee? You have to know that Father will not be pleased when he learns of your role in all of this. You started a war with the enchantresses!"

"She *stole* my husband! She had no right! I will not be ransoming anyone. She stole my husband's heart, so I will do the same with her only child." The Queen's voice was haughty and demented.

Elena's blood ran cold. The Queen was mad. Madame LaBelle might not have truly loved or cared for her children, but if one were to be kidnapped, murdered, and have their heart ripped out... Madame LaBelle would not handle it well. The death and destruction that ensued would be devastating and complete. She would send an undeniably clear message that Harbor Ridge would not tolerate those who would harm their enchantresses. Waverly would never be the same. And the Queen would be made an example of in the most gory fashion Madame LaBelle could devise.

The voices continued just beyond the wall of her cell, but Elena could no longer focus on them. Her heartbeat pounded through her ears as lightning coursed down her arms. Elena rose from her seated position and turned to stand with her back against the cool stone wall. She tried to focus on her breath in an attempt to rein in her powers before she electrified the whole room. When breathing didn't work, she let loose small bolts of lightning, brightening the room in spurts and allowing her to take in her surroundings.

The room was solid stone. No windows, no doors, no apparent seams in the masonry that might provide a way out. It looked as though the room had been built up around her. There was a small drain in the middle of the floor, and another in the ceiling, but otherwise there didn't appear to be any way out. The grate in the ceiling might have been big enough for her to fit through, but she couldn't reach it and the drain in the floor was smaller than her foot.

Mux, she thought to herself, *I need help. I need to find Agon. And Quinn. And Roska. Are they here? Have they been captured too?*

She began running her hands along the stones that built her prison walls. There had to be a way out. The stones were aged, and the mortar was crumbling in parts, so she felt safe in assuming that the prison hadn't actually been built up around her while she'd been unconscious. Which meant there had to be a door or an entrance of some sort.

"Oh, good. You're awake."

Elena jumped with a start, turning on her heel, lightning poised in the palm of her hand. It was the young man. The Prince. He stood before her with a blazing torch in his hand, but Elena couldn't see how he'd managed to enter the room. She had been so focused on her search for a weakness in the walls, she hadn't even noticed that the conversation she'd been eavesdropping on had ended. The Queen had left, and the Prince had somehow entered her prison.

Elena had heard of the Prince, in passing, as a child. He was a couple of cycles older than her, and supposedly as dull and tiresome as his father, the King. As Elena studied him now though, she wondered if those who had spoken so harshly of him at Harbor Ridge had ever actually met him.

He was at least a head taller than she was, with flawless copper-toned skin. His tightly coiled black hair fell across his bright hazel eyes as he looked down at her, his perfectly full lips curled up into a smirk.

Elena closed her mouth with a snap, realizing that she'd been caught ogling the Prince. She cast her eyes down to the scarred and pitted stone flooring. She'd never met royalty before and wasn't sure what the protocol was.

You're a prisoner, Elena chastised herself, *there is no protocol for this.*

"Are you planning on using that on me?" he asked, pointedly staring at the lightning still flashing under her skin and arcing between her fingertips.

"That entirely depends on you, Your Highness." Elena surprised herself with her boldness. She chanced a look up at the Prince, worried that her flippant tongue would get her killed sooner.

Much to her surprise and relief, the Prince was smiling. His eyes sparkled and he let loose the most melodious laugh Elena had ever heard.

"My, aren't you a feisty little firefly?" The Prince chuckled at his own joke.

Elena glared up at him. "Firefly?" she questioned, trying to keep the annoyance from her tone but ultimately failing.

"Yes, Firefly. You know, those harmless little bugs that fly around, lighting up the summer nights. I think it's quite fitting, don't you?"

"If I'm so harmless, why am I trapped in this windowless, doorless prison? And where is my familiar? Where is Agon?" To hells with polite protocol. This arrogant jerk was goading her, and she was not in the mood. Elena let her lightning build under the skin of her exposed forearms, brightening the room to near blinding.

"Calm down, Firefly," the Prince said, lowering his torch slowly and laying it on the ground beside him. When he straightened, he held his arms up in surrender. "Your little rat friend is just fine. One cell over. Screaming like he's possessed and scorching every inch of the place."

"You know telling someone to calm down almost always has the opposite effect, right?" Elena snapped, unleashing small bolts of lightning into the stone floor. "And Agon isn't a rat."

"Listen, Firefly, I can't help you if you kill me, and I'd really like to help you." His words had lost all semblance of playful mockery.

Elena studied his face for a few tense moments, trying to determine if he was being sincere before she relaxed some and turned down her powers. She didn't fully rein in her lightning. It provided far more effective light than his torch, and she wasn't entirely sure the Prince was trustworthy.

"Why would you want to help me?" she asked.

"Because I don't think you're the problem here. And I know that killing you will only make things worse for the whole country."

His bluntness caught her off guard, but Elena couldn't disagree with his logic. Not to mention if he was willing to help her escape, then her chances of getting out of that damned prison cell alive dramatically increased.

"You would go against the Queen?" Elena didn't hold her own mother in high esteem, but she also knew how hard it would be for the Prince to openly disobey his mother.

"If it means stopping a war before it begins, absolutely," he replied simply. "My mother blames yours for my father leaving her bed. She thinks that your mother has bewitched him or some shyt to make him fall in love with her. My mother seems to have forgotten that my father has always had... extramarital relationships. Typically with unwilling servants. Honestly, since my father started visiting your mother, the staff have been much happier and safer. Hells, the whole country has benefitted from their relationship. Except my prideful mother."

The Prince paced the width of her cell while he spoke, repeatedly running his fingers through his curls, clearly uncomfortable with the topic of his father's escapades. Elena appreciated his candor, even if she couldn't return the favor. If the Prince knew that her mother was only using his father for his power and authority in Waverly, she wasn't sure he'd be so willing to help her.

"So what's the plan?" Elena asked. She shifted her position, making sure to keep several paces between herself and the Prince. He might be here to help her, or he might just be playing a part. Befriending her in the hopes of gaining access to any secrets she might have about her mother or Harbor Ridge before the Queen had her heart removed from her chest.

"Well, Firefly, I'm so glad you asked." His mock enthusiasm rang harshly in the stone cell. "I thought we'd just walk out the front door."

He looked so confident; Elena almost missed the meaning of his words.

"Wait, what? You can't be serious." She stared at him, stunned. Gods, was he insane? Or just incredibly arrogant?

"I'm the Prince. Who would stop me?" He took a dramatic bow as if to emphasize his status.

"I imagine your mother would." Elena couldn't believe this man. The audacity. *Mother Goddess, please send me some actual help. Not this foolhardy man-child.*

"Firstly, yes, my mother is the Queen, but she's not really the authority around here when my father is away. I understand in your school women ruled the roost and men were merely playthings. While I find that idea highly intriguing," he waggled his eyebrows at her while yet another smirk played across his lips, "but out here in the real world, the men are in charge. When the King is away, the authority and power shifts to me."

Elena said nothing, stunned into silence by the pure, unadulterated arrogance that the Prince exuded in every word he spoke.

"Gods, it's no wonder the people hate you all."

"Pardon? What the hells does that mean?" The Prince's voice carried a sharp edge.

Mux. She hadn't meant to say that aloud. "Apologies, Your Highness," she said quickly, although not without a sharpened edge of her own. "I only meant that perhaps the people of Waverly would be more inclined to respect an authority that respected them as well."

"Well isn't that the pot calling the kettle? Your people belittle men and use us as breeding stock, yet you have the audacity to be offended by my authority in my own kingdom?" The Prince held her stare, daring her to challenge him further.

If Q were here, this whole discussion would have turned fiery by now. If Roska were with her, he would have opened a civil discourse about the balance of power needed between all gender identities in order to build a thriving community.

Unfortunately, Elena was on her own, and—despite the Prince's seemingly boundless arrogance—she still needed his help to escape and survive.

She held his gaze for a moment longer, then dropped her eyes. *Let him think he's won this argument. For now.*

"Now if it's all right with you, Firefly, I think we should get your little rodent and get out of here." The Prince gestured toward the far wall, indicating that they would be exiting that way, but Elena was still thoroughly confused. It looked to be a solid stone wall. She'd felt all over all the stones in the room and hadn't found so much as a single weak stone. When she didn't move, the Prince chuckled to himself and waltzed across the room. He glanced over his shoulder at her, winked, and pushed his hand through the wall.

What the mux?

"Come along, Firefly. Your rodent is waiting, and we really must get moving." With one hand still hidden within the wall somehow, he offered her his free hand. Cautiously, Elena crossed the room to join him, recalled her lightning from her hand, and gently placed it in his. She felt a wave of heat pass through her, the moment her skin made contact with his, but she quickly brushed the feeling aside. It was probably just a result of her tense emotions. Or a side effect of her reining in her lightning so quickly to avoid electrifying the Prince. It certainly had nothing to do with that gorgeous but arrogant man-child who was now leading her through a solid stone wall and into a second chamber.

The second room was much like the cell they'd just left, with one small difference: this room was riddled with scars and smelled like smoke.

Agon was vibrating with fury in the corner, backing away from the Prince while hissing, spitting, and blasting lightning in all directions.

Elena quickly stepped out from behind the Prince, hands raised, and Agon froze.

Are you all right? she thought to him at the same moment that his voice echoed in her mind, *What the hells is going on?*

Elena walked over to Agon, kneeling before him on the surprisingly warm stone floor. Apparently, if they shot enough lightning into stone, it would heat the room. Good to know, although Elena hoped she'd never need that information in the future.

Agon tossed a quick glance over her shoulder to the Prince who seemed to be nearly towering over them. *Who the mux is that?*

That's the Prince. We're in Riverayn. We were wrong. The King didn't unleash the turmio. *It was the Queen. She had us captured and brought here so we couldn't stop it.* Elena chanced a quick glance over her shoulder to see if the Prince was watching them. He was. *The Prince wants to help free us.*

Why? Agon was rightfully suspicious, as was she. Unfortunately, they didn't have a lot of time to waste debating the subject.

He has his reasons, which we haven't gotten into, but I think we can trust him. At least for now. There's something about him… I can't put my finger on it, but I think he can safely get us out of this damned place and back on the road to Q and Roska.

Agon studied the Prince where he stood, waiting patiently beside the wall as non-threateningly as possible. She could feel him weighing their options, but she knew he wouldn't find an alternative solution to their captivity.

Without another word, Agon subtly nodded to her, then made quick work of climbing up the skirts of her dress and back to reach his perch on her shoulder.

Elena rose and turned to face the Prince.

"Let's get out of here, Firefly." He pressed his hand through yet another wall. She took hold of his other hand for a second time—pointedly trying to ignore the heat that ignited from their joined hands and spread throughout her body—and they were gone.

36

QUINN

T HE SOLDIERS HAD MOVED on, finally. Packed up and headed further west, according to Lyra. Quinn tried to speculate where they might be headed, but honestly, he didn't give a mux. They needed to get to the cave and see if Elena was there. If she wasn't, Q was pretty sure he'd end up punching his father in the face.

Just once.

Probably.

It took nearly a full day for those damn soldiers to actually leave, so they had to wait until first light on the following day to leave the inn. As much as Q wanted to get out of Nexton and back to those damned mountains, it wasn't smart to try and travel at night, in the frost season, with a cold-blooded familiar and a seemingly endless snowstorm. It wasn't quite a blizzard, but by the looks of it, it would be by midnight.

Quinn thought he might actually go insane. He was stir-crazy and cranky, having been stuck in this town for nearly a week. Just sitting around, waiting for the soldiers to vacate. It had been one of the longest weeks of his life. Possibly the longest, if he included just how much sleep he hadn't gotten, worrying about Elena.

As a result, Q was up before the sun, packed and ready to go as soon as Roska and Aiden began to stir in their cots.

"If we leave now, we should be able to reach the base of the mountains by dusk. We can camp in the same spot, hopefully, and start the hike into the mountains tomorrow morning." Q was speaking while forcibly handing Aiden his pack and cloak and helping Roska into his fur-lined cloak.

"Ow, hey, hold on!" Roska jerked away when Quinn nearly smacked him in the head while trying to force a pack onto his brother's back.

"Quinn," Aiden spoke calmly, raising his hands as though he were trying to calm a rabid beast. "We're all anxious to get to the cave. I'm sure Elena is fine. I've seen it. She will be fine. But we won't be if you make us trek out into the frost and snow without even having a proper breakfast."

Quinn felt the fire pool in his palm before he realized what he was doing. The sudden heat shocked him, and he glanced down to find he had nearly set the inn on fire.

Mux.

"Why don't you go outside for a bit?" Roska offered, watching Q with a nervous air about him. "Maybe go hunt with Lyra in the woods. Or just burn a hole in the snow-covered fields. Burn off some of your anxious energy." Roska smirked at his bad joke, but Quinn knew he was probably right. If Q stayed in this inn one more minute, he'd likely set the whole place on fire out of sheer frustration.

Saying nothing, he nodded, tightened his own cloak, and left.

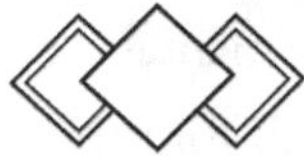

The cold air was a welcome relief from the stifling warmth of the overcrowded dining hall and tavern. Quinn strode purposefully toward the woods, avoiding eye contact and potential small talk with the merchants who were opening their stores. He made quick work of the walk through town, reaching the tree line that surrounded Nexton in a matter of moments.

Lyra, having sensed his proximity, raced to meet him. She caught up to him as he reached the small creek that ran through the woods. It was an offshoot of the river than ran through all of Waverly, starting in the peaks of the Dragon's Teeth and flowing through the country until it reach the Southern Sea.

Are we leaving now? she asked silently.

No, was his only reply.

She didn't ask any more questions. He knew she could feel the heat radiating off of him and see the snow melt beneath his steps. He was a raging ball of pent-up fire, and he needed to find a release. Quickly.

Lyra jumped in his path and then led him down a small, almost invisible, deer trail deeper into the woods, away from prying eyes. She took him to a clearing, where the snow had created a small hill in the center, then she ran up behind him, jumped, and pushed him face-first into the snow.

The sudden cold barely registered beneath the shock he felt at losing his footing and landing so badly. But Lyra knew what she was doing. Quinn loosened the mental grip he'd been holding onto for dear life, unleashing the full force of his fire in the middle of the snow pile. In moments, the pile—that had been nearly up to his waist when he'd entered the clearing—had vanished, replaced by a fine mist in the air and a puddle that soaked the forest floor.

Q rose from the muddy puddle he'd just created, glaring at Lyra. "You know, there were easier, less aggressive ways of doing that." He tried in vain to shake the mud from his clothes.

"Yes, but I thought it was best to be direct. Besides, I didn't want you to burn down the forest, and your eyes were glowing. Seemed like the most effective way to cool you off." Lyra was sitting primly on top of a pile of snow, tail curled around her body and resting peacefully on her feet.

At that, Quinn scraped some of the mud off his stomach and threw it at her. Much to his annoyance, she skillfully dodged his attack, while managing to kick some snow at the same time, nailing him in the face.

Q stood statuesque in the mud for a moment, before he burst out laughing so loudly that he spooked the crows who'd been nesting in the trees around them. He channeled his heat, focusing on the snow on his face, and quickly melted it away. Then, Q had a thought. He focused on his clothing, drawing the heat slowly to his extremities first, drying the mud that now caked his arms and legs until all the water evaporated and the mud turned to dust. Q continued to draw on his heat, keeping it at a low burn rather than a full-fledged inferno, and dried the mud that soaked through his shirt. Once he'd finished drying out his clothes, he looked smugly at Lyra as he brushed the bone-dry dirt from his clothing.

"It's about damn time," she said. "I've been able to control my fire for over a dozen cycles. What the hells took you so long?"

Quinn just smiled. He felt so much lighter, and he was quite proud of himself, and he knew Elena would be too. He needed to find her so he could show off his newfound control.

"Let's get back. I'm hungry. We'll have some breakfast with Ros and Aiden, then get out of this damn town and off to the mountains." Quinn ruffled Lyra's ears as he walked passed her, following the deer trail back to the main road.

Breakfast was quick. Roska and Aiden had already ordered for him, and the food had just arrived by the time Q joined them. They didn't ask about the light layer of dust that still coated his wool shirt. Instead, Roska offered him a cup of black tea and some honey.

"Feeling better?" Aiden teased, sipping his tea and wiping the last of the egg from his plate with a crust of bread.

"Yeah," Quinn said, but he didn't elaborate. Instead, he focused all of his attention on the plate of eggs and bacon before him. He shoveled the food into his mouth as quickly as he could without choking. He refused to be the one they waited on to finish before leaving.

Q could feel Roska's eyes surveying him, maybe trying to see if he was about to combust again, but Q knew his brother would find nothing to worry about. He'd been able to release all the pent-up stress and pressure that had been building since they'd left their father's tower. He was ok again. For now.

You really need to find a better way to deal with your emotions, Lyra chided.

I think I might have. He'd been able to focus his power and slowly release the energy within him to dry his clothes without incident. Q was pretty sure he could do that on command now, and if he were able to regularly, *carefully*, release some of that pressure throughout the day, then he probably wouldn't blow up any more houses, boil lakes, or melt snow drifts.

"Pretty sure" and "probably" don't give me a lot of comfort. He felt Lyra's tail warm where it lay across his feet under the table. When the heat of it got uncomfortable, Q kicked her tail off of his boot, grumbling under his breath about her showing off.

Yeah, she had more control of her powers, but she also had a shyt load of practice. The two of them had been relying on her fire for over a decade. Q had only learned about his powers seven or eight moons ago.

Gods, has it really been that long? It felt like he'd only met Elena a week ago, while also feeling like he'd known her his whole life. Which, when he thought about it, he kinda had. She was their center, and Q knew that if he asked Roska, his brother would feel the same.

Elena had this way about her that made them want to be the best version of themselves.

Watching Roska swoon—because there really was no better word for how he'd been behaving lately—over Brigit sent Q's mind down a path of thoughts about their sister and her potential life-mate.

If she could make him and Roska feel like this, always working hard to make her proud, he couldn't even imagine how it would be for the person she chose to spend her life with. Quinn chuckled to himself. That person would be both the luckiest and unluckiest creature on the planet. Elena deserved nothing but the best, and Q was certain that he and Roska would ensure she got it.

37

ELENA

Elena wasn't sure if she should have been impressed or annoyed at how easily the Prince managed to facilitate their escape. He literally walked them through the prison cell wall, and confidently strode through the castle and out to the stables. None of the guards said a word to them. Hells, most averted their eyes like he was some sort of god. It was equally amazing and infuriating. This man-child was a cocky son-of-a-bitch, literally, and they treated him like the end-all-be-all authority.

They had made a quick stop in what had appeared to be a bedroom that had been converted into a massive closet, in which the Prince had insisted she change clothes. He seemed to think that her simple but practical dress was "offensive to the eyes." Elena had to hold on tight to Agon when the Prince had made that particular comment because Agon was fully prepared to electrocute him and take their chances on escaping without the Prince's assistance.

Instead, she'd changed into another—equally "plain" but considerably cleaner—dress and new boots. Thankfully, they hadn't taken Elena's cloak from her when they'd tossed her into the cell, and she managed to shock the Prince with its magic as the cloak shimmered and shifted colors to match her new forest green dress. Elena took an intense pride in the look of surprise on his face as he watched the cloak change from a deep, almost chocolate brown, to a rich forest green.

In the stables, Elena wandered, petting the horses and trying to look as natural as possible while he spoke to an attendant.

The smell of the stables was warm and comforting. The fresh hay mixed with the natural scent of the horses brought her back to her life in Andover. It seemed like ages ago, she was working in the inn with Amelia, spending time with the girls at the town well, and learning to ride with Quinn. Elena never had much experience with horses at Harbor Ridge, but she felt so much love and comfort around them now. She stood before a sweet old mare, gently running her hand through the horse's mane as her mind drifted back to those days. Tears prickled her eyes as she wondered how Amelia was faring without them. Had her mother's investigators gone back there, searching for her and her brothers? Had they hurt Amelia when they realized the triplets weren't there?

I'm sure she's fine. Agon nuzzled her neck. *She's an impressive woman, and apparently a decent enchantress, especially if she managed to get your mother to leave her alone. I'm sure that even if the investigators showed up, she wouldn't have tolerated anything but formal politeness from them. Amelia is just fine.*

I hope you're right, Elena replied. She couldn't help but feel responsible for any harm that might come to the town because of her and her brothers.

"Where to, Firefly?" The Prince startled her, standing far too close and practically whispering in her ear, his breath hot on her cheek. Elena jumped, nearly spooking the mare. Agon turned to face the Prince, snapping his tiny, sharp teeth. "Easy there, rodent." The Prince took a step back, hands raised in self-defense. "I didn't mean to scare you. Gods, you two are jumpy."

"You would be too if you were trapped in the castle of the woman who wants to rip your heart out," Elena replied, rolling her shoulders in a fruitless attempt to ease some of the tension gathering there.

"There's no need to worry, Firefly." The Prince smiled confidently at her. Was he ever *not* confident? "You are with me now. No one will touch you." He paused, raising a single eyebrow. "Unless you want them too, of course."

"Gods, you are impossible." Even as Elena glared at the pompous Prince, she could feel the heat rising in her cheeks. *Impossibly charming and incorrigible. A dangerous combination.*

"So, where to?" he asked again, a flicker of heat in his eyes. He knew he was getting under her skin, and he liked it. *Muxing ass.*

"I need to find my br— companions." Elena caught herself before revealing the truth about her birth. "The men I was traveling with before your depraved mother had me abducted."

The Prince's eye snapped up from where they'd been studying the horse. "Don't call my mother that," he practically growled at her. The fire in his eyes had switched from the subtle heat of flirting to something else entirely. Elena understood now why the guards didn't give them a second glance.

"With respect, Your Majesty," Elena replied, suffusing her words with all the sarcasm and disdain she had, "how should I describe the woman who had me kidnapped so that she could murder me to punish my mother for *muxing* the King?"

The Prince glared at her a moment longer. He was challenging her, and he expected her to back down. Last solar cycle, his stare would have withered her on the spot, but after the things she'd endured in the last several moons, there was nothing this arrogant princeling could do to intimidate her. She held his stare, refusing to so much as blink, for several long moments.

Suddenly the Prince broke off their staring contest, chuckled to himself, and said to her, "You could just say 'The Queen' like most people do."

"I could have, but I felt the need for a little added rhetoric. My companions are probably worried sick. I need to get back to them. Now." Elena could feel her power building in her palms, dancing under her skin and moments away from arcing across her fingertips. She needed to rein in her anxiety, or she'd spook the horses and create even more trouble. She needed to get out of this damned castle and back on the road to her brothers.

"Well, you've been gone from them for a couple of weeks now," the Prince started.

"*Weeks?* How is that possible?" Elena felt the floor slip out from beneath her. She placed a steadying hand on the mare's neck.

"Ah, that's magic, my dear Firefly." The Prince took a couple of slow, cautious steps toward her, seeming to have noticed her sudden disorientation. "Those prison cells exist outside of time. What feels like moments in there could be hours, days, or even weeks out here." He shrugged nonchalantly. "It's one of the few magical things that Mother actually enjoys."

Elena couldn't breathe. Her heart was racing, palms sweaty, and it felt as though the ground was shaking beneath her feet.

"Careful there, Firefly." The Prince stepped up behind her, gently placing both hands on her shoulders. Agon turned to snap at his hands but stopped when he felt Elena list to the side. She'd lost *weeks*. For all she knew, her brothers were dead. Killed by the Queen's soldiers or the *turmio*. She couldn't do this without them. How was she supposed to do *anything* without them? She needed to find her brothers.

Elena could feel the Prince's hands on her, but the weight of his touch barely registered. He guided her away from the horses, to a bench beside a wall of tack. She sat—more like collapsed—onto the bench, ice suddenly flowing through her veins. She tried to drown out the rising storm of misery and fear that was brewing within her.

"Hey, Firefly. Look at me." The Prince gently lifted her face. "You're ok. Just try to breathe." He moved his hand from her chin to her chest, resting lightly above her heart while his other hand moved from her shoulder to the middle of her back. "Deep breath." When it was clear that telling her to breathe wasn't going to calm her down, he switched tactics. "Tell me, what do you smell right now?"

"What?" Elena gasped between quick, shallow breaths. Her head was spinning, the world crumbling beneath her, and he was asking her about smells?

"Humor me," he said kindly. "What do you smell?"

Squeezing her eyes closed, Elena tried to focus on the scents that surrounded them. "Horse, manure, fresh hay, and something else. Smoky almost."

"Good. That's great. What can you hear?" His hands still rested on her body. The one on her back started slowly rubbing up and down the length of her spine.

"I hear," she paused, taking in the sounds around her, "the horses chewing, stable boys cleaning out the stalls, my heart, and your breathing."

"Excellent, Firefly. Truly, you're doing a fantastic job. Last one, open your eyes and tell me what you see."

Slowly, Elena opened her eyes. The Prince was kneeling before her in the straw and gravel on the stable floor. His dark curls had fallen over his face, partially hiding his eyes from view, but either he wasn't bothered by the obstruction or he didn't want to take his hands off her yet. His eyes were frustratingly beautiful. Deep, dark chocolate pools of endless possibilities drawing her in as she tried to remember what he'd asked.

See. He wanted to know what you could see. Seems like you've calmed down enough now though. We could probably move on. Agon's tone of tight irritation mixed with relief—presumably at her not exploding and setting the stable on fire—brought her back to the present moment. She sat up a little straighter, pulling away from the hand on her chest and feeling an unnerving sense of loss as the heat from his hand left her body. The hand on her back lightened its touch but continued its lazy journey up and down her spine.

"I see a prince, kneeling before me," Elena said, trying to sound cool and collected.

"I've never had any complaints from women who found me on my knees before them." He looked up at her with that cocky smirk again.

"I imagine they were just being kind, Your Majesty." Elena's hands gripped the edge of the bench as she fought the urge to brush his hair back from his eyes. "It's not wise to offend royalty."

"That's a fair point," he said with a nod, his hand still stroking her back as he looked up at her from beneath his curls. "But I have it on good authority that women rather enjoy this particular position."

Elena's face was on fire. She wanted to look away, but his eyes drew her in closer. She leaned toward him without even noticing her movements until Agon flickered his lightning and shocked her—just enough to break the spell between her and the Prince—reminding her of their current circumstance.

"We should get moving," Elena said suddenly. She moved to rise from the bench when the Prince placed both hands firmly on her shoulders. He'd dropped the flirtatious attitude and studied her face.

"Are you sure you're ok? That was a hell of an episode. It's ok if you need more time, Firefly." The genuine concern in his voice was jarring.

Elena swallowed hard and nodded. "I'm fine, Your Majesty. Thank you for your concern, but I really do need to get back to my companions."

"Please, call me Niko. I'm just glad I was able to help. I used to have panic attacks like that a lot as a child. I had a nurse who taught me how to overcome them. It didn't stop the attacks, but she helped me to gain control. Focus on the real, tangible things around me, so that I might ground myself and end the episode more quickly." He offered her his hand. Elena accepted his assistance and rose to stand beside him.

"Does it still happen to you?" She studied her boots, too embarrassed to look him in the eyes.

"Not as often as it used to, but yes. I do still have the odd panic attack now and then." He was still holding her hand, his thumb stroking the back of her hand, creating an unbidden heat in her lower belly.

Elena freed her hand from his grasp, took a deep, cleansing breath, and turned to face him. "Thank you for your assistance. Both in our escape and with this episode of embarrassing emotion. I truly appreciate it." She glanced around the stable, remembering once again that she had lost so much time already and feeling an urgency to find her brothers. "We need to be leaving."

"Right, then," the Prince—Niko—gestured to the horse, "who are we taking and where?"

"While I appreciate your kindness," Elena began, "I can't ask you to come with us." She didn't want to reveal her brothers to the Prince. He might have freed her from certain death, but that didn't mean she trusted him and she *knew* Quinn wouldn't like her traveling with the son of the enemy.

"You didn't ask. I insisted." And there was that cocksure grin again. Much to Elena's dismay, it didn't elicit the same feelings of annoyance that it had before. Now, her cheeks actually warmed under the glow of that smirk.

"My companions will be waiting for me." It was only a half-lie. Her brothers would be waiting for her, she just wasn't sure where.

"Well, then we should get moving, Firefly." The Prince walked over to the mare Elena had been petting moments ago. He stroked the mare's strong neck, then grabbed a saddle and blanket, preparing the horse for the journey.

Where are we going? Agon asked, nosing her cheek to ensure he had her attention.

I'm not sure. I imagine they've found our father by now, but if it's truly been two weeks, they've likely moved on. They're probably going to recapture the turmio *like we had planned.* Elena looked out the stable door, north towards the Dragon's Teeth. That's where her brothers would be going. If they were going to recapture the *turmio*, they would need to get back to that cave. It was the only prison they knew of that could contain such a powerful monster.

There was a map of Waverly hanging on the wall in the tack room. Elena wandered over to it, running her hand along the worn leather, following the flow of the river that cut through the entire country. The river ran along the edge of Riverayn and was the only access Waverly had to the sea. The river also served as a border between their neighbor countries to the west, Rolam and Slyvestris, which meant that Waverly's traders had to travel through foreign land to reach the Southern Sea. Elena traced the river back upstream, to its birthplace in the Dragon's Teeth. That's where they needed to be.

Horses would get them there eventually, but based on the map, it would take at least a week of hard riding.

Elena gritted her teeth. She didn't want to ask the Prince for help, but she was going to need more than a horse for this journey. She took a fortifying breath before she spoke.

"I don't need a horse," she said plainly. "I need a boat. One that is swift and light, that can navigate the river quickly and get me to the mountains. To the source of the river."

Niko's hands stilled from their task of tightening the saddle on the mare. Elena was impressed at how deftly he'd managed to prepare the horse. She had assumed a prince wouldn't know how to saddle his own mount. That's what servants were for, wasn't it? He studied her over the horse's back for a moment, then just as deftly he removed the saddle and blanket. Niko put the tack away and dug an apple out of a nearby barrel, handing it to the mare and patting her on the neck.

"Sorry for the trouble, girl," he spoke quickly to the mare as she muzzled his chest, looking for more treats. "I have boats. Right this way, Firefly." And with that, he turned and walked out of the stable.

38

ROSKA

I T WAS MID-MORNING BEFORE they left the inn and Nexton. Roska had finally gotten the courage to bid Brigit goodbye, and much to his surprise, she'd seemed genuinely disappointed at their departure. It had thrilled him and broken his heart a bit to see the look of dismay in her eyes as she said a kind goodbye to him. For a moment, Roska even thought she might try and hug him. He surprised himself when he realized that he wouldn't be uncomfortable with her touch.

He tried not to dwell on that revelation though. They had much bigger things to focus on, and Roska knew he'd probably never see her again. Instead, he turned his attention to the path before them—both metaphorically and literally—as they hiked through snow-slicked grasslands. He needed to keep his mind on his feet or he would certainly slip and fall.

They didn't speak as they traveled. Trying to keep a "low profile"—as Quinn had called it—meant staying low to the ground and avoiding being seen by other travelers who traversed the road just west of them. Q had informed them that they needed to stick close to the road for now, but out of sight in case there were more soldiers about.

"The road leads into the mountains," Quinn had told them over breakfast. "The problem is that it's the only road that goes north, and it's a pretty popular route for traders and merchants. Before, when Elena and I came through here, it was warmer, and we were able to trek along the river, following the water to its source. Now that the frost is on though, that route will be too dangerous."

Roska had initially objected to this seemingly logic-less thought, but Quinn had elaborated—although he'd seemed annoyed that he needed to justify his choices to anyone—and explained that the river was a strong, quick-flowing beast that wouldn't freeze over entirely in the snow and ice. However, the edges of the river would freeze and it would be hard to tell the difference between what was snow-covered grass along the riverside and what was actually slick, half-frozen water. That is, until one of them stepped on the wrong thing, broke the ice, fell into the water, and drowned or froze to death before the others could get to them.

Roska had a suspicion that Q was exaggerating the danger, and likely their father would be able to use his magic to pull them from the river quickly, but he didn't see the point in arguing. Plus, Roska's time out in the world was limited and his knowledge of the frost's effect on rivers was basically nonexistent. He chose to trust his brother's judgment because he really didn't have a reason not to.

They weren't making very good time, which put both of the boys into sullen, irritable moods. Aiden, however, seemed perfectly content with their meandering pace. He didn't say much, but when he did it was usually poor attempts at small talk. Roska assumed that spending ages alone in a crumbling tower with only a wolf and a magic looking glass to keep him company had driven their father a bit mad.

"Quinn," their father spoke up, breaking the tense quiet. "Do you remember that planting season when you were about eleven, hunting in the woods with Lyra and you fell into the stream?"

Quinn seemed to remember the incident none-too fondly, flinching slightly at the mention of it. "Yeah, what about it?"

"Do you remember what caused you to fall?" From the subtle chuckle and smirk on Aiden's lips, Roska had a sinking suspicion that their father knew the answer.

"I slipped," Q replied shortly, clearly not enjoying this particular line of conversation.

"You slipped? That's it? Come now, son. You must remember what you slipped *on*." Aiden was grinning from ear to ear now.

"Nope."

"Well, I remember," Aiden said proudly. "You slipped on a massive pile of bear shyt." He barely managed to get the words out before giving in to fits of uncontrollable laughter. "Not just slipped though, you muxing slid through the shyt, and landed ass first in the river!"

If they had been trying to remain undetected, Aiden had completely ruined their chances. He was laughing so loudly, with such reckless abandon that it was contagious. Roska couldn't help himself. He pictured a younger—softer but still angry at the world—version of his brother, sliding through a steaming pile of shyt and landing unceremoniously in a river. Roska desperately tried to keep his amusement at bay, but he failed miserably, breaking into out-of-control giggles.

Quinn didn't stop walking. In fact, he lengthened his stride and quickened his pace to put distance between them. Much to his chagrin, however, Lyra had recalled the incident and didn't share in his embarrassment.

"The river was still half-frozen!" she added, regaling them with a play-by-play of the whole scene. "He was in a hurry, hoping to catch this deer that we'd seen frolicking through the trees. Little Q was determined to kill our first deer and bring it back to show off his skills to Amelia." Lyra jumped through the high snow, kicking up bits of ice as she raced to get in front of Quinn, ensuring that he wouldn't miss out on her version of the story.

Q, his path now blocked by his fox, glared down at her and then them with an air of treachery. Roska was worried for a moment that they'd upset him. Quinn could be sensitive about things, and all of Aiden's stories about Q seemed to be stories in which Q came out embarrassed in some way, shape, or form.

Roska held his breath and dropped his eyes to his boots. Suddenly finding the story less funny, he felt guilty at having laughed at his brother's expense.

A massive ball of snow slammed into Roska's head, pieces of snow falling inside his wool shirt as other bits stuck to his hair and face. He looked up, shocked by the sudden, icy attack.

Quinn stood a few paces in front of him. His brother wore the smile of a cat that had finally caught a bird that had been plaguing its master's garden for weeks. Disgustingly proud.

"Oops, sorry, bro," Q added, without a hint of remorse.

Roska stood frozen only a second longer before he dusted off his shirt.

"You know, *bro*," Roska said, not looking up as he shook the last of the snow from his hair. "That wasn't very nice." He didn't look up, but with a quickness and accuracy he hadn't been confident he had, Roska fired a barrage of smaller snowballs from his hands into his brother's stomach.

Quinn fell to the ground with an *oomph* and rolled onto his side, hands wrapped protectively around his middle.

Aiden immediately burst into a new fit of hysterics, tears threatening to freeze on his cheeks.

"If you three are quite finished," came a calm—but clearly annoyed—voice. Aleerah stepped onto their path, commanding their attention and silencing the laughter with one look. "I'm not sure if you all remember what we're *supposed* to be doing, but we have a rather time-sensitive mission to complete. You can have snowball fights and embarrassing story competitions after we stop the *turmio*."

"Aye, you're right." Aiden took a few steadying deep breaths. "Just trying to break the tension, is all. These two were acting like we're going off to the gallows."

"Well if we don't get moving, we'll end up burying all of our loved ones." Aleerah's tone was blunt, massacring all the lightheartedness that they had been feeling just a moment before.

"Aleerah," Aiden chastised. "There's no need for that. We all know what's hanging in the balance here. We know what is at stake. But it doesn't mean that the boys have to feel the weight of the world on their shoulders."

"Whether they acknowledge it or not, the weight is there. Making light of things won't change anything." Aleerah countered.

"Maybe not, but it would make the journey a bit less depressing." Aiden waved his hand, magically removing the last of the snow from Roska's hair and clothes.

Roska walked over to Quinn, offering him a hand to help his brother stand. Aiden then removed the snow from Q with a second wave of his hand.

"She's not wrong," Demoni added from her perch wrapped tightly around Roska's neck. "We have to stop that monster before it kills everyone."

"We know," Roska said, not unkindly. "The weight of this mission is a heavy one, made all the heavier by the knowledge that it's entirely my fault." Roska couldn't look up to meet his brother's eyes, but he felt Q's strong hand rest firmly on his shoulder.

"We can't undo what's been done," Quinn said matter-of-factly, "but we can try to right our wrongs as we go. At least that's what Amelia always tells me," he added with a shrug. He squeezed Roska's shoulder and released him. "Besides, Elena is waiting for us."

And that was the end of it. Q turned on his heel, leading their party onward, through the high grass and toward the mountains waiting ominously beyond the snowy haze of the horizon.

39

ELENA

When Niko said he had a ship they could use, Elena had been expecting a cargo ship or one of the massive—fancy but cumbersome—merchant vessels.

She hadn't been expecting the sleek longship he'd presented her with. It looked like one of the viking ships she'd read about in her study of fables and myths. The long, lightweight boat had been designed to move quickly through shallow water, driven by the power of wind in its sails, or rowed when the wind was not in their favor.

Elena had been thoroughly confused and then undeniably intrigued when Niko had helped her onto the ship, then placed his hands on the steering oar at the stern, and it had begun moving away from the dock, out of the harbor, and into the middle of the river. The sails were still rolled tight along the length of the mast yet they were sailing away from Riverayn at a steady—albeit, rather slow—pace.

She'd stared at him in open-mouthed wonder as he flawlessly guided their ship through the harbor and around the incoming or outgoing trader ships until they'd departed the city.

He'd released the steering oar then, tethering it to the stern to keep them from veering off their intended path. When Niko caught her gaze, as she stood completely baffled by the feat he'd just accomplished, he merely shrugged.

"Blood magic," he'd said, as though that were all the explanation she needed.

It wasn't however, and she spent the next half hour peppering him with questions as to how such magic worked. Much to her annoyance, he had very little by way of answers, and she was left with still more questions.

Between the prison cells and the longships, it seemed the royal family used magic more than the Queen would like their citizens to know. Elena wondered how this magic would be affected by the *turmio*. Would the *turmio* eat the spells that enabled this blood magic to work? Would it simply kill the magic in the royal bloodline? Would it kill the royal family?

Elena didn't know the answers to any of the questions, and she feared they would only find the truth if the *turmio* accomplished its goal and annihilated all magic in the world.

Elena looked out over the edge of the longship as it glided seamlessly through the calm river. They were pushing slowly upstream, fighting against the heavy current of Waverly's lifeblood. The river was the main source of freshwater for the majority of the country and the most popular trade route for merchants. The river itself and its many tributaries were vital to life in Waverly.

As Niko sidled up beside her, Elena barely registered his closeness. She was lost in thoughts of her brothers and worry over the other magical beings who would soon be targeted by the *turmio*. If they weren't in danger already.

"What's on your mind, Firefly?" His quiet tone caught her off-guard. It was completely lacking in the over-confident air he'd had throughout their time in the castle.

Elena didn't take her eyes off the horizon as she spoke. "I just keep thinking that we're too late."

"Too late for what?" Niko kept his voice light, unobtrusive, but she thought she could hear a hint of nervousness in his words.

"Too late to stop the *turmio*. Too late to save the world."

"What makes you think that?" He leaned closer to her, as though worried that others would overhear their conversation.

"I don't know how to explain it." She sighed in exasperation. "I just feel like something is very wrong. My magic has never been incredibly reliable, but I can feel it weakening. Just a little."

Niko's blank stare either meant he had no idea what she was talking about, or that he was trying to be impartial and let her talk without the weight of his opinions or worries. She continued talking because, regardless of what his blank stare meant, she was anxious and she tended to talk too much when she was stressed.

"You know that feeling of working your body just a little too hard? Like you lifted one too many bags of flour and your muscles were pushed passed their limits, just a bit?" He simply blinked at her.

"Right," she said, "maybe you don't know that feeling. Anyway, it's a feeling like something is off. Not quite *wrong* but leaning that way, and you know you have to do something to stop it, but you don't know exactly what."

Niko still didn't speak. Elena's cheeks grew hot and she looked away from him, back over the side of the longship, watching the trees pass by. She'd embarrassed herself. Again. Trying to connect with a prince and explain her feelings—like he would know anything about it. *Stupid girl.*

Stop that—Agon spoke in her mind, but he was cut off by Niko's voice.

"When did you lift bags of flour? I thought the daughter of the most powerful enchantress in the world would never have to do a single moment of manual labor."

Elena balked at his words at first, offended that he thought she was some pampered, spoiled girl, but then she thought for a moment. He was right. When she lived at Harbor Ridge, she'd never done any work outside of her studies. Her first few weeks in Andover with Amelia had had a steep learning curve, both mentally and physically. Elena remembered how emotionally drained and physically exhausted she'd been at the end of each and every day for nearly a full lunar cycle. She'd eventually adapted and now was quite proud of the strength and endurance she'd built up.

Niko didn't know all of her history though. It was only natural that he would be confused to hear she'd been lifting anything other than sachets of herbs or a mortar and pestle.

"I've spent the last two seasons living in a small town, working in their inn." Elena fought the urge to elaborate and tell Niko her whole life story. He was the son of the woman who wanted to kill her. He might be helping her now, but Elena still didn't entirely trust him.

He offered a small hum of acknowledgment but didn't press her on the subject. Elena was grateful for it. She knew if he asked her any questions, she'd end up explaining the events of the last several moons to him, ultimately revealing the truth about her traveling companions and putting them all at risk.

They stood in silence for a while, watching the frosty trees give way to roads, snow-covered houses, and towns. As they passed along the center of the town, several citizens came out to wave to the Prince. To his credit—and Elena's surprise—he didn't blow them off, ignore them, or act like they were beneath him. Prince Niko waved to each and every citizen who called out to him. He greeted them with a welcoming smile and even managed to shake hands with a few of the fishermen who were out on the river in their own boats.

Wow, they really like him, Elena thought, mostly to herself, but Agon replied as though she'd been speaking to him.

Well, he's good-looking—by traditional standards—and comes off as very friendly and open. It would be more surprising if they didn't like him. It doesn't mean we should like or trust him.

Elena reached up and scratched Agon under his chin while he perched on her shoulder. He was right. This could easily be a facade the Prince used when he was out amongst his subjects. Still, she couldn't help thinking that it would be much easier for him to ignore them, rather than going out of his way to be kind.

Elena turned to lean her back against the far side of the ship, watching him wave to the last of the children who had chased their boat along the riverside until the trees started to take over again, marking the end of their small town.

"You are not what I expected," she said, unable to keep the shock and amusement from her voice.

"Oh?" He raised a single eyebrow incredulously. "You thought about me often, did you? What did you expect of your prince then?"

Elena rolled her eyes dramatically at him. "Gods, I was *going* to give you a compliment, but never mind." She turned away from him again, walking to the prow of the ship.

Niko's chuckle hooked her attention, drawing her in. She turned back to face him as he sat in one of the seats that lined the sides of the ship. In her mythology books, the seats would have been inhabited by enslaved peoples or prisoners whose entire purpose was the row until their arms gave out, then they would be swapped out for another batch of enslaved captives. In reality though, with the blood magic that powered the vessel, she assumed the seats were more likely to be used by the royal family and the massive party of courtiers and servants that traveled with them wherever they went.

"What's wrong, Firefly? Did I shatter your biased view of royalty?" Niko stretched his long legs out before him, resting his feet on the empty seat in front of him and angling his body so he could lean his back along the side of the longship.

Elena tried to glare menacingly at him, but she wasn't sure she hit her mark. He held her stare and chuckled again.

"Gods, you are the most arrogant human on the planet, aren't you?" she grumbled, shaking her head in annoyance. She was tempted to flick some of her lightning at him, but Elena knew her aim wasn't perfect and she didn't want to accidentally set the sails on fire instead.

"I don't know. I haven't met everyone on the planet. I wouldn't want to lie to you, Firefly." His mouth quirked up into yet another cocky grin, but Elena felt the heavy weight of truth in his words. He might be an overly self-assured, arrogant prince, but he was an honest man. At least, he would be with her.

You can't really believe him. Come on, *Elena. You aren't naive.* Agon's judgment burned.

No, I'm not naive. You would think that by now—after all we've been through—you could trust my judgment. My intuition. It has never been wrong, and we have always benefitted from trusting it. Elena didn't really mean to snap at him, but she was so muxing tired of having the same argument with him. Ever since they were kicked out of Harbor Ridge, he'd been chastising her for trusting too quickly. She'd had to defend her decisions to him time and again. It was exhausting. *Trusting my intuition has led us to find both of our siblings and gain more control over our powers than either of us ever thought we could. If you won't trust me and have faith in my decisions, then keep it to yourself. I don't want to hear it anymore.*

Elena flicked her eyes to Niko, realizing that as far as he was concerned, she'd suddenly shut down and stopped talking to him. She instantly worried that she'd offended him in some way.

Not because he was a prince—although that definitely was a factor. In truth, Elena was always worried that she would say the wrong thing and upset someone. She'd worried about it her whole life, always watching her words and triple checking every thought before voicing her feelings or opinions. She debated looking internally, uncovering the reason for her trepidation, but that would take precious time and energy that she could expend doing more important things. Like avoiding conflict altogether. Including internal conflict.

Niko was watching her. Studying her as she had been studying him when they'd passed by that town. Embarrassment flushed her cheeks and she broke eye contact with him, picking invisible lint off her cloak.

"No worries, Firefly," Niko's voice drew her eyes back to him. "I know your weasel doesn't like me, but I swear to the Mother Goddess I am only trying to help you. My mother is off her rocker these days, and she needs to be stopped. I don't want to hurt her, but I won't let her hurt anyone else in her misguided attempts to reclaim my father's affections." His gaze was as unwavering as his voice. He meant every single word he said, and he wanted to ensure that she knew that. Elena could practically feel his need for her to believe him radiating off of him. Niko was clearly used to people not taking him seriously, and he was trying to convince her to take a chance on him.

Agon seemed to pick up on the same heavy weight of sincerity in Niko's words because the tension in his body dissipated. He relaxed the tightened grip of his claws in her cloak and repositioned himself into a more comfortable, less defensive stance on her shoulder.

Elena offered him a weak smile. There was something special about this man, and she was torn between leaning into the feelings she was developing for him and running away as fast as she possibly could.

"Thank you for helping us," she told him. The words felt entirely insufficient, but it was the best she could come up with.

"Of course, Firefly. I would never abandon a damsel in distress." Niko flawlessly slipped back into his arrogant prince persona, the heavy seriousness of his previous statements having vanished from his eyes.

She rolled her eyes at him again, then dug through her cloak pockets until she found her waterskin. He'd refilled it for her before they'd left the castle, as well as restocked her pockets with food for the road.

"No, don't waste that." He got up from his lounging position, motioning for her to put the waterskin away. "I asked the servants to pack us a few meals for the trip." Niko pulled a large wicker basket out from a storage space in the hull that she hadn't noticed before. He laid a thick, woolen blanket on the deck and took a seat, beckoning her to join him. Eyeing him curiously, Elena took a seat opposite him on the soft blanket, spreading her cloak out behind her, so she wouldn't sit on any of her pockets.

"Here." Niko handed her a pewter dish from the basket, before loading it down with fresh fruit—oranges, strawberries, and a long, skinny, yellow thing she'd never seen before—a few thick slices of roast, and a roll. Elena placed the dish on her lap, and Niko handed her a goblet of wine.

"Goodness." Elena inhaled the delicious fragrances of the food. "This is amazing." She took an awkwardly large bite of the roast, trying to hide her overly full mouth behind her hand. An unchecked moan escaped her mouth. Niko's eyes widened and his mouth broke into a face-splitting grin. He didn't even have the decency to pretend he hadn't heard her.

"That good? I'll be sure to relay your compliments to the chef upon our return." Niko popped a strawberry into his mouth, grinning like he'd just won some unspoken argument between them.

Wait, what did he say?

Elena choked down the large bite, "What do you mean 'our return?' I'm not going back to the castle with you. I'm meeting up with my br—traveling companions and that will be the end of this." She gestured between them, to ensure he caught her meaning.

"Right. Of course, Firefly. I misspoke." His eyes, however, seemed to say something else entirely. He fully believed that she would return with him to the castle.

Why the hells would she do that?

40

QUINN

L YRA HOPPED THROUGH THE tall, frozen grass before them. Quinn kept close behind her and directed the others where to step to avoid any slick patches of ice masquerading as snow.

Quinn couldn't help but resent Aleerah a bit for putting things into perspective so sharply when they were finally taking a moment to breathe and relax. Everyone knew what was at stake, and he didn't think was it necessary for her to dump icy water over them all when they were just trying to decompress. He understood her logic, but making their trip into a death march wasn't going to make things move any faster or stop the *turmio* any sooner.

I imagine she didn't understand what was happening and thought we were just muxing around. I don't think she meant to bring everyone down. Lyra's voice sounded slightly apologetic in his mind. Like she felt she needed to make amends for Aleerah's lecture. *She's scared and probably thought we were making light of the situation.*

We're all scared, Q countered. *It doesn't mean we can't try to blow off a little steam.*

I agree with you, Lyra replied, glancing quickly over her shoulder to him before bounding over a fallen tree. *I'm just trying to see things from her perspective.*

Q shrugged at that. Aleerah was used to spending all of her time with their scatterbrained—possibly legitimately insane—father. Quinn imagined keeping Aiden on track was a lot like trying to herd chickens or cats. He didn't envy Aleerah her job as keeper of the unbalanced demi-god, but he still couldn't quite excuse her needlessly harsh words.

Lyra had a point; Aleerah was just trying to do what she thought was best. But so was their mother when she separated them at birth, and again when she locked them in that tower for weeks. Not to mention Aiden's argument that he was doing what was best by watching them go through hells and not once stepping in to aid them.

Q was getting *really* sick of people making decisions for him because they knew "what was best." It was a bullshyt excuse to try and control his actions and the actions of his brother and sister to sway the results in someone else's favor.

Mux that.

Quinn decided right there, ankle-deep in the snow in the middle of a frozen grassy field, no one would make decisions for him. Ever again.

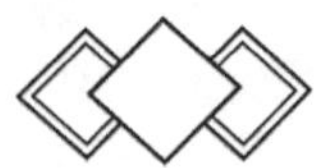

The sun was setting on the second day of their grassland hike when they finally reached the circle of stones that he and Elena had taken shelter in before first entering the Dragon's Teeth. The same stones that saw the three of them sleep together for the first time in their lives—outside of their mother's womb. The stones that had witnessed their defeat and abduction by those damned investigators of their mother's.

If I never see these muxing stones again, it will be too soon.

Quinn was not looking forward to another night sleeping relatively unguarded and exposed to the elements. They'd established a pretty decent routine. Lyra slept with Demoni under her tail to ensure the ice dragon didn't freeze overnight. Roska slept between Q and the fire they'd keep stoked for the night. While Ros always said the cold didn't bother him, Q didn't like the way his brother's lips turned slightly blue after their first night in the forest. He'd decided then that Ros would sleep closer to the fire, to ensure his temperature didn't get too low. It seemed like his brother struggled to maintain his internal temperature almost as much as his reptilian familiar.

As soon as they got to the stones, Aiden dropped his pack against one of the tall stones, pulled out a large cooking pot, and walked off to the river, presumably to collect water from them to cook with or make tea. Roska and Demoni stalked off into the surrounding grass to find any sticks and dry branches to start their fire. Begrudgingly, Q had to agree that traveling with their father had turned out to be quite handy. Q could build a fire in a snap—literally—but he needed something to actually burn to maintain it. Dry wood was harder to come by, now that everything was buried in snow. What wood they did find was often too wet to burn. Aiden was able to evaporate the snow or conjure dry wood for them when they needed it.

Lyra walked in a slow circle around the interior of the stone encampment, using her heat to melt the snow and ice. Quinn came in behind her and scorched the exposed earth. It wasn't the most environmentally friendly option, but it was a controlled burn and it ensured that their campfire wouldn't end up causing a wildfire. Plus, it helped to dry out the formerly frozen ground after Lyra melted the snow into puddles. It was a system they'd perfected over the last few weeks, and it had become second nature to him.

Q couldn't help but smile to himself. It was barely a season ago that he learned he had these powers, now here he was controlling them without any conscious thought. The fire was an extension of himself. Belladonna would be proud.

Wait, what the hells? Why do I care about making that witch proud?

Because secretly you really like her and you want her to like you, Lyra said matter-of-factly. *Don't tell me you honestly didn't realize that.*

Shut it. I do not like her. I barely tolerate her. Quinn hated when Lyra was more in tune with his emotions than he was. It was annoying.

Wow. That's just sad, Q. It's ok to like people, you know, Lyra teased. Her face twisted into a foxy version of a smirk, and Q couldn't help but smile at her.

Oh, yeah, he poked, *you* are definitely the one to teach me about liking people. You have tried to bite, or successfully bitten, literally every human we've come across!

That's not true! Lyra flicked her tail at him, shooting tiny sparks in his direction. *I never once tried to bite Amelia.* At that, she sat in the middle of the stone circle, wrapped her tail primly around her feet, and licked the singed fur clean.

Oh, I'm terribly sorry, Quinn replied. *How rude of me. That's right. Of the dozens, if not hundreds of people we've encountered, you didn't try to bite Amelia—arguably the kindest human on the planet. Good job.*

In my defense, most of the others were people we were thieving or running from. I was biting them for your protection. Ungrateful ass. Lyra didn't even bother looking up from her tail as she responded. Clearly feeling she'd won the argument.

Quinn just laughed. She wasn't wrong, after all. They'd spent much of their life thieving and running. It had been the only way they'd survived for several solar cycles before finding Amelia. It wasn't a history he was proud of, exactly, but Q couldn't help but be impressed with their stubborn ability to survive any situation.

It was why he felt confident in his plan to hijack whatever self-sacrificing mission Roska had in mind. If anyone could survive that, it would be him and Lyra.

Dinner was a quiet, simple affair. Roasted rabbit Q had caught along their travels earlier in the day, travel biscuits, black tea, and the last few carrots that Q had harvested—stolen—from Belladonna's garden. He'd been surprised to see them growing there at all, so far into the frost season, but Castor had explained that Belladonna refused to let the elements dictate what she could eat and when. Her magic kept her garden thriving so she was never subject to the whims of nature. Q would have mocked her for it, but honestly, the carrots were delicious.

"I'll keep watch tonight," Aleerah said, breaking the near silence of their meal. "I'm sorry for snapping at you all earlier."

Quinn couldn't have imagined such a large and fearsome creature looking so dejected. Her head hung low, and she refused to make eye contact with them. "I shouldn't have been so harsh. I'm just worried, as I'm sure you all are. This is the end goal that Aiden and I have been waiting for since before the Age of Fire. It's been nearly an eon of watching and waiting. Knowing it would all come to this eventually." She chanced a quick glance at Q and Ros before adding. "It's been the hardest thing of my life, watching you three grow and knowing that one of you..."

Aleerah let her sentence trail off, but they all knew what she was referring to. The prophecy said "one must fall," and they all knew what that meant.

Aiden rose from his cross-legged seat on the scorched earth and walked over to scratch behind Aleerah's massive ears. "We all understand, Alee, and we accept your apology. Don't we, boys?" Q and Ros both nodded in agreement. "We're all a bit high-strung these days." Aiden continued. "It will all be over soon though. It will be ok."

Q knew his father was trying to comfort them all with his confident words, but he didn't know how ok Elena would be with how things panned out.

I guess we'll find out in a day or two.

41

BELLADONNA

BELLADONNA WAS AWOKEN ABRUPTLY by a curt knock at the door followed by an even more curt, "Headmistress," from behind the closed door. As though the guard thought someone else might answer the door.

"Gods, how do you stand that? I could never get used to that nonsense." Belladonna yawned and stretched, twining her legs around Beatrice's, effectively keeping the headmistress trapped in the bed.

"I imagine you'd get used to it eventually," Beatrice said in a husky whisper as she placed a chaste kiss on Belladonna's lips. "Good morning, darling."

Belladonna watched in silent awe as the sunlight danced along Beatrice's exposed flesh. She reached out to touch it, mesmerized by the closeness of her skin. Ever so gently, Belladonna grazed her fingertips along Beatrice's arm, beginning at her elbow and slowly moving up to her shoulder, then across to her collarbone. Just as she was about to allow her hand to drift lower, another more urgent and insistent knock came.

"Oh, mux everything," Bea muttered quietly. She disentangled from Belladonna's legs, slid into a silk robe that had been hanging on the post at the foot of the bed, and grunted admittance to the guard on the other side of the door.

"Sorry to disturb you, Headmistress." The guard didn't spare a glance at Belladonna as she rose from the bed, wrapping herself in a blanket and casually combing her fingers through her tangled locks. "There's been a development at the wall."

"What sort of development?" Beatrice asked.

Belladonna couldn't help the tingle that passed through her body, coiling just below her stomach. It was quite exhilarating to see Beatrice in command of things. Exhilarating and intoxicating. She sat on the bed, in awe of her enchantress.

"Soldiers have been spotted, ma'am. The seers had a vision of a small battalion heading this way. They estimate the soldiers make it through the woods and within range of the archers by week's end."

"Well, that is irksome. Not surprising, of course, but annoying nonetheless." Belladonna stretched her neck, releasing a series of popping sounds from her spine.

Beatrice spoke to the guard, ignoring Belladonna's comment entirely. "Ready the archers and tell the smithies to prioritize arrowheads for the next couple of days. Make sure we have plenty of ammo to stall the soldiers' advances."

"Yes, Headmistress." The guard offered a quick bow, turned on her heel, and disappeared out of the room, firmly closing the door behind her as she exited.

"Will that be enough?" Belladonna asked in a hushed voice. She knew there were guards stationed outside the headmistress' door at all times, and she didn't want to risk them overhearing.

"We have inferno and cyclone enchantresses at each of the towers, along with some of the best markswomen in the world," Beatrice began. "We have tidal enchantresses along the wall closest to the river, and seismitists on the side that backs up to the mountain. Arrows will be of less use than our magics, but it is likely that our magics will continue to fail us as the *turmio* grows, so we need to be prepared for anything."

Beatrice looked exhausted, and they'd only been awake for a few minutes. All the tension that Belladonna had helped to release from Bea's body was back in full force.

Belladonna rose from the bed, holding the blanket around her shoulders with one hand while she offered the other to Bea. Beatrice took hold of the proffered hand as though it were a lifeline and she was a sailor lost at sea in the middle of a hurricane.

"It will be all right, Bea," Belladonna promised. It wasn't a promise that she could realistically keep, because it was entirely out of her control. Still, it felt like the truth. "Your children are strong. Powerful. They will be able to stop this thing, and we will halt that arrogant Queen's attempts at a hostile takeover." She squeezed Beatrice's hand firmly, to emphasize her words. "Everything will work out."

Beatrice pulled Belladonna into her arms, wrapping the witch in a strong embrace. "Mother Goddess, I truly hope you're right."

42
ELENA

"**H**OW MUCH LONGER DO you think it will be?" Elena asked for about the hundredth time that morning.

She'd fallen asleep shortly after they finished their meal the night before. She hadn't realized just how exhausted she was until she woke up and Niko informed her that she'd been out for nearly twelve hours. The sun hadn't even woken her. In an effort to let her rest, the princeling had erected a small tent over her with a second blanket, shielding her from the elements and the glaring sunlight.

Niko offered her a steaming cup of coffee. "I imagine we'll be at the base of the mountain by sundown. We'll have to hike the rest of the way on foot."

"We?" Elena asked, taking the cup and warming her frozen fingertips against the thick ceramic dish.

"Aye, *we*," he said with a cocksure grin.

"You can't be serious." Elena hid her smile behind the cup, taking a long, grateful sip of the beverage.

"What's wrong with me coming along? I can't, in good conscience, free a young lady from my mother's prison, only to leave her to hike into the pit of hells alone." Niko placed a hand across his heart, feigning shock at the mere suggestion.

"Gods, you're impossible." Elena failed to quell the smile that lit up her face.

Gods, you both are. Agon's exasperation was palpable as he stretched out on the sun-drenched deck.

Elena rolled her eyes and turned to watch the scenery as they sailed past. They were moving at an impressive speed, the trees all mixing into a blur of white and green. She'd long since lost track of where they were, never having traveled before being kicked out of Harbor Ridge. Elena's concept of Waverly was limited to the Dark Woods, Andover, the inn in Nexton, and the section of the river that ran from Nexton to the Dragon's Teeth. She strained to recall her geography lessons, but Elena had never been very good with maps, and the instructor had been a harsh and unforgiving woman. The second Elena had finished her basic lessons, she'd refused to go back. She could recall a very simplistic image of the map in her head, but she had no idea how far they'd traveled so she couldn't even guess how much farther they had to go.

One thing Elena knew for certain, though, was that Niko was absolutely *not* going with her into the mountains to find her brothers and father. And he sure as hells was *not* going to help them stop the *turmio*. It wasn't his responsibility. It was hers. Hers and her brothers alone.

Not to mention Q would hate the princeling.

Because they're too much alike, Agon observed.

What are you talking about?

You know what I mean. The cockiness. The arrogance they use to hide just how self-conscious they really are. Q does it because he truly thinks he's unworthy of good things. The Prince does it because he doesn't feel like he's earned *the things that he has.* Agon rolled onto his back, exposing the slightly lighter fur of his underbelly.

How can you tell? Elena studied Niko's profile as he adjusted their sails. She wanted to see what Agon had seen in him.

It's in the way he watches you. He's constantly checking to see if you're smiling when he makes a joke. He wants to show you that he's more than just a prince. That he's a capable man. I'd be willing to bet you are the first girl he's ever met who didn't immediately swoon at the sight of him.

Elena watched the Prince a moment longer, then looked away. She replayed the last day with him and realized Agon was right. Niko was constantly watching her reactions to him. She wasn't exactly unkind to him, but she wasn't really paying much attention to a lot of what he did or said. Too preoccupied with the impending end-of-the-world looming just beyond the horizons. Niko must have interpreted that as her being disinterested. It wasn't that she *wasn't* interested in him; she just had bigger issues weighing on her.

Still, she caught herself watching him when he wasn't looking more than she would've liked to admit. Elena's experience with men was almost as limited as her experience with travel, but her time working at Amelia's inn had enabled her to see all sorts of relationships and dynamics between couples. She loved seeing the adoring looks in the eyes of happy couples and would daydream about having that for herself one day. As a child, Harbor Ridge had drilled into all the students that there was no such thing as "happily ever after." Elena had started to realize that that wasn't the truth. One of her favorite couples, the Millers, had been mated for over fifty years, and they still showed the same love and affection to each other as the young newly mated couples.

"We're making good time," Niko said, drawing Elena out of her memories. "Are you sure your companions will be there?"

"No, but it's the only place I can think of." Elena looked dejectedly upstream. "I don't know where else they might go, but I know we have to end up here. It seems like the safest choice. If they aren't there yet, then they should be soon. Right, Agon?"

Agon didn't respond. Somehow, the little weasel had fallen asleep, belly still exposed, stretched out in the sun like he didn't have a care in the world. Like the magic wasn't on the verge of annihilation.

Lucky.

"Tell me something, Firefly," Niko said, coming to sit across from her on one of the many benches that lined both sides of the longship. His knees narrowly avoided touching hers, and Elena swore she could feel the heat of his body through her skirts.

"What do you want to know?" Elena asked nervously.

Niko shrugged. "Something weird. Something funny. Something no one else knows."

Elena thought for a long moment, rifling through memories trying to find a funny one or a weird one that was innocuous enough that it couldn't be used against her.

That seems a little defensive. Agon's voice was a mixture of light-hearted condescension with a dash of concern.

Elena didn't bother responding to him. Instead, she settled on a memory and spoke to Niko. "When I was little, maybe eight or nine solar cycles old, I used to play hide-and-seek with my nanny. Agon and I would hide in cabinets, under beds, even the older girls' wardrobes if we could get into their rooms." Niko's face broke into a grin, enthralled by her story and clearly enjoying the idea of little Elena sneaking around the school. "There was one day, when we were playing in one of the study halls, that Agon and I managed to find one of my mother's secret passageways that run throughout the castle. We didn't know what it was, of course, but we were curious and quickly forgot about Nanny Maureen and our game." Elena paused in her story, remembering the feel of the cold stones on her bare feet as she and Agon had crept down the dark passageway. Agon had only just started learning to control his lightning and attempted to use it to light their way. Elena vividly remembered the way his blue lightning crackled, echoing down the seemingly endless hall. She glanced up from her hands to find Niko staring at her, a slightly puzzled and concerned look in his eyes, so she quickly jumped back into her story. "We followed the passageway for a while. It seemed to go on forever until we heard these weird sounds. I'd never heard sounds like that before. Rhythmic scraping sounds, grunting, someone swearing and calling out for the gods and Mother Goddess."

Elena's cheeks heated as she relived the memory. *Why the hells had she picked* this *story to share?* She shook her head, hoping to shake loose her embarrassment as well. "We followed the sounds to an opening hidden behind a tapestry. When I peeked out from behind it, I saw one of my mother's guards with a man I'd never seen before." Elena's voice was a hushed whisper, barely able to get the words out.

This was *definitely* the wrong story to tell.

"Well...?" Niko prodded after several moments of stilted silence. "What happened?"

"What do you mean 'what happened?' They were... you know." Elena's cheeks were on fire. She stared at her knees, unable to meet his eyes.

"You know what?" She could hear the smile in his voice. Niko knew what they were doing, he just wanted to hear her say it.

Muxing ass.

"You *know*. I don't need to say it." Elena tried to hide her embarrassment behind the hair that had fallen loose from her braid. If she didn't look at him, maybe he wouldn't notice the flush of her cheeks or sense the butterflies swarming in her stomach.

"I have no idea what you're talking about, Firefly. I'm just an innocent young prince. I can't even imagine what a man and woman might do alone in a room together." He was teasing her and thoroughly enjoying himself.

Elena looked at him now, trying to make her face as menacing as possible.

Niko burst out laughing. "Come now, Firefly. No need for the grumpy face. Watching you squirm is easily the best part of my day."

Elena glared at him for a moment, then she leaned forward, boldly placing her hands firmly on his thighs just above his knees. Her face was so close to his that their exhales mingled, and she watched his gaze flick from her eyes to her lips. Slowly, purposefully, Elena licked her lips, enjoying the power she felt as his eyes traced the route her tongue had just taken. She took a slow, deep breath, inhaling the scent of fresh linen, pine, and just the slightest hint of sweat that wafted from him. Niko's eyes flashed quickly to hers before returning their focus to her lips. Elena leaned forward just a hair more, her nose practically touching his. She smiled.

"If you wanted to watch me squirm," she whispered, "you could have just asked."

Niko leaned into her, brushing his nose against hers, attempting to close the distance and let his lips finally make first contact with hers. Just as his soft lips grazed hers, Elena released the lightning she'd been holding at bay in her fingertips, shocking both of his thighs and causing him to fall backward on his seat, slamming his back against the bench behind him.

Elena cackled with laughter as Agon literally rolled across the hull, unable to contain his amusement.

"Ah! What the bloody hells was that for?" Niko shouted after he managed to right himself. He rubbed his thighs vigorously, as though he could rub away her shocks.

"I just wanted to watch you squirm for a moment," Elena said, not even bothering to contain her glee. "You're right. This was definitely the best part of my day!"

43

ROSKA

THEY'D WOKEN WITH THE sun, relieved themselves, and left the rocks as fresh snow had begun falling. Roska pulled his cloak tighter around his neck. He really needed to get a hooded cloak. Although, realistically, he wouldn't have the need for it much longer.

Roska was resigned to his fate. The ritual required a sacrifice since all magic comes with a cost. He knew it had to be him who paid the price. If not for his foolish and misguided actions, the *turmio* would never have been released in the first place. He couldn't let his siblings pay for his mistake.

Demoni was curled up around the stone Q had just heated for her, riding in his pack and likely reading his thoughts. She didn't want to die any more than he did, but she'd agreed to the plan without argument. She felt just as responsible as he did, and this was the only way they could make it right.

That didn't mean they weren't both terrified.

The ritual was a series of banishing and binding spells meant to attract, capture, and contain the *turmio* in what Aiden called "The Nothing." Roska had been too nervous to ask more about The

Nothing. He didn't really want to know. He just wanted to get it over with, yet he desperately wished they could delay indefinitely.

He'd spent the majority of their hike convincing himself that he was making the right choice, even as thoughts of Brigit kept infiltrating his mind. Roska hoped she would forget about him because he hated the idea of her missing him.

Assuming she would. She's probably grateful that you're gone now. Roska flinched at his own dark thoughts.

Don't think like that. Demoni's voice drowned out the negative words that were clouding his mind. *Brigit likes you. She will be sad that we're gone, but it will be ok. We are worthy of her affections. Don't let the Brotherhood's mind-warping thoughts take that away.*

It doesn't matter anyway. We'll never see her again. Roska followed Q's footprints in the snow, keeping his eyes on the slick road before them. He didn't want to think about Brigit. He didn't want to wonder what might have been. There was no point. He had more important things to focus on.

"You have all the ingredients for the ritual, don't you, Father?" Roska asked, forcing his mind to focus on the tasks that lay before them.

"Aye. I collected most of what I was lacking while we were at Belladonna's. Bought the last few herbs at a stall in Nexton yesterday. We are as ready as we'll ever be." Aiden sidestepped a large boulder that must've fallen from the mountains and continued speaking. "When we first get to the cavern, I'll get everything set up. The *turmio* won't know we're there at first, but it will come quickly when it senses the strength of our combined magics. Hopefully, it hasn't gotten too powerful since its release. Last time..." his voice trailed off. It was a long moment before he spoke again, his voice raw with barely contained emotion. "Last time, it was fully corporeal and killed several of my companions before we were able to contain it." He quickly wiped his cheek, pushing away the unwanted emotions. "Back then, the *turmio* had been left unchecked for several solar cycles, so it had plenty of time to feast and grow. This time, it has only been free for a few lunar cycles. It should be easier to capture."

Roska tried to take comfort in his father's words, but they didn't offer much solace.

"How did magic survive then?" Q shook snow from his hair, then pulled the hood of his cloak to cover his head and shield his face. "I thought the muxing thing was supposed to eat magic and kill everything with powers."

"The gods stepped in," Aiden said plainly. "Ages ago, the gods were far more 'hands-on' in their approach with this world. There were hundreds of demi-gods as proof of the constant interactions the gods and goddesses had with this world. I was part of an army of nearly a hundred demi-gods tasked with stopping the *turmio*. By the time the battle was over, we'd lost seventy-seven of our brethren."

Roska froze in place, staring at their father's back as he continued walking down the road into the mountains.

Seventy-seven dead, just to capture one monster? Gods, what have I unleashed upon this world?

"Come on, Ros," Quinn said, placing a steady hand on Roska's shoulder and giving it a comforting squeeze. "We have to keep moving."

Roska followed behind Aiden as he led them into the Dragon's Teeth. The road quickly devolved into a rough path through the jagged stone mountains, made all the more challenging by the snow and ice. More than once, one of them slipped or slid across the frozen rocks. After the third time Roska had slipped and nearly taken Aiden and Quinn out with him, Q decided to take the lead. He and Lyra used their heat to melt the snow and ice on the path, carving a safe passage through the mountains.

"That really is quite the handy skill you have there, son," Aiden admired.

"Yeah, thanks." Q's face seemed to redden at the compliment. Roska knew that his brother didn't like their father much, but he appreciated that Q seemed to be warming to Aiden finally.

They didn't speak much as they hiked, too focused on keeping their pace without falling to their death. There was a heaviness in the air that had nothing to do with the snow falling harder and faster with each passing moment. They knew that they wouldn't all be walking out of the Dragon's Teeth when this was all over.

"The entrance to the cave is just ahead," Quinn said over his shoulder.

"Aye, Aleerah is already in the tunnels that lead to the cavern. It seems a family of bats had taken up residence in the cave entrance. She spooked them—and herself, but don't tell her I said that." Aiden chuckled lightly, trying to brighten the darkness that followed them as they trekked deeper into the mountains.

Roska said nothing. He didn't trust his voice not to betray his fears. He knew he was doing the right thing, but he currently lacked the over-confidence that he'd felt the last time he'd entered this space.

On his last visit to the cavern, Roska had used a different entrance, so when they rounded the final ridge and he faced "the mouth within the teeth" as prophecy had called it, he was stunned into stillness.

"You... You walked into that?" Roska raised a shaking finger, pointed at the seemingly endless abyss that lay open before them. The entrance was fringed with intensely sharp-looking stalactites and stalagmites, making the cave look like the mouth of a vicious beast.

"Yeah," Quinn said with a shrug. "Didn't have a lot of other options, did we? Fair warning though, when we walked in last time, the entrance sealed up, trapping us in the cave and forcing us to move forward." Q looked at Roska, seeming to see the terror in his eyes, and added, "Nothing to worry about though. It just means we have to keep moving forward, which we have to do anyway."

Q was right. Magical creatures were getting sick and possibly already dying because of this monster. Moving forward was their only option. Roska offered a weak nod and followed his brother into the ominous black abyss.

44

QUINN

JUST AS BEFORE, THE cave entrance had sealed behind them as soon as they'd all crossed the threshold. Quinn didn't find it any less unsettling this time as he had the first time he'd entered the cave with Elena. This time, however, he was more prepared for it and called the fire into his palm so he could light their way. Lyra took up the rear, keeping a flame on her tail so they wouldn't get lost or lose any members of their traveling crew.

No one spoke as they crept farther into the mountain's core. Q wasn't sure if it was nerves that kept his brother from speaking, or if Ros was regretting his intended plans.

While he didn't know exactly what Roska and Aiden had planned, Q knew it was some sort of stupid, self-sacrificing bullshyt that Roska intended to die doing. Lyra had finally told him that she was willfully ignorant of Aiden and Roska's plan. She had literally run away when they were making the plan so she wouldn't have to lie to him. He appreciated that in so much as he didn't like the idea of secrets between him and his familiar, but he was thoroughly pissed that she hadn't learned their plans so that he could stop it.

I didn't run, she corrected him in his mind. *I simply asked them to stop talking for a couple minutes while I went upstairs.*

Q rolled his eyes at this comment. The speed of her movement didn't matter. It was the fact that she'd allowed them to make plans behind his back that pissed him off.

From the moment he'd learned he had siblings, Q had appointed himself the role of Big Brother. He had no idea if that was fair or even remotely accurate, but he couldn't deny the strong urge he felt to keep them safe. Regardless of birth order, it was his job to protect them, not the other way around. He didn't know what Roska had planned, but he fully intended to stop him, or—assuming Roska's plan was the only option they had—take his brother's place.

As they crept quietly into the cavern, the yawning chasm in the center of the space called to him. Drawing him in. A sudden wave of nausea rose within him, giving Q a sense of worms crawling around his insides.

Lyra quickly placed herself between Q and the chasm, herding him like a sheepdog guides its flock, away from the edge of the gaping abyss that would happily swallow him whole. Aleerah waited for them on the far side of the cavern, sitting next to Roska's abandoned cart of ritual shyt. Apparently, no one else had ventured into the cavern to scavenge the items they'd left behind when he and Elena had first escorted Roska out of the mountain as their prisoner.

The hole in the center of the ceiling provided plenty of light in the cavern. Quinn extinguished his flames, staring up at the sky. He vividly remembered the last time he'd been here. Watching the black cloud swarm from the chasm, through the gaping hole, blocking out the light as it had escaped into the world. And now they intended to bring it back here. Stronger and potentially in a physical body.

Mux everything.

With a casual leap, Aleerah crossed the chasm and laid down beside Aiden.

"Everyone on," she said, indicating that they should all climb onto her back.

Cautiously and as gently as possible, Roska, Aiden, and Quinn all positioned themselves along her spine. Lyra, naturally, refused the ride. Instead, she got a running start and jumped smoothly across the chasm as though she'd done it a thousand times. Aleerah chuckled at her boldness. Quinn couldn't help but smile with pride at his nimble little fox. With two massive bounds, Aleerah cleared the chasm again, landing with ease beside Lyra and the makeshift altar.

Aiden hopped down from Aleerah's back and quickly got to work setting up the altar for his own ritual. Q watched him pull multiple jars and sachets from his pockets. With a snap of his fingers, Aiden conjured a heavy black cauldron which landed with a loud thud, echoing throughout the cavern and making Q's ears ring.

"Oops, sorry about that, lads. Probably should've thought that through a bit more." Aiden offered them a small, amused smile. Quinn and Roska, who had both thrown their hands over their ears, glared at their father while they lowered their hands slowly.

"That seems to be an ongoing theme with you," Q grumbled. He considered tossing a small fireball at their father but figured that wouldn't be helpful. Not to mention, Elena didn't approve when he threw fireballs at people.

Sometimes Elena takes all the fun out of things. Even when she's not here. Sparks flared at the tip of Lyra's tail, but she managed to keep them to herself.

Yeah, but she's a good person, and we could learn a lot from her, Q reasoned. He didn't feel the need to be as good as Elena. Honestly, he wasn't even sure he was capable of being *that* good. Still, asking himself, "What would Elena do?" had stopped him from committing violent acts more than a few times since she'd been gone.

Lyra rolled her eyes at him—an impressive feat in a fox—but quelled her sparks before she set anything on fire.

Aiden finished setting everything up. "Roska, I will need your help with these spells. You've performed this sort of magic before, and I know you'll be able to handle this with me now. Quinn, once we get started, the *turmio* will sense our presence and our intentions. It will be coming for us. I need you to hold it off as long as you can. Burn it up. If it has managed to reform a body, it will channel its powers through its hands and eyes. Blind if it you're able. Aleerah, I'll need you with Lyra and Quinn. Demoni, you will have to stand guard, as the last defense, over Roska and me while we work."

Everyone nodded as Aiden assigned their roles. Q didn't like taking orders from Aiden, but he knew it was smart to follow the advice of a man who'd lived for ages and had dealt with this creature before.

"Elena should be arriving any minute," Aiden added, glancing toward the opening they'd come through earlier.

They all paused and watched the entrance for a few moments, hoping to see her appear at his words.

No such luck.

"Well, she should be here soon. Hopefully, before the *turmio* arrives so she can help defend us while we complete the ritual." Aiden shrugged and turned to face the cauldron. "Lyra, would you be so kind as to start a fire for the cauldron?"

Lyra flicked her tail at the pile of dry wood within a stone circle Aiden had conjured and the flames took hold in an instant.

"Splendid." Aiden smiled at the firefox. "Here we go!"

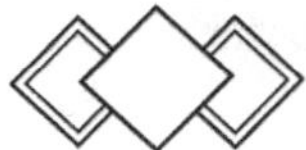

Time passed painfully slowly. Seconds felt like hours as Quinn watched Aiden and Roska begin the ritual out of the corner of his eye. He kept most of his focus on the sky still visible through the gaping hole in the cavern ceiling.

His heart pounded in his chest, seeming to echo in his ears. Flames danced nervously on his fingers, quickly spreading up his arms. Q was once again grateful for their father's magic. Aiden had taken it upon himself to spell Quinn's clothing, making it immune to his fire. He would never burn through his clothes again.

Not that you'll be alive much longer to enjoy it.

The voice that reverberated in his mind wasn't his own, nor was it Lyra's. This voice was ancient, gravelly, and enraged.

Who the hells are you, and why are you in my head? Quinn raged in return.

You know exactly who I am, stupid boy. Your efforts are pointless. You cannot stop me. You cannot trap me. You cannot kill me. The demon's voice raged in his head. Quinn flinched as the words grew with power and anger.

You don't belong here! Q yelled back.

I have been here since the birth of this world. I will be here at its death. It is you who does not belong.

The ground began to shake as the voice in his head grew louder and louder.

"It's coming!" Aiden shouted. "Get ready!"

The cavern plunged into darkness as the black swarm flooded in through the opening above them.

Quinn's fire surged, engulfing his entire body in flames as he faced off with the vaguely humanoid black mass before him. Throwing fireballs and shooting long blasts of flames at the demon, Q offered silent prayers to any deity that might be listening. Pleading for help and good fortune, and willing himself to stay alive long enough to allow Aiden and Roska the time they needed to finish the ritual and save the world.

45
ELENA

THE MOUNTAIN QUAKED BENEATH her feet as Elena and Niko ran through the tunnels that led to the cavern. She was too late. The sounds of a battle raged within the heart of the mountain. Elena could hear Q's cries of rage echoing throughout the mountain.

"You have to go back!" Elena yelled at Niko over the sounds of the fighting.

"Like hells! I'm not letting you out of my sight," he shouted in response.

Elena didn't have a chance to argue, as the mountain shook again and the tunnel began collapsing around them. Niko reacted quickly, shoving Elena forward as the ceiling of the tunnel fell on top of him.

"NIKO!" Elena cried. She rushed over to the pile of stones, trying desperately to dig him free of the collapse. "Niko! Please say something."

"I'm all right, Firefly." Niko's voice sounded strained and distant. "I didn't get hit, I'm just stuck."

Elena started shoving the larger rocks away, attempting to clear the passageway and reach him.

Elena, we can't stay here! Your brothers need us. Hells, the world *needs us!* Agon sparked as he jumped around on the tunnel floor behind her. The sounds of the battle were louder still, and Elena was able to feel the heat from Q's fire turning the cavern into an oven.

But, we can't just leave him! Elena looked frantically over her shoulder, toward the fight, while still struggling to clear the tunnel for Niko.

We have to. He says he's not hurt. We can come back and save him after all this shyt is over. Agon didn't say what they were both thinking.

Assuming they survived the fight.

"Niko!" Elena called. "Niko, I'm sorry. We have to go help my brothers." She didn't even try to hide the truth of the situation anymore. "I'm sorry I lied to you, and I'm sorry we didn't get to know each other better. You seem like a really wonderful person." Elena choked back a sob as she turned away from the princeling. "I'll come back for you."

With that, she turned, scooped up Agon, and ran as fast as she could towards the cries of her brothers.

"Elena, wait!" Niko yelled, but she couldn't hear him. She was already in the thick of the battle, praying for safety and success.

Elena rushed into the room, barely taking a moment to assess the situation. Quinn, whose entire body was on fire, stood toe-to-toe with a massive humanoid creature. The creature almost seemed to be made of smoke itself, except that it could—and did—take a punch. Flaming punches, as it were, over and over.

"Elena!" Quinn didn't seem surprised by her arrival. If anything, he seemed relieved that she was finally there. Like he'd been waiting for her.

Elena channeled all of her magic into her hands, feeling the lightning dance across her skin, flare in her eyes, and course throughout her whole body.

Quinn continued pummeling the creature with blow after blow of fiery punches, while the creature attempted to grab hold of him. Elena didn't know what it would do once it grabbed him, but she refused to let it achieve that goal. Agon jumped from her shoulder and slunk stealthily across the cavern until he reached the creature's feet. With a quick thought to Elena, she understood what he was doing. In a moment of flawless synchronicity, Elena and Agon unleash their lightning on the creature—hers aimed at its head, while Agon's took out its legs.

The creature let out an unearthly cry, its legs buckled beneath it as its hand gripped its head.

Without missing a beat, Lyra pounced onto its back, digging her teeth into its smokey neck, dragging it to the ground. The firefox shook the demon's neck so violently that Elena was surprised its head didn't completely detach from its body.

Agon wrapped himself tightly around one of the creature's legs, continuously shocking it and making it impossible for the creature to stand up.

Elena rushed to Q's side, seeing him nearly collapse at the edge of the chasm.

"Are you all right? Where are you hurt?" she asked in a rushed voice. She wasn't sure how long Lyra and Agon could keep the creature down. "What the hells is that thing?"

Quinn seemed to be gasping for air, but Elena couldn't see any blood or obvious injuries. "I'm not hurt," he said between labored breaths. "Just winded. It takes a lot to be a fiery ball of rage." He nodded to the creature, still struggling to rise. "That's the *turmio*."

Elena inhaled sharply. *That's the* turmio? *Gods, how many magical beings had to die for it to create this smoky form?*

"Aim for the head," Quinn continued. "Roska and Aiden are in the middle of the ritual to trap that son of a bitch. We just have to keep him occupied long enough for them to finish the spells and shyt."

Before Elena could respond or even take a moment to register that her father was so close, the creature—the *turmio*—threw Lyra from its throat and kicked Agon across the room. They both landed in a heap on the floor beside what appeared to be the unconscious form of a giant wolf-bear hybrid.

Enough! Foolish children! An enraged voice vibrated throughout the cavern, shaking the walls and knocking small rocks from the ceiling. Elena threw her hands over her head to protect herself from the falling debris. *You cannot stop me!* It roared, opening a gaping hole in front of its smoky head, blacker than anything Elena had ever seen.

The *turmio* inhaled deeply through its yawning maw. For a moment, nothing seemed to happen, but then she felt it. Elena's magic began to fade. Her lightning sputtered out on her hands, disappearing from her skin and leaving her feeling hollow.

Quinn's fire had vanished as well, his eyes returning to their normal forest green, a panic spreading quickly across his face. The *turmio* was devouring their magic. Agon and Lyra lay motionless across the cavern, but Elena could see the magic fading from them as well. She was surprised to realize that they weren't fading away entirely, as she had expected them to. Familiars were created entirely by magic, so it made sense that without magic, the familiars would cease to exist. It struck her as odd, as her vision darkened a bit, that Agon would still be with her. She couldn't feel him in her mind anymore. For a split second, she thought he was dead, but exhaled a sigh of relief when she saw his tail twitch. He might not be connected to her anymore, but he was still alive.

As their powers faded, the *turmio* grew more and more solid. It shifted from a thick, faceless humanoid creature into a man. Skin as pale as fresh snow, with eyes as black as death itself. The *turmio*—now fully corporeal—stalked toward them, his shiny black boots echoed through the suddenly silent cavern.

Faintly, Elena could hear Roska and Aiden working their spells, chanting in some language she'd never heard before. She prayed they were nearly done. Elena didn't think she or Quinn would survive fighting the *turmio* without their magics.

"You really thought you could stop me?" The man's voice was as smooth as silk and dripping with venom. "Don't you know who I am?"

"You're a muxing demon, and you belong in hells," Quinn spat.

With a wave of his hand, the man flung Quinn across the chasm. He landed with a thud against the far wall of the cavern, falling limp to the floor.

"Quinn!" Elena shrieked. She rose to face the monster, desperately wishing she had even the faintest hint of her powers to slam into that demon's flawless porcelain face.

The man clicked his tongue and raised his hand. "You are the enchantress I've heard so much about then?" He posed it as a question, but she knew he didn't expect—or want—an answer.

Without warning, Elena felt her feet lift from the ground. The *turmio* crooked his finger, drawing her now-weightless form closer to him. When she was within reach, he grabbed her throat. Her hands flew to his wrists, clawing at his skin, trying to free herself from his grip.

"What makes you so special, huh? You don't seem all that unique to me." He held her at arm's length, entirely unphased by her attempts to get free. He turned her slightly from one side to the other, inspecting her.

Elena's vision began to narrow as she struggled to catch her breath. She kicked out at the *turmio* but her legs were too short to make contact, and she was quickly losing the ability to focus on anything.

Elena felt the floor rush up to meet her as her vision faded to black.

46

ROSKA

ROSKA RUSHED TO THE edge of the chasm, hurling sharp icicles at the *turmio*. The man had been so distracted with Elena that he hadn't seen the shard of ice Roska had thrown until it skewered his arm, forcing him to drop Elena.

"Go! I've got this." Aiden called out, still focusing on the magics building before him. The ritual was *almost* complete. Roska just needed to buy him a few more minutes, and get the monster into position.

Roska raced around the edge of the chasm, shooting sharp, arrow-like sticks of ice at the *turmio* as he hurried to Elena's side. The *turmio* quickly got over its shock at the unexpectedness of Roska's attack, turning to face him and opening his mouth wider than should have been physically possible. Roska heard him start to suck in a deep breath, but his reflexes were too quick. Roska speared an ice arrow right through the *turmio*'s throat and out the back of his head. The *turmio* dropped in a heap on the floor instantly.

Roska ran past it and slid to a kneeling position beside Elena. He gingerly lifted her head into his lap, brushing her hair from her face and checking her pulse.

Her heart was still beating. She was alive. He exhaled a breath he'd been holding since she'd arrived in the middle of the fight.

"Elena?" He spoke softly, not wanting to startle her but needing her to wake. "Elena, I need you to open your eyes." Roska watched on bated breath as her eyelids started to flutter. "Praise to the Mother," he sighed.

"Roska." Elena's voice was rough, likely a result of the *turmio*'s violent handling.

"Yes, *tyttö*, it's me. You're going to be ok." He brushed her hair from her forehead and placed a gentle kiss at her hairline. Unbidden, tears began to fall from his eyes, landing quietly on her upturned face.

"I'm all right," she said to him, taking his hand in her own and offering a reassuring squeeze. With her other hand, Elena reached up and brushed the tears from his cheeks, resting her hand on his face and holding his gaze.

Across the chasm, Aiden shouted, "It's ready! We need to move him. Can you bring him around?"

Roska helped Elena to her feet, then walked over to the slumped form of the *turmio*. Ice arrow to the head or not, the creature could not be killed, only contained. Roska hauled the monster to his feet, pulling one of the *turmio*'s limp arms across his shoulders while Elena took hold of the other arm, taking on as much of the dead weight as possible. Carefully, they made their way along the edge of the chasm to the other side of the cavern with Aiden and Quinn.

Much to his relief, Q was already sitting upright, although he looked thoroughly disoriented, his eyes unfocused and befuddled.

Aiden met them at the chasm, taking the weight from Elena and leading the way to the cauldron. They dumped the seemingly lifeless body of the *turmio* on the ground beside the chasm, returning to the cauldron to complete the final step. Aiden had explained that the *turmio* would not willingly go into The Nothing, and would likely need to be pushed or dragged into it. Roska had accepted that he would be the one to travel into The Nothing with it, as penance for having been the one to release it in the first place.

Q had figured out their plan, at least to a point. He knew that Roska planned to sacrifice himself. He didn't know how Q had figured it out, but it didn't matter now. Q was temporarily incapacitated and unable to stop him. Roska would be able to redeem himself and save the world from the demon he'd unleashed. He would finally be able to make things right.

"We need to surround him with these herbs," Aiden said, tossing sachets of herbs to Roska and Elena. "Don't be stingy, either. We need to make sure this shyt sticks."

They each spread the herbs liberally around the monster, encircling him in the herbs meant to bind and banish.

"Perfect. Now, Roska, since you were the one to unleash it—no, none of that self-pity. We all do things we regret. Since you released it, it will be more powerful if you are the one to seal it back in." Aiden guided Roska to stand before the creature, handing him the incantation on a slip of parchment and a sharp blade. "I'll be here with you, adding my powers to the spell, but you need to be the one to actually cast it. Are you ready?"

Roska held the parchment in shaking fingers, his eyes solely focused on the shining tip of the blade in his hand. He knew in that moment that he would never be ready. He spared a quick glance to Quinn as he sat leaning unsteadily on the wall of the cavern. Then Roska looked to Elena, tears streaming down her face. Elena knew what needed to be done. Roska had to assume she'd learned about binding rituals and banishments in her studies at Harbor Ridge. She would know that the ritual would be risky, but that was the price to seal the *turmio* into its enteral prison. As much as she cried for him, Roska trusted that she knew this was the only option. Roska doubted she knew just how high a price he would be paying to undo his wrongs. She offered him an encouraging smile without bothering to wipe away her tears.

Roska began the incantation. He felt his power flow through him and saw the teal light glow from his eyes onto the parchment in his hands. He spoke the words with a strength and confidence he didn't feel. His mind flashed to Brigit for a moment, but he forced the thought away. She would be better off without him anyway.

Demoni slithered up his leg, making her way over his middle and wrapping herself protectively around his neck.

The *turmio* began to stir. Roska watched in muted horror as the hole in the back of his head healed itself and the monster sat up in the circle of binding herbs.

"No!" he roared, shaking the cavern walls. "I will *not* go back there!" He jumped to standing, pushing with all his might against an invisible wall created by their binding spell and reinforced by the herbs.

Roska kept chanting, he couldn't stop the incantation or it would all be for naught.

Elena took a step closer to him, laying her hand on his shoulder and sharing what little energy she had left with him. The *turmio* had consumed much of her power, but Roska could still feel a glimmer of it within her as she maintained contact with him.

"Release me, you arrogant children." The *turmio*'s demands fell on deaf ears. No one would be releasing that monster ever again.

That was one of the changes Aiden had made to the ritual. He sealed the banishment with blood magic. The only people in the world who could release the *turmio* again would be blood descendants of the triplets. They would be able to ensure that no one would ever free it again.

The *turmio* smashed his fists into the invisible wall, over and over. Roska knew the binding herbs wouldn't hold forever, he just needed them to hold long enough for him to finish the incantation.

Roska took the sharp dagger to his palm, slicing the skin and allowing his blood to drip and mingle with the herbs that surrounded the *turmio*.

Just a few more lines, Demoni's thoughts of encouragement pushed him forward.

As he finished the last words of the incantation, the floor beneath the binding circle cracked. The spell containing the *turmio* dissolved with a deafening hiss, freeing the demon once more.

Calmly, the *turmio* stepped across the now-useless circle of herbs. He pushed one hand in the air toward Aiden, throwing him across the chasm effortlessly. Aiden smashed into the stones and landed in a heap next to Aleerah, Lyra, and Agon.

"You truly thought you could stop me?" The *turmio* cackled maniacally. "*Me*? I'm pure power incarnate." With a flick of his wrist, Roska felt himself lift off the ground and hover above the floor. "I really should thank you, boy. If not for you, I'd still be trapped in that hells. The Nothing. The name doesn't do it justice. I'm almost disappointed that your ritual failed so spectacularly. I might've enjoyed watching you suffer in the endless abyss." He shrugged as a cruel smile spread across his face. "Oh well. I guess I'll just have to make do with stealing your powers and absorbing all the magic of this world. I've always wanted to be a God." The *turmio* laughed proudly, flinging Roska into the wall beside Quinn. Demoni held her place around his throat, helping to brace his neck upon impact, but the pain still radiated through him in a violent wave. Roska heard something crack along his left side. A sharp pain burst through, and his breathing became painful and labored.

I think he broke one of your ribs, Demoni assessed.

We have to stop him! Roska struggled to stand but was unable to get his feet beneath him, much less to stand upright and fight an increasingly powerful demon. His vision blurred, the pain in his lungs nearly blinding him.

"It's almost sad how close you came to stopping me, only to fail." The *turmio* took another step toward Roska and Quinn.

With a sudden ferocity, Elena leapt onto the *turmio*'s back, stabbing him repeatedly in the chest with a dagger Roska recognized as the one Quinn had given her all those moons ago. She shrieked like a demoness, slamming the blade into the *turmio* over and over.

The monster roared in rage and pain, spinning violently and trying to throw Elena off its back. She wouldn't let go though, gripping tighter, wrapping her legs around his waist with one arm holding tight around his neck and pulling him farther backward. Toward the chasm and The Nothing that awaited him.

Agon appeared out of nowhere, latching onto the *turmio*'s leg and sinking his viciously sharp teeth into the sensitive tendons at the monster's ankle.

The *turmio* cried out in pain, lost its balance, and fell backward into the chasm. Taking Elena and Agon with it into The Nothing.

The last thing Roska heard before the blackness enveloped him was the sound of his sister's screams as she vanished from their world.

See how this story ends in Reign and Ruin.
Available wherever books are sold.

ACKNOWLEDGMENTS

I've been staring at a blank page for a few weeks now, trying to write the *perfect* acknowledgments for my second book. Isn't that silly? There's no such thing as "perfect." You'd think my years of deconstructing that "ideal" in my head would have broken that mentality by now, but clearly, it hasn't.

I have had so many wonderful, supportive people in my life. I'm quite lucky in that regard. Support came from unexpected places. I've had old friends from high school buy multiple copies for members of their families, and rope their friends into buying copies too. I've had family members buy *several* copies to give to their friends as gifts. My brother-in-law got into a bidding war with my uncle and cousin at a family reunion to win a signed copy of Storm and Flame at the family reunion. Honestly, the outpour of support has been overwhelming. You are the ones who make this possible. You are the ones who give me the motivation to keep going, keep writing, keeping publishing. I couldn't—or wouldn't—do this without you.

This is all to say that I am so stunned by the love and support my books have received. I'm so grateful for you.

I'd also like to throw an extra thanks to my former work-wife and accidental (but perfect) critique partner, Melissa. You might recall her from the acknowledgments in S&F. She has been my eternal cheerleader when I'm doubting myself, and my emotional support human when I need to push myself out of my comfort zone and talk to bookstore owners so my books can be on their shelves. She also had a great deal of input in shaping Beatrice and Belladonna's relationship. Navigating uniquely LGBTQA+ relationship problems was an interesting challenge for me and Melissa helped me to make these characters real and relatable. Beatrice's redemption arc wouldn't be possible without Melissa.

47

ABOUT THE AUTHOR

Mallory lives in Texas with her husband and their two young boys. She spends her days home-schooling and full-time parenting. Her nights, and any free time she manages to carve out during the day, are devoted to reading and writing.

If you enjoy these stories, please make sure to leave reviews on your favorite sites. That's the absolute best way to help spread the word about Elena, Quinn, and Roska. Thank you so much! I'll see you in the next one!

www.ingramcontent.com/pod-product-compliance
Lightning Source LLC
Chambersburg PA
CBHW021211310726
48971CB00006B/1520